She stared into he
want you to think I was

"Only if you believed the CIA tried to kill Tom because he knew the truth behind the Kennedy assassination." I gave her a smile, hoping again to get one from her in return.

She offered that twitch at the corners of her mouth. I had the feeling if I ever got a fill-blown smile from her, it would unhinge my knees. Her expression turned somber. "Can I tell you something you really will think is crazy?"

"Sure."

"Sometimes I hate Tom for having his accident and for what it did to us and to our lives."

"That doesn't sound crazy." I'd done it, too. *Amy should have waited at the hospital for me.* "It's normal to think that sometimes. As long as it doesn't become the only feeling you have for him."

Her eyes held a pained look. "If he'd only called me that night and told me he was too tired to drive, I would have gone for him, and none of this would have happened."

"You're putting the blame on yourself." I had a master's degree in it. *If only I'd been at the hospital on time...* "You can't do that. Not too long ago, you told me I wasn't responsible for Amy's accident. And you're not the least bit responsible for Tom's."

She sipped from her cup. "I've told myself that a hundred times, but sometimes I can't help thinking I am."

Illegal Maneuvers

by

David A. Freas

Illegal Maneuvers

Cover Art by *The Wild Rose Press, Inc.*

The Wild Rose Press, Inc.
PO Box 708
Adams Basin, NY 14410-0708
Visit us at www.thewildrosepress.com

Publishing History
First Edition, 2021
Trade Paperback ISBN 978-1-5092-3589-6
Digital ISBN 978-1-5092-3590-2

Published in the United States of America

Dedication

To my parents, Foster and Emma. I wish you were still
here to share my joy.
To my family, Linda, Laurel, and Colin. This book is as
much yours as mine.

Acknowledgments

My parents, Foster and Emma instilled a love of reading and words in me from my earliest days. That love made me look at books and think I could do better.

My family, Linda, Laurel, and Colin, were my primary sounding board, brainstormers, and surrogate characters when I needed help translating the ideas in my head to accurate words on the page. And they understood that for me, taking writing supplies on a vacation was as necessary as clothing.

Marty and Pam and Andi and Bill believed in me and encouraged me from the start of this journey, when I doubted I'd be good enough to make it to the end. And they called me on it when I tried to get away with less than my best. Katie, Jim, Janet, Paula, Thorsen and Neva continue that support.

Pennwriters members – a more diverse group with so much in common doesn't exist anywhere on this planet – have taught me so much in so many different ways that to list you individually would take volumes.

Mickey, my beta reader, caught mistakes I missed in 300 read-throughs.

Ally Robertson, Lori Graham, and Rhonda Penders at The Wild Rose Press took a chance on me and, with a massive dose of patience, made a dream come true.

Thank you all for making this book possible.

Chapter 1

04/04/2003 – First Meeting

Cold air chilled the sweat on my arms when I entered Lou's Tavern, craving a beer after working late. The day had been a warm one for early April, and a cold brew would cure what ailed me.

Lou's was a good place to go for a drink. Clean, fairly well lit, and relatively quiet—except for the perpetual clack of pool balls from the back room—it was the epitome of what a neighborhood bar should be. I recognized most of the people there, if not by name, by face.

Not so the woman a few stools away with a tall empty glass in front of her. She had long dark hair and a trim figure in black from shoulders to soles. The big diamond on her finger shot sparks of fire, and everything else about her signaled polish, refinement, and money. She didn't fit in with Lou's blue-collar patrons, a Rolls-Royce in a Dodge showroom. She raised her glass and waggled it. "Another, please."

The glass slipped from her hand and fell on its side, spilling ice and the dregs of her drink on the bar. She put her hand over her mouth for a second. "Sorry."

Lou said, "No problem." He picked up the glass and wiped the spill away. "I think you've had enough."

"I want another one." Demand in her voice before

she added a kinder, "Pleashe," the ess mushy.

"No, ma'am." Lou didn't tolerate drunks, even classy lady drunks.

"Pleashe?" Her alto voice took on a wheedling tone. "Juss one more."

"I'll call anyone you want to give you a ride home. But I won't sell you another drink."

"Fine. I'll go someplache that will." She slapped a twenty from her purse on the bar and slipped off the stool. Her weight came down on one tipped heel, and her ankle rolled. She grabbed the bar to keep from falling. Her purse hit the floor, spewing its contents. She raked everything back in and tracked a tottering path towards the door.

"Dan." Lou shot me the 'go after her' look. Four years ago, I'd staked him the money he needed to buy the place when the old owner hung up his bar towel. If the woman turned herself or someone else into coffin filler, it could cost Lou and me a ton. I nodded and got to my feet. The possibility of getting sued wasn't all that had me moving. Why would a woman like her pick a place like Lou's to drink herself to oblivion? Spotting a wallet under her stool, I scooped it up and went after her.

She was trying to fit the key into the lock of a dark blue Lexus LS and not getting it. She turned at my approach and backed against the car. "Wha-what do you want?"

"Nothing. I—"

"Here." She held out her car keys. "Take it. I won't call the cops."

My scuffed boots, worn jeans, faded flannel shirt, and D-J Auto Renewal cap clearly said carjacker to her.

"I don't want your car. I just want—"

She thrust her purse at me. "There's sixty dollars in there. It's all I have. Please don't hurt me."

I raised a hand, palm out. "Whoa. Hurting you is the last thing on my mind. And if I wanted your money, I'd already have it." I showed her the wallet. "You missed this picking up the stuff from your purse."

She snatched it from my hand and staggered a step sideways. I caught her by the arms before she nosedived into the paving. "Maybe I better drive you home."

She backed out of my grasp and stuffed the wallet in her purse. "I can drive myself."

She stood a few inches shorter than my six-four. Without the heels, she'd go maybe five-eleven. I couldn't see her eyes in the dim light of the parking lot, but guessed they'd be some shade of brown to go with her dark hair. "No, you can't. You can't even get your car door unlocked."

"Because it's too dark out here to see the damn lock."

I lifted the keys from her hand. "And didn't think to try this." I thumbed the remote.

She gave a little start as the car's locks popped and the interior lights came on. "Give me my keys." She made a weak swipe for them and missed, then eyed me, her head cocked to one side as if she was evaluating me. "Have you ever been in a car crash?"

The question stopped me for a moment. "No. Why?"

"I wonder what it's like to smash into a tree." Her voice had a dreamy tone.

"I don't know, and I don't recommend trying to

find out. You might kill yourself."

"Maybe I want to," she snapped then repeated slowly and sadly, "Maybe I want to."

All the more reason she shouldn't be driving. "I'd better take you home so you don't."

She pressed her mouth into a defiant line.

"Look, I'm the unofficial designated driver for this bar. I want to see you get home safe. That's all. So it's either me or a taxi. Take your pick."

"Neither. Give me my keys. I can drive myself home."

"You try, I'll call the cops before you reach the corner."

"You wouldn't."

"I would." I waggled my cell phone to emphasize how serious I was.

She swayed then staggered to keep her feet under her. I caught her before she fell. "Still think you're fit to drive?"

Resistance slowly drained out of her, and she shook her head. I tapped the button to lock her car and tucked her keys in my pocket, led her to my Toyota pick-up and helped her in. She had the polish not to recoil at its grubby interior. Getting behind the wheel, I started the engine. "Where do you live?"

She held off a second or two before she said, "Millers Run Road."

A back road of gentle curves and rises and dips with not many homes on it, farm houses mostly. She didn't look like the farmhouse type. "That's where you live?"

"It's where I want to go."

"You have a friend who lives there? Or—"

"Just take me there. Please."

"Okay." I pulled onto the street. "What's your name?"

"Why do you want to know?"

I shrugged. "Just making conversation."

"What's yours?"

"Dan Gallagher."

"Stephanie. Stephanie Mercer."

"Hi, Stephanie. Nice to meet you."

She looked out the window. "Please don't ask me any more questions."

I didn't. She didn't say anything either, staring out the window, until we'd traveled a couple miles along Millers Run Road. Then she straightened in the seat. "Slow down."

I was doing the speed limit, so it couldn't be that, and she didn't look like she was getting ready to toss her cookies. Better to know. "You feeling sick?"

"Just slow down. Please."

I slowed. A hundred or so yards farther on, she blurted, "Stop! Stop here! Stop! Stop!"

Maybe she did have to puke. I braked, expecting her to yank open the door and lean out. She sat up straighter instead and stared into the darkness outside her window. The spot was nothing special. The almost full moon lit a slight curve, no berm to speak of, a drainage ditch with trees and low scrub beyond. No houses anywhere in sight.

The lights from the dash picked out a tear sliding down her cheek. After a few moments, she sighed and slumped in her seat. "You can go now."

I put the truck in drive. "Where to?"

"Glenwood Heights. Thirty-seven Elm Circle."

I held in the whistle forming on my lips. Glenwood Heights was the high rent district. Make that very high rent. Stephanie definitely hadn't belonged in Lou's.

Things weren't adding up. "What's so special about that spot back there?"

She shook her head and stared out the window. I turned my truck around in a driveway and headed back to Schuylerton. As we passed the spot again, a light went on in my head. Something happened here, something that hit her hard. My guess was a car crash. If that was the case, her reaction made sense. An intersection in town hit me the same way.

Fifteen silent minutes later, I drove the gently curving streets of Glenwood Heights. Thirty-seven Elm Circle was a big stone and glass—lots of glass—ranch house with neat little shrubs lining the foundation and a pair of mature maples in the front yard. A white basket weave fence extended from the corner of the garage to the property line, probably enclosing an in-ground pool. Houses in Glenwood Heights had them the way houses elsewhere had floors.

Stephanie got out of my truck as soon as I stopped in her driveway and walked toward a low flagstone porch, steadier on her feet than when she'd left Lou's. I tailed her anyway. Sensor lights snapped on as we neared the porch, illuminating white wicker furniture with thick flowered cushions. Metal wind chimes tinkled crisp notes in the breeze. She whirled around. "Why are you following me?"

I stepped back a pace. "Just want to make sure you get inside safely."

"I'm fine." She pawed through her purse for a second or two. "Where are my keys? Don't tell me I lost them."

I tugged them from my jeans pocket and held them out. "Here."

She jerked them from my hand and turned toward the door. Seconds later, the keys hit the porch. "Dammit!"

I picked them up. "Let me." I unlocked the door, pushed it open, and returned her keys. "There you go. Can I make a suggestion? Drink a big glass of water before you go to bed. And another one if you wake up in the night. You won't feel so rocky tomorrow morning."

She hesitated as if she wanted to say something then stepped inside and swung the door shut. I stopped it before it latched. "It's none of my business why you want to kill yourself—"

"I never said any such thing."

"Yeah, you did. Right after I said you could if you hit a tree."

She looked away.

"Next time you get an idea like that, call me instead." The words were out before I could stop them. I handed her a D-J Auto Renewal business card from my wallet. "Or if you just want to talk. I'm a good listener."

"Thank you, no. I'm fine." She returned my card, shut the door, and set the lock.

I slipped the card between the door and jamb then got in my truck. I started it and sat there a minute, puzzled by why I'd offered to listen to her problems. I shrugged it away. I'd probably never hear from her again.

Three weeks later, she called me.

Chapter 2

04/24/2003 – Coffee Shop Meeting

A few minutes after seven that evening, I entered Pete's Perk, a coffee shop between a dollar store and a yard goods place in a block long strip mall at the west end of town. Stephanie sat in a booth at the back and raised a hand when she spotted me. I slid onto the opposite bench. She had on a black dress with half sleeves and a square neckline. I'd guessed wrong on her having brown eyes. They were dark blue with specks of silvery gray, and her hair had a chestnut cast to it. She said, "Thank you for agreeing to meet me."

When the waitress came, we ordered coffee.

"I never thanked you for returning my wallet and driving me home that night. And I want to apologize for being terribly rude to you and to thank you for your kindness and for bringing my car to me the next day."

I'd had one of my guys haul it from Lou's lot to her home on our rollback. "Happy to help."

"I don't know how I would have gotten it otherwise. I felt too wretched to do anything all day. I didn't heed your advice about drinking water before I went to bed. I want to thank you, too, for not taking advantage of my inebriation. I don't usually drink that much."

I waved that away. I'm not the kind of guy who

puts the moves on a drunk woman. The big diamond and fancy wedding ring on her hand made her off limits anyway.

"And speaking of that," she fished a small package from her purse, "this is for you." She pushed it across the table.

"Hangover cure tablets?"

"The next time you see me getting drunk in Lou's, drive me home again and make me take two of those. Please?"

"I have a better idea. The next time you feel like getting smashed, call me instead."

"Then your offer still stands? To listen to my troubles? It's okay if you'd rather not. I shouldn't be dumping them on you."

"It still stands."

The waitress delivered our coffees. Stephanie added cream and sugar to hers. "Why did you offer anyway?"

I'd done a lot of thinking about it since that night despite my best efforts to put it out of my mind. "You looked like you needed someone to talk to. It's a lot less dangerous than trying to uproot a tree with your car." I smiled, hoping it would pull one from her.

She managed a small twitch of the corners of her mouth, nothing more. "It is." Her spoon made sharp tinks against the side of the mug as she stirred. "The night you drove me home was the six-month anniversary of my husband's death."

"I'm sorry."

"Tom's not dead the way people usually think of dead, but he might as well be." She kept stirring her coffee long after the sugar and cream had mixed. "He's in Oakhurst Care Center in a coma." Her voice was flat with sadness. "He was in an accident—"

The hard little kernels of pain forever living deep in me began to throb. "Where you had me stop on Millers Run Road."

She nodded once. "He was a lawyer at O'Reilly, Styles, and McNamara. He'd been working long hours, he was tired, and he'd gone for drinks and dinner with some people from the firm. The police said his car went off the road and hit a tree." She told it in a rush as if saying it fast would make it hurt less.

I remembered the incident vaguely. It had made the front page of the *Sentinel-Tribune*, a long article with a big picture of a Caddy on its roof and a smaller one of EMTs wheeling him to the ambulance.

"I visit him every day and sit by his bed and hold his hand and talk to him and hope and pray one day, he'll say something or squeeze my hand to let me know he's still there and maybe one day he'll wake up. The doctors say he never will, say he'll be like that until he really dies. Then in the next breath, they say miracles happen and there's a chance he could recover." She stopped talking.

I sipped my coffee and waited, a tad sorry now I'd offered to listen to her troubles. She was hitting a little too close to my core. At least she had the possibility of things turning around. It would never happen for me.

"It gets so hard to sit there day after day and talk to him, not knowing if he'll ever get better. But I can't stop believing he will, so I keep going. Sometimes I get so tired of the futility of it all, I want it to be over." She lifted the spoon from her cup and laid it on a napkin. "I'd reached that point that night. I wanted to end it all."

"And if you had, and Tom comes out of his coma one day, you wouldn't be there to see it happen. Or what if you hadn't died, had ended up like Tom?"

She glanced away for a moment, a sure sign she'd thought of that. "Then I wouldn't know I was like him. I wouldn't know anything. And that in its own way would be an end to it." She gazed into her coffee cup for a long time. "I was being selfish, wasn't I?"

I thought she was but kept it to myself.

"I feel like I'm in limbo, like I'll be sitting with him, talking to him, and holding his hand until the day *I* die. I hate feeling as if I'm watching him fade away inch by inch. Sometimes, I wish he would die so it would be over with, and I could move on with my life. Then I hate myself for even thinking it."

"Understandable. It's a tough thing to have to live with."

Her downcast expression lifted for a moment, as if I'd offered her absolution from such thoughts. "Sorry to unload on you."

"Better than running into a tree." There was more to the story than she'd told me. I knew it but didn't press her for it.

We talked for two hours that night and when we parted, I told her she could call me any time day or night for anything. The next day I questioned why I'd offered. I hadn't done anything miraculous at Pete's Perk, had merely listened to her talk.

Why had she turned to me? Doesn't she have any friends to support her? Or was last night's meeting her opening move in some kind of game she hopes to run on me? Every emotion I'd seen that night on Millers Run

11

Road and in Pete's Perk last night rang true. And nothing she'd done or said smacked of a con. I didn't think she was setting me up for something. Still, until I knew for sure, I intended to stay on my toes.

But maybe I was worrying for nothing. Maybe last night was the last I'd ever see of her.

It wasn't.

Over the next five weeks we met a half dozen times, always in the evening at one of the dozen or so coffee shops and small diners scattered across Schuylerton. Once or twice, I managed to say something to raise her spirits. Mostly, I simply listened.

She was thirty-four, Tom thirty-six. She'd grown up near Pittsburgh, he outside Allentown. They met her freshmen year at the University of Pennsylvania. The bond had been instant and strong, and neither one dated anyone else afterward. They married after her graduation, and she worked while he attended Cornell Law School. After they moved here, she earned a master of psychology at the local university, then went to work part time as a counselor at the county-funded mental health clinic in town and volunteered at Safe Haven, the local women's shelter. She liked the work, but it had become even more important to her since Tom's accident, giving her something to do to keep from going crazy in the too big house full of never-to-come-true plans and dreams.

She said thank you at the end of each meeting. At her car after the fourth one, she added a hug. At the end of the sixth, she followed it with a quick, light kiss on my cheek.

I thought about her often in the time between our meetings, trying to understand why she had turned to me and why I went every time she called. Partly it was because I enjoyed talking to an attractive woman. Who wouldn't? And Stephanie certainly was attractive. Not an eye-popping, stop-me-in-my-tracks fox, but a subtly beautiful woman who looked more so each time we met. Plus, I loved to hear her talk. Her alto voice sat on my ear like honey on my tongue.

But mostly I went because I worried some night she'd feel as she had that night at Lou's and would kill herself instead of calling me. The thought she might filled me with a small irrational knot of dread I couldn't dispel.

Chapter 3

05/28/2003 – Dinner And Discussion

Just before seven-thirty I parked my black '61 Pontiac Ventura—my first restoration—in the lot behind Mitchell's, two slots down from Stephanie's Lexus.

Every town has at least one high-class restaurant. In Schuylerton, PA, it's Mitchell's on Second Street. A dozen years ago, Mitchell Harding bailed on the eat-you-alive world of the New York City restaurant business for a saner pace of life in rural Pennsylvania. New York's loss was Schuylerton's gain.

Stephanie had called that afternoon, inviting me to dinner. Dinner at a high-class restaurant looking at her or dinner at Lou's looking at him? No contest. Lou was one ugly dude. Plus, it had been a week since I'd seen her, and my worries about her had risen a couple notches.

I opened her door and offered her an assist from her car. "Sorry I'm late. I got tied up with something at work."

"It's fine."

She looked gorgeous in a black dress, dark stockings, black heels, and a necklace and dangling earrings of small black stones in a dark silver setting. "I definitely would have been on time if I'd known I'd be dining with one of Dior's models tonight."

A faint touch of a smile again, as if she wanted to smile but couldn't quite manage it. "And I didn't know I'd be dining with someone from GQ."

I wore tan slacks, a yellow-pinstripe blue shirt, yellow and blue tie, navy blazer, and burgundy Dan Post cowboy boots. I did look sharp, but I'm hardly GQ material. My face was a standard one with gray eyes, a nose, and mouth below brown hair, nothing special about it. "You'll never see me on the cover."

"Stop it. You're a handsome man, Dan Gallagher."

That she found me so was a pleasing surprise. As we crossed the parking lot toward the restored hundred-and-thirty-year-old two-story house, she asked, "Have you ever eaten here?"

"It's one of my favorite restaurants."

"Really?" She stared at me with wide eyes. "Please don't take this the wrong way, but I never pictured you as the fine dining type."

"'There are more things in heaven and earth, Stephanie, than are dreamt of in your philosophy.'"

"A Shakespeare quoting body shop owner. You intrigue me."

"That's nice to hear." *And why did it feel so good?*

"Tom and I loved to come here, but I haven't since his accident. I thought it would be too painful to come to a place that meant so much to us."

I found it pleasing, too, that she felt comfortable enough to be here with me. But I hoped it wouldn't backfire, stirring hurtful memories for her.

We stepped onto the full-length porch—a great place to have a drink on a nice day—and I opened the maroon door. Mitchell's décor is golden oak, dark red seating, and red and gold carpeting, lit by many large multi-paned windows during the day and subdued lighting at night.

The hostess, Mitchell's wife, Arianna, greeted us both by name and had the good taste not to react to my presence at Stephanie's side. She said our table would be ready in a minute and invited us to have a drink at the bar or on the porch while we waited. We picked the porch. After the waitress served us, I asked, "How are you doing?"

Stephanie waved her free hand as she tasted her Rusty Nail. "We are not going to talk about me or Tom or his accident tonight. Other than knowing you're one of the kindest men I've ever run into, I know hardly anything about you. I invited you to dinner so I can get to know Dan Gallagher."

I sampled my Maker's Mark Old Fashioned. "Not much to know. Local boy to the core. Born here, grew up here, lived all forty-two years of my life here, work here."

"Oh, no. You're not getting off that easy. There's more to you than that. D-J Auto Renewal isn't a regular body shop. It's a nationally known auto restoration business."

I smiled to remove any sting from my words. "You've been reading up on me."

She smiled too, a small, tentative grin, as if she wasn't sure how to do it. Even so, it brought a life to her face that hadn't been there before, making it truly beautiful. "I wanted to know more about you."

"And what did you find out?"

"I'd rather you told me. Start with D-J Auto Renewal. Are cars the only thing you restore?"

"And trucks. Any make, any model, any year, but we specialize in ones from the mid-fifties through the early seventies."

"What does that involve?"

"In a nutshell? Before a car even comes into the shop, I evaluate it and decide if it's worth restoring. Some are too far gone. Once it gets to the shop, we tear it down until nothing is bolted to anything else. We return each part—even the nuts and bolts—to like new condition or replace it then rebuild the car from the ground up. In about a year, the owner has essentially a new car."

Arianna approached us, menus in hand and a smile on her face. "Mrs. Mercer, Mr. Gallagher, your table is ready. If you'll come this way, please."

She led us to a table, a waiter on our heels. Light classical music played softly alongside muted conversations. I didn't need to read the menu to know what I wanted. Nor did Stephanie. We ordered New York strips well done. I like a woman who eats meat. When the waiter asked about the wine, Stephanie said it was my call. I chose an Australian shiraz, and the waiter hurried away. Then Steph asked, "How did you get into doing restorations?"

I finished my Old Fashioned. "When I was a kid, I was always hanging around Clark Richards's body shop down the street from my house, fascinated by his ability to turn smashed up cars into beauties again. I took auto body shop in high school, and my buddy, Jay Winters, and I went to work for Clark after we graduated. Couple years later Clark said he was ready to retire and would sell us the business if we were interested. Jay and I said yes, even though we didn't know the first thing about running a business, and changed the name to D-J Auto Body. With lots of guidance from Clark, we made a go of it."

A woman and man stopped at our table. The woman said, "Hello, Stephanie."

She was a petite, blue-eyed, curly haired blonde in a dark green dress, her voice a silky soprano. The man, a head taller than she, had brown hair and eyes and a lean runner's build in a dark blue suit. I pegged both to be about Stephanie's age. She introduced them as Jeff and Lisa Styles, friends since Tom's law school days, and introduced me as her friend. I liked the sound of that and smiled at her to let her know I did.

Jeff leveled a disapproving gaze at me. "You own that...car restoration business on Covington Road, right?" His tone equated it with sewer work.

"That's me. You the Styles in O'Reilly, Styles, and McNamara?"

"No." He stroked his tie into place, looked away, and cleared his throat. "Not yet. That's my father." He took Lisa's arm. "Our table's ready. Good to see you again, Stephanie. Nice meeting you, Dan." His tone said it was anything but.

After I okayed the wine, the waiter poured for both of us. Stephanie sipped then held up her glass. "This is perfect. You know your wines."

"Only enough to get by without making a fool of myself."

"You do better than that. You have excellent taste." She swallowed more wine. "Now how did you go from a regular body shop to one specializing in restorations?"

"One day, a guy asked us to restore a car he owned, a '58 Chevy Impala like the one Ron Howard drove in

American Graffiti. He liked our work so much, he told his friends about us, and before long we were doing more restorations than routine repairs. So we changed the name again and stopped doing repairs." I paused for a swallow of wine. "At first, we only did the body and farmed out everything else. Bit by bit, we added them, now we do it all in-house except for a few specialized things like re-chroming parts. By ninety-one, we'd run out of space at Clark's and moved the whole operation to Covington Road."

"And you two still run it together?"

I shook my head. "The year before we moved, Jay started spending every weekend in Atlantic City. It was okay when he was gambling his money there. When I discovered he was gambling the shop's money as well, I bought him out and kicked him out."

"That had to be hard for you. But it probably saved your business."

The memory of the confrontation still sat in my head as bitter as scorched coffee on my tongue. "It was, and it did."

As the waiter served our entrees, I glanced toward the Styleses' table. Jeff was glaring at us, the same disparaging expression on his face. The moment our gazes met, he looked away.

Steph said, "Tell me more about the restoration business."

And I was off and running. Who doesn't enjoy talking about their life's work? Turning a dog into a diamond was the most thrilling—okay, the second most thrilling—thing in the world to me. Stephanie seemed to find my describing it as fascinating as I found the process itself. I feared I was monopolizing the conversation and tried several times to change the topic, but she insisted I tell her more. Running out of things to say about the time I ran out of food on my plate, I said, "Stop by some time, I'll give you a tour."

Our waiter cleared our table and asked if we wanted dessert. After we ordered 4-layer chocolate cake and coffee, I excused myself to the men's room. Turning away from the urinal, I came face to face with Jeff Styles, anger flickering in his eyes. "What are you doing here?"

He had to ask? "Taking a leak."

He folded his arms across his chest and scowled at me.

"I mean at Mitchell's."

I avoid confrontations whenever possible, but I wasn't about to let someone I met minutes ago intimidate me either. "Having dinner." I stepped around him to the sink.

He let out the exasperated sigh of a parent dealing with a willful child. "Why are you here with Stephanie?" He said each word carefully as if I was dense.

"She invited me."

"How did you become friends with her?"

I yanked towels from the holder and dried my hands. "We ran into each other." I discarded the towels and stepped around him again.

He grabbed my arm. "I want a better answer than that."

I wrenched free. "You're not getting one." I opened the door.

"Wait."

I let the door swing shut.

"Are you aware of Tom's situation?" The ire had drained from his tone. "That he's in a nursing home in a coma?"

"Yep."

"Stephanie has enough turmoil in her life right now. She doesn't need another complication." He reached for my arm again then thought better of it. "So tread lightly."

"I always do." I stalked out.

An uneasy expression filled Stephanie's face, as if she now regretted asking me to dinner. Maybe she'd gotten sick of hearing about D-J. Or maybe having her friends see us together, expecting they'd give her a hard time over having dinner with me, had upset her. She gazed at the tablecloth, picked up her wine glass, set it down, scanned the room, adjusted her silverware. "Dan...I—"

The waiter set out our dessert and coffee. She eyed her cake for a second then downed the last sip of her wine, inhaled and exhaled a breath. "Dan, I owe you an apology."

"For?" I lopped off a bite of cake and stuck it in my mouth.

"All I ever do is unload on you about Tom's accident."

"You don't have to apologize for it."

"I do." She paused. "I know about Amy. About her accident."

Ten years ago, a drunk behind the wheel of a delivery truck ran a red light and T-boned my wife's car. He never saw the light, never slowed down, had plowed into her at forty miles an hour, killing her instantly. That she hadn't suffered for one second was the only softness in the hard kernel of pain deep in my soul.

"Dan, I'm so sorry for your loss." Stephanie squeezed my hand lightly. Her eyes held compassion and curiosity. "Was what happened to Amy why you were so adamant about driving me home from the bar?"

I laid my fork by my partially eaten cake and nodded. "I failed Amy." I inhaled a deep breath. "I promised myself after it happened, I'd never let anyone down that way again."

"If the driver who hit Amy was drunk and ran a red light, how did you fail her?"

"I was supposed to pick her up. We were going out to dinner. A quick meal at Burger King before she went back to the hospital—she was a nurse—to pick up some overtime. I wasn't there to get her, so she headed to the shops." I paused, sighed. "I was still there because I was working on something I could have easily picked up the next day, but I wanted to finish it." I shook my head sadly. "If I'd just dropped it…"

She squeezed my hand again. "You are not responsible for Amy's death. If you'd picked her up, the truck driver still would have run the red light and might have hit you. And both of you might have died."

Rationally, I knew she was right, but I'd never been able to forgive myself for not being at the hospital in time to pick Amy up.

"Then you wouldn't have been here last month to save me."

That earned a small softening of the one hard kernel of pain I carried. Nothing would ever soften the other kernel, the one still granite hard after all those years. I stared at my half-eaten dessert to hide the agony remembering always put on my face.

"Dan?" Stephanie squeezed my hand a third time. "What is it?"

Only two people knew that after years of trying, Amy was ten weeks pregnant when she died—her Ob-Gyn and me. I'd never shared it with anyone else. As much as part of me wanted to tell Stephanie, I couldn't. I stared at my plate for another second. "Nothing. I'm okay." I felt like a cad for keeping the whole story from her.

"Oh, Dan." Stephanie's voice carried a hurt matching my own and her eyes glistened on the edge of tears. "All I ever do is bemoan Tom's accident, and every time must remind you of Amy." She squeezed my hand again. "I am so, so sorry."

"You didn't know. And it's been a long time, so it doesn't hurt too bad anymore. It's more like...like an old injury that flares up every so often."

"Every time I talk about Tom." She plucked a tissue from her purse and dabbed her eyes. "Why didn't you tell me?"

"You didn't need my woe on top of your own." I took her hand. "It's okay. Really. I can handle it." I'd handled it then by pouring myself into D-J Auto Renewal until nothing mattered but D-J. I'd kicked Jay, my life-long pal, to the curb when his gambling threatened it instead of offering to help him overcome his addiction. All to keep the pain of losing Amy and our child at bay.

"I promise I won't bring it up again." She gripped my hand tight. "But if you ever want to talk about her or anything," she managed a small smile, "I'm a good listener."

I smiled back and returned her grasp. "It's a deal."

"Lisa came over while you were in the men's room and asked me about you, wanting to know how we met and what we were doing here."

"Jeff cornered me there, asking the same things. What did you tell her?"

"The truth. That you'd done me a favor, and I was treating you to dinner to thank you. Then she asked if you knew about Tom and, after I said you did, warned me to be careful about letting you too far into my life because you might have an ulterior motive."

"I got the same from Jeff. Are they always so nosy about your business?"

"Not until tonight. I think they're concerned because they've never seen me with anyone but Tom."

In the parking lot, we exchanged the hug that had become part of our meetings. Stephanie appeared in no hurry to end it this time and I was certainly in no rush. Jeff and Lisa Styles, crossing the lot to their car, saw it.

Their sour gazes could have curdled powdered milk.

Chapter 4

05/29/2003 – A Lawyer Visits

I was in my office the next day, working up an estimate for restoring a '67 Olds 4-4-2 hardtop when Nora Wynn, secretary extraordinaire, buzzed me on the intercom, interrupting my calculations. "There's a man here to see you, Dan."

"Be out in a minute."

D-J Auto Renewal operates out of a two-hundred-thousand square foot main building and six ten-thousand square foot ancillary buildings on the northwest edge of Schuylerton. I finished my calculations then stepped from my office into the showroom fronting the main building. A black '57 Chrysler 300C, a light blue '63 Studebaker Avanti, and a red '65 Ford Mustang fastback were on display. Every car we restore gets exhibited for a month before we return it to its owner. A linebacker in a black topcoat dripping with buttons and straps stood by the Avanti.

He looked like a man with a car he wanted restored. "Can I help you?"

He turned. Under the topcoat, he had on a navy suit, white shirt, light blue tie with gold crowns, and shiny black tassel loafers. Signs he had money. Even better. He was maybe an inch taller than my six-four and ten pounds over my two-forty. "Are you Daniel

Gallagher?" His rich baritone voice commanded attention.

"Yep. What can I do for you?"

"Holland Carter of O'Reilly, Styles, and McNamara." He held out a business card.

He wasn't merely Holland Carter, he was Holland J. Carter, III, Esq. *Well, isn't he a somebody.* Carter was about my age with wavy light brown hair, dark brown eyes, a broad nose, and a square chin and smelling of Stetson cologne. What did a lawyer with Tom Mercer's firm want with me? I'd bet it had nothing to do with restoring a car.

"May we speak in private?"

I waved him into my office and circled my desk. "What can I do for you, Mr. Carter?"

He took a chair facing me, lifting his pant legs to save the crease over his knees, and shot me a smile of expensive orthodontia. "I believe you are acquainted with Stephanie Mercer, Mr. Gallagher."

So not a car restoration. I wasn't surprised. No great mental leap to figure out Styles told him we knew each other. But why was he prying into it? "I am. What about her?"

Another smile, this one a predator spotting prey. "What is the nature of your relationship with her?"

"Why do you want to know?"

"That I'm curious will suffice."

Not good enough. "None of your business." I stood. "I'll show you out."

Carter leveled a scowl at me then let it fade. "Hear me out, please, first." He pressed his fingertips together. "Tom Mercer was a valued member of the O'Reilly, Styles, and McNamara family. After his unfortunate accident, we took Stephanie under our wing, so to speak. I am inquiring into your relationship with her pursuant to her best interests."

I sat again. "And her best interests are?"

"This past six months have been very painful for her. I'm trying to protect her from further hurt."

Then where the hell were you the night she wanted to kill herself?

"So I hope you will understand why I would like the names of several people—three should do—who can vouch for your character."

Had Stephanie asked him to do this? I doubted it. I'd call her and ask, but didn't have her number. The one time I'd asked for it, she'd changed the subject. I never asked again. "I'll give you one." I jotted a name and number on a pad, tore the page off, and handed it to him.

"Frank Morrison is your attorney?"

"Yep."

"He's a good man." Carter folded the paper and tucked it into an inside pocket. "I'm sure he'll vouch for you." He matched up his fingertips again. "However, I also would not be performing my obligation to Stephanie with due diligence if I did not request some proof you have no interest in her money. Your W-2 from the last two years will suffice."

"Not going to happen."

The scowl flashed across his face again quickly replaced by a stern glare. "If you don't comply, I will institute legal proceedings to compel you to."

"We'll see about that." I dialed a number then hit the speaker button. After the second ring, a voice said, "Graves and Morrison, Attorneys-at-Law. How may I direct your call?"

"Hi, Betty. It's Dan Gallagher. Can I steal a minute of Frank's time?" D-J had restored a '63 Corvette split-window coupe for him. He always had time for me.

"Sure, Dan. No problem. Please hold."

Carter's eyebrows rose.

A moment later, the phone clicked and a tenor voice said, "Hi, Dan. What's up?"

Carter's eyebrows went up again.

"You're on speaker, Frank. I need your advice on something. You know Tom Mercer?" A rhetorical question. Frank knew every lawyer in the county. "I struck up a friendship with his wife a month or so ago. Now I have a lawyer in my office, wanting to see financial proof I'm not after her money and threatening legal action if I don't."

"Did you show him anything?"

"Nope."

"Good. Who's the lawyer?"

Carter cleared his throat. "Holland Carter of O'Reilly, Styles, and McNamara, Frank."

"Holland." His cool greeting said Carter wasn't on his Christmas list. "Is this a legal matter you are pursuing on Mrs. Mercer's behalf?"

"No. I'm only—"

"Is Mrs. Mercer of sound mind and in full control of her mental faculties?"

"Yes."

"Did she ask you to obtain this information?"

"As I explained to Mr. Gallagher, I'm acting in what I feel are her best interests."

"That isn't what I asked, Holland." Frank's tone turned cold. "Did she specifically ask you to inquire into Dan's financial status?"

Carter straightened in his chair. "Well…no. I felt it would be prudent to determine Mr. Gallagher's friendship with her is not a ruse for financial gain."

"You have no legal authority to view Dan's financials, and you know it. If you want to see them, get a warrant. If and when—emphasis on if—you get one, come see me. Go about it any other way, Holland, and I'll be on you like a starving wolf on a lamb. Do we understand each other?"

"Yes." Chastised schoolboy in Carter's tone.

"Good. Better yet, drop the idea entirely." Frank hung up.

"There's your answer, Mr. Carter." I jabbed a finger. "And there's the door."

Chapter 5

06/02/2003 – Mutual Aid

My phone rang minutes after I got home four days later. I tossed the work shirt I'd just shed into the hamper and picked up.

"Dan, can you meet me for dinner?"

Heaviness in Stephanie's tone caught my attention. "Is something wrong?"

"Nothing major. I just need…can I lean on your shoulder for a while?"

"When and where do you want my shoulder?"

A small, weak chuckle. "Now, if you can. At Three Brothers?" A family-style diner noted for great food in generous portions at a good price.

"Sure. Twenty minutes?"

"That's fine."

I grabbed a quick shower and headed for the restaurant. Stephanie pulled into the lot seconds after I did. She had on a gray silk blouse, black pantsuit, and low heels. I'd never seen her in anything other than black and shades of gray. Maybe she wore them as a sort of mourning for Tom or simply favored them the way Nora favored yellow. Her walk toward me mirrored her tone on the phone, but her tired expression lifted for a moment when she spotted me. "I hope you don't mind eating here. I need comfort food, not fine dining."

"Comfort food works for me anytime."

After our waitress scurried off with our drink orders, I patted my shoulder. "Start leaning."

A weak try at a smile then a sigh. "It's been a bad day, start to finish. My first client—a woman I've been counselling on alcohol addiction—arrived reeking of liquor. Then I overheard a clerk on the phone revealing privileged information about a client to a friend, so I had to report her to our manager. I hated to do it because she's a single mother barely making ends meet, and she'll lose her job over this. But I had to do it. Patient confidentiality is an unbreakable rule."

"I've had to can a few people myself. And I hated doing it just as much."

Our waitress returned with our sodas and took our orders. I swallowed some Coke. "What else?"

"When I got to Oakhurst, they were prepping Tom for transfer to the hospital. He was having trouble breathing, and his doctor thought it might be the start of pneumonia. It happens a lot with people in his condition. I've been at the hospital all afternoon while they ran tests."

"And?"

"They won't know for sure until tomorrow. Right now, they're treating him as if it is."

"I'll hold good thoughts it isn't."

She touched the back of my hand, a silent thank-you. "His doctor says every time he gets it, it will be harder for him to fight it off. One day he won't be able to, and it will kill him. It scares me because I don't want to lose him. Then I think it would be a relief because I would never again have to see him the way he is now." She looked down for a moment. "Then I feel guilty for thinking it."

"Don't beat yourself up for thinking any of those things. They're all perfectly normal."

The waitress served her salad and my soup. Stephanie stirred the greens on her plate but didn't eat any. "I know. I guess I simply needed to hear someone else tell me."

I spooned clam chowder into my mouth. "I'd say a wasted patient, a rule-breaking employee, and Tom coming down with pneumonia add up to a bit more than 'nothing major wrong.'"

She nodded and took a bite of salad. We ate in silence until the waitress served our entrees. Then Stephanie asked, "How was your day?"

"Routine. But I had a visit from one of Tom's co-workers, Holland Carter, Thursday." I salted my fries and spread steak sauce over my sirloin.

She let out a low sound, part groan, part growl.

Her reaction startled me. "You don't like him?"

"He's..." She circled her fork in the air, as if it would help bring a description to mind.

"He's not just Holland Carter, he's Holland J. Carter III, Esq."

"Exactly!" Her eyes brightened. "What did he want?"

"Financial proof I'm not after your money. He didn't like it when I wouldn't show him any, even threatened to get a court order forcing me to."

She pared a thin slice from her grilled chicken breast. "I didn't ask him to do that, I swear. If I wanted to know, I'd ask you directly."

"And I'd tell you."

"Everyone at the firm's been wonderful about helping me with anything I needed." She shook her head. "But Holl has taken it further, seeing himself as some kind of protector saving me from people hoping to take advantage of me."

"That's me according to him."

She rolled her eyes. "That is not you."

"There's more going on than that. He wanted to know the nature of our relationship and didn't like that I wouldn't tell him."

She was silent for a second or two. "I think he views you as competition."

"Competition?" I carved off a bite of steak and chewed.

"Not to sound vain, but for me," she said softly. "I think Holl has ideas beyond protecting me from con artists. I think he hopes if he plays my hero," she hung air quotes around the word, "I'll fall in love with him and marry him if Tom should die."

I couldn't blame Carter. Stephanie Mercer was a captivating woman. A sudden and surprising twitch of jealousy flitted through me. Still, I suppressed a laugh at Carter for thinking I was in some kind of duel with him for Stephanie.

"He's called a couple times a month since Tom's accident, asking if he could do anything for me. He even suggested the last time he called that if Tom remains in a coma much longer, I should think about divorcing him so I can 'move on to the next phase of my life' in his words." She shook her head. "I would never do that to Tom."

"It's none of my business, but if Tom would die, what would you do?" My heart thumped hard waiting for her answer, surprising me.

"I never thought about it." She drank some soda. "I suppose get on with my life." She took a bite of baked potato and chewed it slowly, marking the end of that topic. "What I do and who I spend time with is none of Holl's business. I'll talk to Jeff Styles tomorrow. Holl won't bother you again."

"No need. I took care of it."

"I'll talk to Jeff anyway. To make sure it doesn't happen again."

Chapter 6

06/03/2003 – Another Lawyer Visit

The following Tuesday, Jeff Styles got out of a dark blue Lincoln Town Car as I parked my truck near the door to D-J Auto Renewal after lunch. He was maybe an inch shorter than I was in a beige topcoat, tan suit, pale green shirt, navy-and-gold stripe tie, and cordovan wingtips. "May I speak with you in private, Dan?"

Stephanie had told me he might pay me a visit. I led him across the showroom to my office and waved him to the seat Holland Carter filled last week. "What's on your mind, Mr. Styles?"

"Jeff, please. I understand a colleague of mine, Holland Carter, was here last week, inquiring into your relationship with Stephanie Mercer." He stroked his tie. "Stephanie did not request he do that."

"I know."

"I hope you will accept my sincere and heartfelt apology on behalf of Holland and of O'Reilly, Styles, and McNamara for his behavior."

"Accepted." I leaned over my desk. "Now I want to know why he did it."

"I honestly don't know."

"How did he find out Stephanie and I were meeting?"

"That was my doing, and I do apologize for it." He repeated the tie-stroking gesture, clearly uncomfortable. "He overheard me that morning telling my father I saw you having dinner with her at Mitchell's the night before."

And visited me the same afternoon. Carter hadn't wasted any time. Moving so fast made me seriously doubt he only had Stephanie's welfare in mind.

"I must admit I was surprised to see you with her there. And a bit curious, too. It's why Lisa and I wanted to know the nature of your relationship with her."

"Carter should have talked to you before coming here."

"He should have, yes. He can sometimes be…impetuous." Styles sighed as if Carter wore on his nerves. "Again, let me apologize for his actions."

"The next time he's impetuous, I'll contact my attorney about legal action against him and your firm."

"Frank made that clear when he spoke to Graham McNamara Thursday morning. And Graham made it clear to Holland." Styles raised a hand. "I assure you he will not approach you again." He ran the hand down his tie again. "I am not here solely on behalf of O'Reilly, Styles, and McNamara, Dan. My motive is personal as well. My goal is to protect Stephanie from further harm of any nature."

Where had I heard that line before? "Mine, too."

He pondered that for a moment. "Good. In that regard, there is an issue I wish to bring to your attention, one where you can be of great benefit to her."

I was all for anything that would help her.

Jeff leaned forward in the chair. "She has expressed the opinion that Tom's accident was no accident, that he was forced off the road."

She'd never said it to me and the possibility had never crossed my mind. "Was he?"

"The police investigated his accident thoroughly and found no evidence it was anything other than a tragic and horrific accident caused by Tom falling asleep at the wheel. You would be doing Stephanie a great favor—and I would personally appreciate it—if you would discourage her from thinking otherwise."

His tone said I'd damned well better do what he said. I don't like people telling me what to do. "What if she's right?"

"She isn't. And clinging to that erroneous belief only prolongs her suffering."

I wondered why he didn't want Stephanie questioning the cause of Tom's accident. "How do you know it isn't easing her suffering?" I rocked back in my chair. "I'll make you a deal. I won't encourage or discourage her, will let her believe what she wants."

"I strongly suggest you see the wisdom of my position and act accordingly."

I pointed to the door. "And I suggest you find your way out."

Chapter 7

06/06/2003 – "Am I Crazy?"

I was in Jansen's Floral & Garden Center shortly after they opened Friday, picking up a bouquet.

Nora Wynn has been with D-J since shortly after the restoration business first took off. And saved my butt more times than I care to count. Every year, on the June day we hired her, I bring her flowers.

I was almost to my truck when a dark blue Lexus entered the lot. A small rise of hope it might be Stephanie's stirred in me, but I tamped it down. There were at least a dozen dark blue Lexuses in town so the odds said this one wasn't hers. I waited anyway to see who was driving it.

The Lexus stopped and my hope came true when Stephanie got out. She spotted me on her way to the door, angled toward me, and waved. I waved back and thought the faintest hint of a smile touched her lips. She called out, "Hi, Dan," as she neared me.

"Hi back."

She had her hair in a ponytail and wore a dark gray tee, black capri pants, and black sneakers. Somehow, she made those casual clothes appear elegant. "What brings you here?"

I showed her the bouquet. "Flowers for my secretary." I told her about Nora. "You?"

"Shopping for flowers and small shrubs for the yard. Do you have any suggestions?"

"Sorry. I don't know a fir from a fir-sythia."

Another trace of a smile. "You mean a *for*-sythia?"

"Them either."

The trace lingered as she pivoted away then almost immediately about-faced. "Do you have time for a cup of coffee?"

"As soon as I get these to Nora, sure."

"Morning Mug in half an hour? I should be done here by then."

"Works for me."

I gave Nora her flowers and made a sweep through D-J's shops to see if anything needing my attention had come up. Nothing had. They rarely did. My crew is that good.

Stephanie was waiting at Morning Mug when I arrived. Standing in line at the counter, she asked if Nora liked the flowers, and I asked if she found any shrubs. Nora did, and she had. After we ordered, she asked if Jeff Styles had come to see me. I gave her the Cliffs Notes version of our conversation but skipped the part about Jeff ordering me to toe the party line regarding the cause of Tom's crash.

"Two large regulars, jumbo blueberry muffin, jumbo chocolate chip muffin." The counter girl set a tray in front of us.

"This is on me." Stephanie handed the girl a ten before I could touch my wallet. Doctoring her coffee with cream and sugar, she suggested instead of sitting in Morning Mug, we stroll the two blocks to a small park on Jackson Lane since the day was a nice one, sunny and mildly warm. The girl behind the counter handed me a cardboard tray holding our muffins. Once we hit the sidewalk on Mulberry Street, Steph said, "Would you do something for me?"

"Name it."

"All my friends call me Steph. I wish you would, too."

"Gladly." I downed some java. "Why didn't you tell me you thought Tom had been run off the road?"

She eyed me with surprise. "How do you know that?"

"Jeff told me. Why didn't you?"

She stared into her cup for a few steps. "I didn't want you to think I was crazy."

"Only if you believed the CIA tried to kill Tom because he knew the truth behind the Kennedy assassination." I gave her a smile, hoping again to get one from her in return.

She offered that twitch at the corners of her mouth. I had the feeling if I ever got a fill-blown smile from her, it would unhinge my knees. Her expression turned somber. "Can I tell you something you really will think is crazy?"

"Sure."

"Sometimes I hate Tom for having his accident and for what it did to us and to our lives."

"That doesn't sound crazy." I'd done it, too. *Amy should have waited at the hospital for me.* "It's normal to think that sometimes. As long as it doesn't become the only feeling you have for him."

Her eyes held a pained look. "If he'd only called me that night and told me he was too tired to drive, I would have gone for him, and none of this would have happened."

"You're putting the blame on yourself." I had a master's degree in it. *If only I'd been at the hospital on time...* "You can't do that. Not too long ago, you told me I wasn't responsible for Amy's accident. And you're not the least bit responsible for Tom's."

She sipped from her cup. "I've told myself that a hundred times, but sometimes I can't help thinking I am."

Steph's easy, athletic gait meshed well with my long-legged stride. Amy had taken such small steps, walking together meant either I'd hobbled along like I was in leg irons or she'd scurried like a running dachshund.

We waited at the corner of Fourth and Mulberry for a truck coming down Fourth. Steph broke a piece from her blueberry muffin and popped it in her mouth. "Do you think I'm crazy for believing Tom's accident wasn't his fault, that something happened to make him hit that tree?"

"Nope. It's perfectly normal to seek other answers when the ones you have don't sit well." I had. I'd never found any.

"It wouldn't change what happened to him, but I think I could live with it easier if I could put at least some of the blame on someone or something else."

I pried loose a chunk of chocolate chip muffin, chewed, and swallowed as the truck rumbled by then drank from my cup as we crossed Fourth. "Why do you think something else caused it?"

"Because Tom was too careful a driver. He's never had an accident or even a speeding ticket. If he was too tired to drive, he would have called me to pick him up or had someone else drive him home."

We stopped for a car backing out of a driveway, and she snitched another piece of her muffin. As the driver pulled away, he waved. We returned it then strolled on. "You're sure of that?"

Steph washed the bite down with a swallow from her cup. "Absolutely. Tom wasn't one bit macho in that regard. If we were at a party two streets from home and he felt the least bit tired, he'd have me drive. Or maybe it was a hit-and-run. Or maybe it was road rage."

I broke off another chunk of muffin. "Could be either one, I suppose."

"Do you want to hear the craziest thing of all? Sometimes I think somebody intentionally ran him off the road."

Her tone was so sure, I considered she might be right, that Tom's crash might have been more than a simple accident. "Do you have anyone in mind?"

She was silent for a bit. "I can't think of anyone. Everyone at work liked him and we got along well with our neighbors."

The park on Jackson Lane was nothing elaborate, a few trees, a few benches, and a pair of paths forming a sinuous X. We picked a bench under an oak near where the paths crossed and nibbled and sipped for a minute before I asked, "How did Jeff Styles know you thought Tom had been run off the road?"

Stephanie swallowed a bite of muffin and a long drink of coffee before she answered. "Lisa insisted I go with them to OSM's Christmas Party last year. After dinner, she asked me how I was doing. I was feeling especially blue that night—it was our first Christmas apart since we became engaged—and I let it all out. Everything, including that."

"How did they react to it?" I popped the last of my muffin into my mouth.

She ate more of hers and took a sip of coffee. "I don't recall Lisa saying anything. But Jeff insisted I was wrong. He said the police were positive Tom's accident was his fault, that he'd fallen asleep, and I had to accept it. I was in such a funk that day, I'm surprised I even remember what they said."

Odd that Jeff had told her not to question what caused Tom's crash, had not questioned what put his best friend in a coma himself. "That the only time you said anything about it to them?"

Another mouthful of her coffee before she nodded. "I never mentioned it again."

"You tell anyone else you thought Tom had been run off the road?"

"My parents and Tom's." She finished her muffin. I sensed she was weighing her next words, considering how I might react to them. "They know some...people in high places. I called them all." She sounded apologetic, as if turning to heavy hitter friends was wrong. "I didn't tell them I thought he'd been run off the road, but I asked if they could do anything to get the police to look at Tom's accident again."

"I'm guessing it didn't get you anywhere."

She shook her head. "They all tried, and they all said the police were very cooperative, but they all were given the same answer: no evidence it was anything other than a one-car accident."

The Schuylerton PD was small but highly professional. "Why do you believe it wasn't?"

"I...feel it." She set her cup on the bench and pressed both hands against her chest. "In here."

Chapter 8

06/11/2003 – A Late Night Call

Steph called me minutes before midnight five days later. In gasping words, she begged me to come to her house.

A rock of dread formed in my stomach. "Ten minutes."

I raced to her home with my gut clenched, my heart thudding, my mind churning with worry, and screeched my Pontiac to a stop in her driveway eight minutes later. Dim light filled the windows. I sprinted to her door. Before I could knock, it flew open.

I barely recognized Steph. Her hair was a disheveled mop, her eyes puffy and red, her nose just red, and tracks of tears marked her cheeks. Her body trembled with tension. I stepped into her marble floored foyer and did the only thing I could think of, wrapping her in a big hug. "What's wrong?"

She clung to me as if I was the only flotsam in an empty ocean and broke into soft sobs. "I feel…like I'm…falling…apart."

I tightened the hug. "Not happening." I eased us into the living room and over to a couch, sat us down, rocked her gently, and whispered soothing words.

After about five minutes, her tears stopped. She kept her head nestled on my shoulder until her breathing calmed. "Thank you."

"No problem." We sat in silence for a minute. "Did something happen to Tom?"

"No." She sat up and massaged her temples. "It's me. I'm so...frustrated, I could scream." A touch of anger rose into her voice. "And so mad I can't think straight. I've tried everything I can to get the police to reinvestigate Tom's accident and gotten nowhere. This evening, Attorney General Moreholt—an old family friend—told me he couldn't help me either." Despair replaced anger. "I don't know who else to turn to." Her words tumbled out faster. "I keep looking for some sign Tom's recovering and never see one, and our anniversary is next Saturday, and it all got to me, and I went to pieces."

"Why didn't you call me before it got this bad?"

"I didn't want...I'm always afraid I'm taking you away from something important."

"Nothing that can't wait." Because I still harbored the low-key fear that if I didn't meet her, I'd read she'd killed herself in the next day's paper.

She touched the back of my hand, the silent thank-you gesture I'd come to know so well, then raised her head from my shoulder. "I feel silly now having dragged you over here so late because I couldn't keep it together."

"I said you could call me any time for anything. Meltdowns qualify." Even at the nadir of my lowness—when it finally sank in I'd lost Amy and our child in the crash—I had never thought of killing myself. Because I didn't give in, I could help Steph hold fast, too. "Has anything like this ever happened to you before?"

She glanced at her folded hands for a long moment

then shook her head.

Her response said otherwise. "It has, hasn't it?"

A whispered, "Yes."

"You definitely need a break. Is there a family member or friend who can sit with Tom for a day or two to give you a breather?"

She shook her head again. "Tom's father had a stroke two years ago, and travel is difficult for him. He's an only child, so there's no one else in his family. And my family...we had a falling out, so they won't help. And I would hate to impose upon a friend."

"I think you need a change, even if it's only for a day. The next time you feel things building up even the least bit, you need to skip a day before it gets this bad again."

"I can't do that to Tom."

"For your own sanity, you need to take a day off—a day where you put Stephanie first—now and then. If you don't, you're going to have more episodes like this."

She nodded once. "I'll think about it. I promise I will."

I eased my arms from around her. "You going to be okay now?"

"Could you please hold me a little longer? No one has in a long time."

I put my arms back in place. She returned her head to my shoulder and leaned against me. "You have no idea how good this feels."

Better than good from my side. I chased the idea from my mind. I couldn't let myself get used to it.

As the tension seeped from her, I scoped out the good-sized living room. I don't know Chippendale from

Hepplewhite but I could tell everything here was top of the line. The room looked straight out of *Better Homes & Gardens* yet had the same inviting aura of warmth and comfort as a cozy den.

Below a lamp on the end table next to me sat a photo in a gold frame. Tom and Steph on a cruise ship. He stood about six-one or so with a lean build, black hair and straight eyebrows, and a softly angular face with nicely scaled features. I could see one reason Steph had been drawn to him. He was a handsome man.

After about five minutes, she lifted her head from my shoulder. "I think I'll be okay now."

She eased away from me, I stood, and she walked me to the door. There, she gave me a fierce hug. "Thank you."

I slipped my hand behind her neck, impelled by a sudden urge to kiss her. I caught myself in time and removed my hand from her neck before the urge could run amok. "Glad I could help."

The feel of her nestled in my arms stayed with me all the way home.

Chapter 9

06/12/2003 – The Wrecked Cadillac

I didn't know what drove me to look into Tom
Mercer's accident. Maybe it was the suffering it had put
in Steph's life. Or her belief it wasn't his fault. Or Jeff
Styles telling me it was. Maybe I'd been curious since
she first told me about it, and seeing her so torn up last
night jacked my curiosity to the max. Maybe I just had
some kind of white knight urge to rescue her from the
dragon of despair, a knight-errant on a quest to right the
wrong done to her.

I drove to the *Sentinel-Tribune* office the next
morning and asked the receptionist how I'd go about
finding an article from April of last year. She directed
me to the Archives Office where a lady set me up at a
computer. "Type in whatever you're after—a name, a
place, an event—click on SEARCH, and you'll get a
list of every article pertaining to it arranged by date."

I typed in 'Tom Mercer' and got forty hits. The
first was a photo op of Tom being admitted to the
county bar in 1995. I scrolled down the list. A mix of
cases he handled before the local court and charity
events he and Steph attended until I hit the one dated
October 5, 2002. *Local Attorney Seriously Injured In
Crash.*

I clicked on the entry and the article I remembered

filled the screen. I skimmed it then printed it. The last three articles were short follow-ups over the next week. *Local Attorney In Coma After Crash. Police Say Attorney Ran Off Road. Attorney Remains In Coma.*

I printed them out, paid for the copies, and left the paper. Being a car guy, I wondered what happened to the Cadillac Tom had been driving when he crashed. Back at the shop, I started calling the half dozen salvage yards in the county. I hit pay dirt at Toland Salvage. Fred said the Caddy had been hauled to his yard and thought it might still be there. He said he'd check and call me back. Five minutes later, he said he had it.

I drove to Fred's, and he led me across the rutted muddy yard to the Caddy. To my left, metal squealed as a crusher reduced a car once someone's pride and joy to a three-by-three metal cube. The Caddy's trunk lid was gone, probably to a body shop repairing a similar Caddy. I circled the bronze DeVille, taking in the damage. Roof crushed just enough to jam the doors and scuffed from front to back, windshield and rear window shattered, right side scratched and peppered with small dings, left side fenders and back door creased and scraped, wheels gouged and scored, driver's airbag deployed. "Where's the driver's door?"

Fred lifted his Quaker State cap and ran his hand over his short gray hair. "Had to scrap it. EMTs bent it all to hell getting the driver out."

I pointed to the raked left side. "How did all this get here?"

Fred replanted his cap on his head. "Got me. Mebbe when it rolled? Mebbe scraping along a tree when Acme Towing pulled it out."

The damage didn't line up with either one, and dark smears on the bronze paint said another car sideswiped the Caddy. The DeVille's left rear corner was caved in, the taillight lens gone except for a few shards clinging to the frame. "What happened here?"

"No idea." He raised his thick shoulders into a shrug. "Heard the guy'd been drinkin' 'fore he crashed. Maybe he backed into something leavin' the bar? Be my guess anyway."

I switched on the small digital camera I'd grabbed from my desk before leaving for Fred's yard and circled the DeVille again, snapping pictures—lots of them—of the damage. Back in my truck, I read the article on Tom's crash and studied the accompanying photos with more care. The article said the Caddy had rolled onto its roof after going off the road and dropping its right wheels into the drainage ditch. The photo showed the Caddy upside down, its nose nudging a tree. The *Police Say Attorney Ran Off Road* article added only that the police thought Tom fell asleep before crashing.

I compared the articles on Tom's crash to the photos I'd taken of his car. The crash unfolded in my mind, and I could match most of the Caddy's damage to how the crash played out. But not the damaged left rear corner or mangled driver's side.

I read *Local Attorney In Coma After Crash.* The article reported Tom hadn't been wearing his seatbelt and had been found with his head and shoulders against the Caddy's roof, the deflated airbag draped over his face. *Jesus.* Why didn't he push it aside? Maybe he'd been rattled or possibly unconscious.

I fired my truck and drove to Millers Run Road. Rolling slowly along it, I tossed glances between the roadside and the picture in the paper until I found the match. I parked my truck a few yards past there and walked back. Using the *Sen-Trib*'s photo as a guide, I stood where Tom's Caddy had left the road and studied the crash site for a few minutes, trying to visualize the car on its roof. No way a tree raked the Caddy's side as Acme Towing pulled it out. And I couldn't spot anything that would have damaged its rear bumper and taillight. Something wasn't adding up.

Driving away, I considered visiting Tom Mercer at Oakhurst then decided against it. What would be the point? He couldn't answer my questions. And I couldn't read his mind.

Back at D-J Auto Renewal, I headed for the paint shop. Gene Parilli, my head bodyman, was sanding the side of a '63 Ford Galaxie fastback. I waited until he shut off the pneumatic sander and ran a hand over the panel before I said his name.

He tugged the paper mask covering his nose and mouth down and shoved his goggles onto his forehead. "Hey, Bossman, what's up?"

I showed him the digital camera. "Got some photos for you to look at, tell me what you think."

"Okay." He slapped the sanding dust from his hands and arms and brushed it from his black hair as he walked outside then lit a Newport and took the camera. "What am I looking for?"

"You tell me." Driving back to the shops, I'd reached a fairly solid conclusion about what had happened to Tom, but I wanted Gene to confirm it. Or show me where I went wrong.

He cycled through the pictures. "It's a total." He shifted his gaze to me. "Why're you showing me pictures of an oh-one Caddy? You don't even like them cars."

"Gonna make it into a four-door ragtop."

"You're kidding, right?"

"Nope." I held my serious expression for a bit then grinned.

Gene broke out one of his own. "Geez, you had me going there for a second, Bossman. So why you really interested in it?"

"I'm curious what happened to it." I pointed to the camera. "What do you see?"

Gene scrolled through the pictures again. "Hit something. Rolled over. Landed shiny side down, knocked the roof out of plumb."

I handed him the *Local Attorney Suffers Serious Injuries In Crash* and *Police Say Attorney Ran Off Road* articles. He skimmed through them then looked at me. "Okay?"

"You see anything that doesn't line up?"

"Yeah, maybe." Gene cycled through the pictures one more time, pausing at a couple. "The bang on the back corner don't go with the rest of it. Might have happened in the crash, but I don't think so. I could tell you better if I saw the car."

"It's at Fred Toland's place. Go check it out, tell me what you see."

Chapter 10

06/16/2003 – How It Got That Way

Gene tapped on my office door Monday morning, strolled in, and dropped into a chair by my desk. "Looked at that Caddy at Fred's Saturday like you asked."

I laid aside the bill I was reviewing, curious what he found. "And?"

"You still got them pictures?"

I lifted the camera from a desk drawer and passed it to him. He turned it on and searched through the pictures then reversed the camera so I could see the one of the Caddy's left rear on the LCD screen. "It don't show up real good here, but there's some scuffs on the bumper where it's pushed in. That's how the taillight got busted, not when it rolled."

I took the camera and studied the picture then pressed the zoom button to enlarge it. The scuffs showed as short scrapes on the corner of the bumper. I checked several others shots I'd taken of that corner of the Caddy. The paint transfer was visible in every one, a dark smear on the bronze. I chastised myself for missing it when I looked the Caddy over.

"Check out driver's side."

I advanced to that picture. "I saw that before. It's all scraped up. Like he got sideswiped."

"That's what happened. If it'd just gone off the road and rolled, it wouldn't be all beat up."

I set the camera down. "Maybe he did the sideswiping. He'd had a couple drinks before he crashed. And he was tired. Maybe he scrubbed along a light pole or something."

"Scratches and scuffs aren't right for that. They'd show direction, front to back or back to front, whichever way he was moving. Like when you scrape your arm along concrete. These go both ways like him and the other car did *this*." He held his hands up, flat and edge to edge and rubbed them back and forth against each other. Picking the camera up, he clicked to another image in the memory. "It shows up better in this photo. See what I mean?"

I enlarged the picture on the LCD. "Now I do."

"Him and another car were trading paint." Gene was a big NASCAR fan, so their lingo peppered his talk. "Go to the next picture."

A shot of the left rear door. "What about it?"

"See those dark smudges on the panel?"

I studied the picture. *How the hell had I missed them?* "Yeah."

"They're donuts." Another NASCAR term. Arcing black streaks from the tires of the other car rubbing against the Caddy.

I set the camera on my desk then tapped it. "What do you think happened?"

"Start to finish? I'd say another car popped the back corner. Could have been accidental. Guy goes to pass the Caddy, cuts it a little too close, clips the back bumper. Could have been the Caddy driver pissed the guy off somehow. He gets alongside the Caddy, they rub doorhandles, the Caddy goes off the road and rolls."

He'd read Tom's accident the same as I had. Now to ask the question I'd been chewing on for two days. "Could the other car have run the Caddy off the road intentionally?"

Gene mulled that over for a bit. "Once they bumped doors, the Caddy could have swerved away and wrecked. But, yeah, the other car could have shoved it."

"Either way, there'd be damage to the other car?"

"Oh, yeah. Front bumper and all down the passenger side. And it was red."

"How do you know?"

"It don't show in the pictures, and you probably missed it 'cause that side of the Caddy was in shadow when you looked at it, but in the light, those smears on it are dark red. Found a paint chip, too, in the seam between the rub strip and the panel on the back driver side door. Spent some time last night going through my color binders, lookin' for a match. Haven't found it yet. I'll keep looking."

Chapter 11

06/17/2003 – Challenging the Chief

Andy Cummings, Schuylerton's Chief of Police, and I met at the Burger King on Poplar the next day. We went way back, as in to first grade. Andy's tall and lean with deep-set brown eyes and sandy hair and moustache, both with tinges of gray. He had on light gray slacks, a white shirt, blue tie and blazer, and black cop brogans.

We hadn't seen each other in a couple months, so with Whoppers, fries, and shakes on the table between us, we did the 'What have you been up to lately?' thing. When it wound down, Andy asked, "You said you wanted to see me. What's on your mind?"

"You remember a crash last October where Tom Mercer ran off Millers Run Road and parked his Caddy on its roof?"

"October fifth. I worked it." Andy regularly pulled routine patrol shifts. "What about it?"

"What happened?"

Andy chewed through a bite of his Whopper. "Mercer fell asleep, went off the road, and rolled it."

"Anything at the time make you think it was anything other than that?"

"Why are you asking?"

"His wife told me she didn't believe he fell

asleep." Not quite how she'd worded it, but close enough for the moment. "She said he was a careful driver, never had a wreck, never even had a speeding ticket."

"How do you know her?"

"Met her a couple months back."

Andy washed down the last bite of his Whopper with a slug of shake. "Look, she's a nice lady who got a shitty deal. I wanted to believe her when she said hubby wouldn't fall asleep and crash, but everything pointed to that and nothing else."

"Such as?"

"He'd been working all kinds of crazy hours for several months prior, and he and some other lawyers from his firm hit the Roadhouse for drinks that night. Tired guy with a couple drinks in him is a prime candidate for nodding off at the wheel, I don't care how good a driver he is."

"She ever say anything to you about someone running him off the road?"

He sucked up more milkshake. "Situation like that—young couple with the world at their feet, and suddenly it's all in the crapper 'cause of something he did—it's natural for her to want someone other than him to lay the blame on. Doesn't mean it happened that way. And all the phone calls in the world won't change it."

"Phone calls?"

"January, I started getting calls from some big guns—state representatives and senators, a superior and a supreme court judge, had one last week from the attorney general himself—all asking me to reopen the investigation. I told every one of them to bring me some evidence, and I'd be happy to. None of them ever did." He finished his shake. "You want coffee?"

"Always."

I disposed of our trays while he was at the counter. Andy returned with two large coffees, set one in front of me, and peeled back the tab on his. "What's got you asking about Mercer's accident?"

Time for me to step onto some thin ice. Andy was a good cop, and I didn't want to accuse him of slipping up at Tom Mercer's crash, but I was about to question whether he had. "Evidence. You know my head bodyman, Gene Parilli? He looked at Mercer's Caddy the other day and found some things on it that say another car was involved."

"What things?"

I laid the folder of photos from my camera on the table, opened it, and spread the photos out. "Busted taillight, paint transfer on the rear bumper where it's pushed in, and damage all down the left side."

Andy studied each one. "He could have crunched his bumper backing out of a stall in the Roadhouse's lot. Tired plus booze equals messed up judgment. The damage down the side could have happened any time— a week, a day before he crashed—and any place. On the street, in a parking lot, maybe even in his own garage."

I shook my head. "Gene knows crashes. He says the crunched taillight came from a car popping Mercer's Caddy there, like maybe the driver clipped it pulling out to pass Mercer. He thinks Mercer swerved when the other car was alongside him, they sideswiped, Mercer over-corrected, went off the road, and into the tree."

"A hit and run?"

"Could be. Could be Mercer sideswiped the other car as payback for clipping his bumper and ended up getting the short end of the stick."

"I don't recall anything that made me think there might be another vehicle involved." He ran a hand over his face. "Maybe I missed it."

I had always admired Andy's ability to admit he might be wrong.

He took another big slug of coffee and swallowed it in several parts as he thought. "I need to take a second look at Mercer's Caddy."

Chapter 12

06/21/2003 – Spreading the News

I was in my driveway Saturday morning, washing the metallic light blue '66 Pontiac LeMans I'd restored for Amy. It was going to be my birthday present to her the year she died. My shop guys were putting the finishing touches on it when she was killed.

A maroon Ford Crown Victoria stopped at the curb, and Andy Cummings got out bearing a tray holding two Pete's Perk coffees. His bland expression offered no clue if he was here to pat me on the back or smack me upside the head. He came up the driveway as I rinsed the suds off the trunk of the LeMans before turning as if I was going to douse him with the spray.

"Hosing down a police officer is a misdemeanor. Ruining Pete's Perk coffee is a felony. Or should be." His weak smile said whatever's on his mind was serious.

I lowered the hose. "I definitely don't want to ruin their coffee."

"Gee, thanks. You got a couple minutes?" He flicked a glance at the LeMans. "Or you want to finish that first?"

It was a few minutes after nine in the morning, so my oak tree would shade the driveway for another hour or two. "I have time."

He followed me into my garage and set the tray on my workbench. He handed me a cup, peeled back the tab on his, and swigged. "Looked at Mercer's Caddy after I talked to you yesterday. You and Gene called it right. Somebody popped it in the back end then Mercer and the other guy banged doors." He shook his head ruefully. "I missed it that night."

I propped a hip against my workbench and sampled my coffee. "What happens now?"

"Since I have evidence, I can justify reopening the investigation. The State Police Crime Lab is taking the Caddy to do a full work up on it."

"Think they'll find anything?"

He downed more coffee. "If there's anything there. Meanwhile, I'll go over the original accident reports, see if I overlooked anything." Another rueful head shake. "I really dropped the ball there. I saw a car off the road on its roof, no other car around, made the jump to it being a one-car, never thought it might be anything but." His tone said he was disappointed with himself.

I wouldn't beat him up further. "What about other cops that night? They agree with you?"

"Parker and Wyzkowski? I don't recall either one saying maybe it wasn't a one-car. Either they missed it too, or were afraid to disagree with the boss." Andy offered a wry grin. "Gonna have to talk to them about that." Another long swig of coffee then he shook his head. "Damn! I should have looked Mercer's car over more thoroughly. Should have listened to Mrs. Mercer, too. Should have figured she wasn't calling me all the time just to hear herself talk."

"It's called being human, Andy. It's what makes you a good cop."

"Doesn't make being wrong go down any easier. I gotta make this right. For the Mercers as well as for myself. You interested in helping?"

"Absolutely."

"Parilli said there'd be damage—maybe heavy—to the right front corner and passenger side of the car that hit Mercer, said it was dark red, and he's looking for an exact match, right? You mind calling around to other body shops, see if any of them remember having a dark red vehicle damaged like that come in the week or so after Mercer crashed?"

"Happy to."

"And that's all you do." He raised a warning finger. "No poking around in this thing."

"There's no law against me asking questions about Mercer and his accident."

"It's not an accident. It's a crime, a hit-and run. If Mercer dies any time within a year of when it happened, it's at least vehicular homicide." He aimed a finger at me. "You do anything to screw my investigation up and, friend or not, I will skin you and hang your tanned hide on my wall." His cell rang. "Cummings." He stepped a few feet away from me and listened for a bunch of seconds. "I'll be there in five." He put the phone away. "Duty calls." Snapping the cap on his coffee cup, he strode toward his car.

"You going to tan my hide if I tell Steph the news?"

He faced me, walking backwards. "Be my guest. But let me know what she says."

I finished off my coffee, wishing again I had Steph's number so I could give her the good news. No, this kind of news merited delivery in person. She might be at the mental health clinic or Safe Haven or maybe running errands this morning. I'd have a better chance of catching her at home this afternoon.

After lunch, I showered and headed for Glenwood Heights. Making the turn onto Elm Circle, even before I could see her house, I knew somehow Steph was home. That spooked me a little.

The minute her house came into view, my gaze locked on her kneeling in the grass, weeding the flowerbed on the shady side of the house. My breathing hitched, and my heart did a little tap dance against my ribs.

Blooming flowers and shrubs splashed color along the house and across the yard. Darkened mulch showed she'd been watering, and a hose snaked across the grass, dribbling wet onto the flagstone walk.

She stood as I pulled into her driveway. She had on a charcoal tee and baggy black shorts. Her legs were long and tan, and her hair was gathered in a messy bun at the nape of her neck. Amy wore her sandy locks that way often, and many times my undoing it and finger-combing the tangles out led to making love. I wondered if unraveling Steph's chestnut tresses would do the same then pushed the thought away.

Her eyes brightened, and the flicker of a smile touched the corners of her mouth. She strode toward me, stripping off her gloves. "What a pleasant surprise. What brings you here?"

"News about Tom."

Worry darkened her eyes as she wiped a sheen of sweat off her brow. "Good or bad?"

"A little of both."

The worry faded as she dried her hand on her

shorts. "Would you like a glass of iced tea? It's fresh this morning."

"Sounds good."

She motioned for me to follow her through a gate in the fence to a patio facing her pool. I sat on a wrought iron chair at a matching table shaded by an umbrella. She disappeared through the slider door, returning a few minutes later with a pitcher and two ice-filled glasses on a tray. She slipped onto the chair facing me, poured, and passed me a glass then gazed at me with wide, nervous eyes. "What did you learn?"

"The day after you had your bad night, I looked at Tom's car. Gene Parilli, my head bodyman, looked it over as well." I hesitated. What I said next would confirm Steph's belief but might be hard for her to accept. I drank from my glass. The tea was super sweet, the way I liked it. "We found damage we both believe shows another car hit his. I showed what we found to Andy Cummings. He's my friend as well as the police chief. He looked at Tom's car, too, and he agrees with us."

"I told him it couldn't be Tom's fault." Tears rose in her eyes again. "Why didn't he listen to me?"

"Cops are human, Steph. They make mistakes. Everything Andy saw that night pointed to a one-car accident, so he never looked beyond that. He's upset by that and sorry he didn't listen to you, but he's fixing that now. He's going to move heaven and earth to find what really happened."

"I assume that's the good part." She stiffened as if bracing to take a blow. "What's the bad?"

She wouldn't want me to beat around the bush. "Tom's accident may not have been an accident.

There's no proof yet, but it's possible whoever hit him did it intentionally to force him off the road."

Her hands trembled, and I took her glass from her and set it on the table. After a moment, her hands steadied, and she dabbed tears from her eyes with a napkin. In a voice raspy with hurt, she said, "What happens now?"

"The State Police are taking his car to their Crime Lab to go over it for evidence. Andy'll reinvestigate Tom's accident, review all the reports, and probably talk to the people he talked to at the time. So he may be in touch with you."

"And what good will that do?" she said glumly. "It's been eight months. People won't remember what happened. Will the State Police even be able to find any proof someone ran Tom off the road after all this time?"

"Andy says they're good. If there's any evidence to be found, they'll find it. Between them and Andy, they will find out what happened to Tom. I'm helping, too. Whoever hit Tom's car didn't get off scot-free. He had damage to his car around the front end and down one side. I'm going to contact all the body shops in the area, ask if any fixed a car with that kind of damage in the weeks after Tom crashed."

Her eyes brightened with hope. "Do you think one of them repaired the car that hit Tom's?"

"Possibly. But whoever hit Tom could also have had his car fixed by a guy working out of his garage."

Her shoulders sagged fractionally. "So we might never find out who hit Tom."

"Don't say never. Now that we're sure another car was involved in his crash, it's a matter of finding out who the driver was. We're coming at it from two directions. One of us will find something."

"And when you do all that, then what? It won't make Tom whole again."

She had me there.

Chapter 13

06/23/2003 – The Lowdown

I slid onto the stool next to Frank Morrison at the counter in Abe's Deli. The hole-in-the-wall hoagie place was his favorite lunch spot. He gathered a huge Italian sub in a two-handed grip, took a bite, then hurriedly dabbed oil from his chin before it could drip onto his crisp white shirt.

I had called him earlier that Monday and asked if we could meet for a few minutes on a personal matter. He'd said he'd be in at Abe's at one.

A waitress stopped in front of me. "Getcha?"

"A number eleven, meat, cheese, and lettuce only, and a Dr. Pepper, please."

"Be a minute." She headed to the prep area.

Frank wiped his chin again. "What's on your mind, Dan?"

"How well do you know Stephanie Mercer?"

He shot a glance at the girl making my hoagie. "Let's move." He carried his plate and soda to one of the four tiny booths at the rear of the deli.

Once I sat across from him, he said, "I thought you might want to know more about her after your go-round with Holland Carter. I called Graham McNamara after I talked to you and read him the riot act about Carter's behavior."

"I heard you did from Jeff Styles the next day. Thanks."

"It's what I'm here for. I also put a flea in Graham's ear about Holl questioning your financial status."

"Good. Thanks." Several years before I kicked Jay Winters out, I'd invented an improved cruise control. One of the big three automakers had bought the patent rights for more than the combined GNPs of several third-world countries. I don't advertise it.

Frank sipped root beer. "How exactly did you meet Stephanie Mercer?"

"She was in Lou's one night two months ago, decimating his stock. I drove her home so she didn't wipe out a family of four driving herself."

"Smart move on your part. If she had, the legal implications for you and Lou could have been serious." He bit off more hoagie, mopped his chin, and chewed. "No kidding. What can you tell me about her?"

"What do you want to know?"

"Anything you can tell me."

"Well, let's see." Bite. Blot. Chew. "She grew up in Sewickley, which if you don't know, is a very, *very* wealthy suburb of Pittsburgh, with all the perks associated with the lifestyle. Large homes on large lots, chauffeurs, private schools, piano and dance lessons, the whole nine yards. Attended UPenn, where she met Tom. They married after she graduated then lived in Ithaca while he was at Cornell Law, came here in ninety-four when he joined OSM. She's charming, witty, cultured, but also very down to earth, never puts on airs because of her background."

"And Tom?"

"You couldn't find a nicer guy. Like Stephanie, he came from money—Mercer Steel and Iron—but never lorded it over others or looked down on those who had less. He told me once he got a bigger rush out of helping Joe Average get justice than winning a million-dollar suit for Walt Wealthy."

"Like you."

"Well…" Frank glanced down and cleared his throat. "Yeah. Unlike me, however, he was a brilliant lawyer. Before his accident, talk around the courthouse water cooler was he had a lock on becoming a full partner at OSM this year and landing a seat on the bench in the next ten. His accident was a tragic loss for the legal community. An even more terrible one for Stephanie." He paused to glance at me. "You know what that's like."

I nodded. I imagined Steph's pain less than a year after Tom's accident was as acute as mine had been that long after losing Amy.

"Why this sudden interest in the Mercers?"

"Steph and I've met a bunch of times since I drove her home. She doesn't think Tom's accident was his fault, thinks something or someone ran him off the road. I've found evidence backing her up."

"And you suspect she did the running off?"

The waitress parked my hoagie and soda in front of me. I waited until she retreated. "It's been in the back of my mind. I'm looking for reason to believe otherwise."

He ate a bite of hoagie, wiped his chin, and held up a forefinger. After he swallowed, he said, "Has she given you reason to think she did it?"

"I'm trying to cover all the bases."

"I can't think of any reason why she would want to harm Tom."

"No gossip or rumors about trouble in their marriage?"

"Not that I ever heard." A stop for a taste of his soda then he took his cell from a pocket. "But maybe Carol knows something I don't. Let me ask her."

I tackled my sandwich, every bite an exercise in jaw stretching, while he talked to his wife. After a couple minutes, he closed the phone and tucked it away. "Carol says the only talk about Stephanie and Tom's marriage was envy over how good it was, and that Stephanie running Tom off the road is as likely as the sun setting in the east. So I would say unless you encounter some irrefutable indicator of her involvement, you're safe in assuming she is free of culpability in Tom's accident."

That was good enough for me.

Chomp. Swipe. Munch. "Carol says Stephanie was asking about you, too. She ran into her at Bon-Ton several weekends ago and she asked Carol what kind of person you were." He smiled around the straw as he sucked in soda. "Carol told her you were a no good, rotten, worthless bum who couldn't be trusted as far as she could throw you."

I grinned. "Sounds about right."

"Actually, she told Stephanie you were a terrific guy with a big heart who would be a great friend." He studied me through a longer drink of soda. "Dan, I'm not trying to pry into your private life, but is there something going on between you and Stephanie Mercer?"

I swallowed a bite of hoagie. "Nothing's going on.

Nothing more than...friendship, I guess you'd call it. Like I have with Nora, like you have with Betty."

"As long as that's all it is."

Yet deep down inside I carried the faint hope it would turn into more than that. "You said Tom was going to make partner at OSM. Any chance someone there was jealous about that?"

"I want to say no, but I honestly don't know. I don't know the internal dynamics at OSM." Frank checked his watch. "You need anything else? I don't want to cut you off, but I gotta run. Client meeting in ten minutes."

"Can't think of anything."

Frank stuffed the last bite of hoagie in his mouth and washed it down with the last of his Pepsi. "If I come up with something, I'll let you know." Picking up his paper plate and empty can, he edged out of the booth.

I mulled over what he'd said through the rest of my lunch then drove to the Schuylerton police station. The former carriage house sat behind the Schuyler mansion, now Schuylerton's City Hall. I sat down facing Andy across his desk. "I need a favor."

"Depends on what it is."

"What can you tell me about Stephanie Mercer?"

He leaned back in his chair. "Wondered when you'd get around to asking."

"Meaning?"

"When I told you I agreed Tom Mercer had been wrecked intentionally, you never asked if I thought she did it."

"Do you?"

He twitched a micro-shrug. "I need evidence

before I can say."

"So what can you tell me about her?"

"She didn't pop up on my radar, which means my guys haven't had a lot of contact with her." He rocked forward, snagged a folder from the right side of his desk, and opened it. "A minor fender bender in ninety-six, a couple traffic violations, and some parking tickets is all. No record of complaints involving her. State Police stopped her for speeding twice. That's all I have on her." He closed the folder. "You want me to dig deeper, I can."

"I'd appreciate it."

"It may take some time." He eyed me for a second. "You thinking she had something to do with her husband's crash?"

"I want to make sure she didn't."

Chapter 14

06/30/2003 – A Welcome Visitor

Monday, I was back in my office after my early afternoon swing through the shops when Nora said over the intercom, "Dan, there's a woman here to see you."

I didn't get many women seeking D-J's services but I'd had a few wanting a car restored, sometimes as a present for their husband or boyfriend, so I wasn't thrown off track by Nora's words. "Be right out."

However, Steph standing by the white '65 Plymouth Barracuda in the showroom threw me. A black blouse and boots and charcoal jeans looked like haute couture on her. The breezy day had ruffled her chestnut hair, leaving a lock hanging by her eye.

I jammed my hands in my jeans pockets to remove the temptation to brush it back into place. "Hey there. What brings you here?"

She raised the carry-out cups from Morning Mug she held in each hand. "I thought maybe you could use a little restoring."

"The fuel that powers my engine. Thank you." I took one from her and motioned her toward my office. "Please tell me you didn't drive down here just to bring me coffee." Not that I'd mind if she did. Anything that got me a chance to see her was great by me.

"I did." She entered my office and beelined to my

picture wall, scanned them, and pointed to one. "Is that Jay Leno?" Awe in her voice.

"Yep. With the first car we did for him. We've done two more since then."

She pointed to another picture. "Meryl Streep and Clint Eastwood?"

"Unh-hunh. The truck behind them was in *The Bridges of Madison County*. We restored it for the owner."

"I had no idea." She stared at the photo for a second then sat in a chair facing my desk and lifted a gift-wrapped box from her tote. "I also came because I wanted to give you this."

The box was about four by five by three, the wrapping paper red-and-gold with a black oval sticker reading *Fiore Jewelers*. I peeled away the paper, revealing a dark blue SEIKO box, opened it, and sucked in a breath. Inside was a titanium chronograph with a bright blue face. Tucked under it was a note. *For all the time you've given me.*

I stared at it for several moments, feeling a half a step behind myself until I managed a lame, "Steph, it's beautiful. And I am deeply touched. Thank you. But it wasn't necessary."

"You've given me the one thing I can never return—your time. All the hours you spent listening to my troubles you could have spent with friends or doing something you wanted to do or simply relaxing."

"I was doing something I wanted to do with a friend. That night in Lou's parking lot, you wanted to kill yourself. If I can prevent that, I'll give you every hour I have to do it."

"You already did what no one—not even some

very powerful people—could do: you got the police to believe me." She laid her hand atop mine. "That means more to me than you'll ever know."

I slipped the watch on. "Then thank you again." I smiled at her. "Spending those hours with you was a better than fair trade."

She gave me the faint hint of a smile before ducking her head. "I also have a favor to ask. Months ago, you offered to show me around. I'm here to collect on that. If this is a good time."

"It is." I stood. "Come on."

As I escorted her across the lot to the disassembly building, an almost overwhelming sense of joy filled me. She cared about me, was interested in me and what I do, touching me to the core of my being. And sending a flash of confusion through my head. Emotions like joy died with Amy.

I opened the side door to the disassembly building. "Here's where it starts. Every car we restore comes here first." I waved toward the men tearing down a platinum '67 Buick Gran Sport. "These guys take it down to a pile of parts except for the engine, trans, and differential. They get torn down in the drivetrain building. The body and frame go to the body shop and the rest go to other sub-shops, where they get restored." I introduced her to Grant Hixson. "He's in charge of this restoration. This car is his baby until it rolls out the door."

Steph eyed the mound of parts growing as the Buick shrank. "How do you keep track of everything?"

"Two-fold. First, every car gets assigned a project number." I showed her the tag on the Buick's engine, sitting on a wheeled rack. "Every part on the car gets that same number." I led her to a computer terminal on the workbench. "Secondly, as each part or component makes its way through the restoration process, the people doing the work enter daily progress notes." I typed in a number and the record for a '59 Mercury Monterey sedan came on the screen. "As of yesterday, this car's about halfway through the process. The mechanicals—brakes, steering, and suspension—are restored, the engine, transmission and differential are about half done, the electrical system is refurbished and ready to install, the body's ready for primer, and the seats have been reupholstered."

I guided her through the upholstery, drivetrain, frame, electrical, and body shops, explaining what happened in each one. An hour later, we were back in the main shop where a crew was finishing up a '71 AMC Javelin. "From here this car goes to the showroom out front for a month then back to the owner."

"I never realized restoring a car was such an involved process. I thought you...I don't know...just fixed up the body and painted it."

"That's all some shops do, but the good ones do like we do." I realized I was trying to do the same thing with Tom's accident. Tearing it down to nothing but pieces so I could put it back together the way it should be.

"And you do it all in a year start to finish?"

"About that. Some take longer if they're rare and parts are hard to come by, or if there's a lot to do on the car, like if the body's riddled with cancer and needs a lot of metalwork, or if the company that does our re-chroming is backed up."

She looked around as we strolled toward my office. "I never expected the place to be so clean and bright, either. I pictured dim light and grimy floors and men in greasy coveralls."

Maybe in the good old days. "Keeping it clean cuts down on accidents and injuries. And when you restore cars for people like Jay Leno and Reggie Jackson, sending it back with grubby fingerprints all over it won't fly. So, except for the sterility part, we're more like an operating room than a garage."

Outside my office door, she said, "Thank you for showing me around. I truly enjoyed it. I imagine you have a lot to do, so I should be going." She hesitated a moment. "Can you spare me another minute first?"

"As many as you need. What's on your mind?"

"Since I met you, I've been feeling better about where I am with Tom and his condition. It doesn't weigh me down the way it used to because I can turn to you when it gets to me. But my unloading on you all the time has to wear on you as well. The Fourth of July is this weekend and I'd like us to do something fun for a change. Unless you have plans."

"I don't." Waxing my Ventura could wait.

"Then I'm inviting you to a swim and cookout at my house. Unless you'd rather do something else."

"Swimming and a cookout sound perfect to me. And maybe the annual fireworks display at Schuyler Park at sundown?"

"Definitely! Swimming, a cookout, and fireworks it is."

"What time and what can I bring?"

"Around noon. Nothing but a bathing suit and yourself."

Chapter 15

07/04/2003 – Swimming and Fireworks

The previous four days had crawled by slower than the week before Christmas when I was a kid.

Steph answered my knock wearing black jogging shorts and a charcoal UPenn tee. As she led me through the house, she said, "Dan, I'm sorry."

"For what?"

"I should have asked before now if you're seeing someone. If you are, she can't be too happy about you spending the day with me."

"Not a problem. I'm a free agent." Had been since Amy's death. I'd never met anyone I wanted to spend the rest of my life with. Although that had been changing lately.

She sighed relief. "And I never asked you if you like to swim or if you can swim. I just assumed you'd enjoy it on a hot summer day."

"I can dogpaddle with the best of them. Even if I didn't swim, lolling around a pool sounds like a great way to spend the holiday." *And spending it with you makes it even better.* I needed to stop thinking like that, especially about a married woman.

"If you need to change," she pointed to a hallway off the kitchen, "the bathroom's the second door on the right."

"Nope." I slapped my shorts lightly. "Just have to shed these."

"Me, too." She grasped the handle to the slider between the kitchen and the patio then turned to me. "There's one condition: No talking about Tom today. If I start, stop me."

"You got it."

She pulled the slider open and we stepped outside. The day was an ideal Fourth of July, hot and sunny, a tad humid, and with a touch of a warm breeze. I set down the small duffel I'd packed then stripped off my street clothes, watching Steph discard her tee and shorts as I did. Under them, she had on a black maillot. Something about a beautiful woman in a swimsuit—be it the most modest one piece or skimpiest bikini—captures a guy's attention. Steph was a beautiful woman and her suit was only moderately demure. I wouldn't have noticed the house next door exploding.

At the edge of the pool, we basked in the sun for a moment before she said, "Race you."

I hit the water a second later, chasing her freestyle. We touched the far wall in a dead heat. She said, "Again," and shoved off.

Another tie. She shouted, "One more time."

I won by a hand at the shallow end. She palmed her hair back from her face. "You lied to me!" Her light tone said she wasn't angry. "That was no dogpaddle! You're a great swimmer. I won medals in high school and college and couldn't beat you."

She was stunningly beautiful with no makeup, her wet hair plastered to her skull, and water beaded on her skin, prisming the sun's rays where they hit the drops right. "I had to impress the SI swimsuit issue cover girl."

"I'm not her. I'm—"

I touched her cheek. "More beautiful than her."

Our faces were inches apart, her gaze locked on mine. In another moment, we'd kiss. I could see the same thought in her eyes. Anticipation tingled through me like a low voltage electrical current. She held my gaze for another second then looked away and took a step back. Good thing she did. Otherwise, I would have crossed that small gap and kissed her. Dismay and relief filled me. Dismay we hadn't kissed, relief we hadn't crossed a line we shouldn't even go near. I kept plenty of space between us as we swam and played in the water.

We climbed out of the pool after an hour and Steph raided her fridge for cold beers. She eyed me intently as she handed me a Molson Ale then sat facing me across the wrought iron table. "Are you feeling okay?"

Over the months we'd been meeting, I'd become increasingly drawn to Steph, stirring feelings mirroring the ones I'd had for Amy after I met her. And today, stirring temptations that were hard to resist. "Yeah. Why?"

"You seem...different somehow...like something's bothering you."

"Nothing." *Other than wanting to hold you and kiss you and knowing I shouldn't.*

A long pull from her bottle. "You're in a different frame of mind than you were earlier. Did I do something to upset you?"

You were going to kiss me and I wanted you to and you didn't. I told her a version of the truth. "Sometimes I get thinking about things I shouldn't and can't shake them." Time to change the subject. "Did I see you coming out of Monica's one day last week?" Monica Reese owned a high-end dress store in downtown Schuylerton.

Steph nodded. "I was picking up my dress for the Safe Haven Women's Shelter fund-raising dinner. Was that you blowing your horn at me?"

"Yep."

"I thought it looked like your truck, but I couldn't see who was driving."

"It was me." I sipped my Molson. Nothing like a cold beer on a hot day. *Safer to think about that.*

"I saw your name on the shelter's gold donor's list at the dinner, in memory of Amy." Gold donors gave a thousand dollars or more. "It was very generous of you."

"She believed strongly that a woman in danger should have a safe place to go. She had a friend in nursing school who didn't. Her boyfriend killed her."

"I almost lost a friend the same way." Steph shifted her gaze to her bottle for a moment. "Have you ever gone to one of the shelter's fundraisers?"

"Not really my thing." I slugged back some ale.

"I'm on the board of directors, so attendance is expected. If Tom is still…incapacitated next year, would you escort me?"

"Sure." When the time came, I'd make an excuse not to go. I wouldn't dare. A woman as beautiful and desirable as Steph in an evening gown would be too hard to resist.

We swam and played in the pool and lazed on deck chairs, cooled off in the water and warmed in the sun until the afternoon was gone. Splashing around brought us inches apart way too often. I managed, barely, to keep my growing desire to kiss her in check each time. From the unease on her face, Steph had the same problem. Sitting knee to knee at the small patio table, dining on barbequed chicken and baked potatoes, wasn't any easier. How much longer could we walk the line without crossing it? Dinner over, we dressed for the fireworks. Steph picked light gray shorts and a black polo. Was there anything she didn't look good wearing?

I kept a polite space between us as we strolled into Schuyler Park and found a spot on a small rise. The growing throng nudged her over until she stood in front of me. Her hair smelled of coconut and flowers. As the second burst filled the sky with arcing spots of light, a shift in the crowd staggered her, and I gripped her waist and pulled her against me to keep her from falling. She gazed back at me as she drew my arms around her. And there it was again, the consuming desire to kiss her, not a quick polite peck on her cheek, but a long lingering one on her lips. The same desire was in her eyes as well. She saved us again by turning to watch the next shower of colors but kept my arms pinned at her waist. I felt like the guy who had the hottest girl in school as his prom date.

The show, as always, was magnificent, and we oohed and aahed along with everyone else at each impressive burst. With the last one fading to trails of smoke, spots lit up the American flag in the center of the park. The crowd faced it, the Schuylerton High band struck up the national anthem, and everyone sang along, their hands over their hearts. As the last notes faded into the night, Steph shivered.

"You okay?"

She nodded, dabbing at tears gathered in the corners of her eyes. "Whenever I hear the Star-Spangled Banner, I get chills and tear up. You probably think that's silly."

"Not one bit. I get them, too."

I took her hand so we wouldn't get separated in the milling, jostling mob surging toward the parking lot. She held it until we were almost to my car, long after the chance of being split up had passed. At her home, I walked her to her front door, where she said, "Thank you for a wonderful day. I had a great time."

"I did, too. And it was your idea, not mine. So thank you for the wonderful day."

Again, we were an inch apart. This time, we closed the gap. The kiss was gentle and sweet and it went right to my core, setting my heart roaring in my chest. It was too long by half and too short by miles. We pulled apart, looked at each other, looked away. We'd crossed that line, regretting we'd taken the first step toward something that never could be.

I shouldn't have let it go that far. The attraction I'd been holding in check not only all day, but for months, had finally bested me.

"Well...goodnight, Dan."

"Good night, Steph."

I could feel her lips on mine all the way home.

Chapter 16

07/05/2003 – Trouble, Questions, and Answers

I left my house the next morning as the sun rose, the sky paling from black through purple and lilac to blue. I planned to spend the day taking photos. Snagging a drive-through breakfast at McDonald's, I cruised back roads outside town, looking for shots. Ten minutes later, I stopped, hauled out my Nikon digital camera, and snapped several pictures of a farmer working his field, his tractor and spreader silhouetted by the rising sun. On another road, I took some of a teen and a Border collie herding cows into a pasture. I also captured horses grazing in a field, ducks on a pond, crows circling a cornfield, a dog resting but alert under a tree in a yard, and anything else catching my eye.

By four that afternoon, I'd filled two memory chips with images. I was hungry as well since I hadn't stopped for lunch. One of Lou's jumbo cheeseburgers, a side of hash browns, and a cold Yuengling would cure it. I packed up my camera and aimed my truck toward town.

A little over an hour later, my belly no longer empty, I parked in my driveway. I swung around the front of my house, gathered my mail from the box, and entered the front door. Mixed in with the bills and credit card offers was a small manila envelope. No stamp, no address, only my name in black ink. I dropped the other letters on the dining room table then pried open the envelope's metal tabs.

Inside were maybe twenty photos. I stared at the first one for a second or two then thumbed through the rest, the sick feeling in my stomach growing with each one. They all showed Steph and me together, and each had a broad red X over my image. At the back of the pack was a note—STAY AWAY FROM HER—in block red letters on white paper the size of the photos.

I called Andy.

He arrived ten minutes later. In my den, I showed him the envelope. He worked his hands into thin cotton gloves before he picked it up by the edges and tipped the pictures out onto my desk. He studied each one then, again touching only the edges, laid it aside. When he'd gone through them all, he tapped the stack. "You want to tell me what's going on between you and Stephanie Mercer? Let's start with the whole story of how you two met."

I told him about running into her at Lou's and how that had evolved into meeting from time to time to talk.

"Looks like someone doesn't approve." He sifted through the pictures to one of Steph hugging me and one of her bussing my cheek. "And like you're doing more than talking."

"Just a 'thank you' hug and peck on the cheek after one of our early meetings. Nothing more." Yet each photo felt like a violation of a more intimate moment.

Andy laid two pictures of Steph and me face to face in her pool in front of me. If expressions were actions, we were about to lock lips for the rest of the day. "This looks like it's leading up to a whole lot more than a 'thank you' peck to me."

"It didn't." *Not for several hours, at least.*

He eyed me for a second. "You say so. You said you touched these." He teased the photos and note back in the envelope. "You ever been fingerprinted?"

"Nope."

Andy slipped the envelope into an evidence baggie and stripped off his gloves. "Let me get my kit out of the car and take yours for elimination purposes."

The moment he left the room, my phone rang. "Dan?" A tremor in Steph's voice.

I knew what put it there. "You got pictures of us together?"

"About two dozen. How did you know?"

"I got them, too. Where did you find them?"

"In my mailbox when I got home a few minutes ago. There's a red X covering your face in each one. Dan, someone's been watching us." Raw fear in her voice. "Who?"

"I don't know." Holland Carter came to mind. "Was there a note with the pictures?"

"Yes. It says, 'Stay away from him.' What do we do?"

"Andy's here now looking at mine. We'll swing by your place soon as we're done. Don't touch them any more than you have to. Without looking through them, do you remember any of the shots?"

Andy came in, saw me on the phone, and signaled he'd wait in the hall by jacking a thumb over his shoulder. I motioned him in.

Steph said, "They're all of us. Walking to our cars. Hugging. Me kissing your cheek. At Jansen's. Outside Morning Mug. Your shops. In my pool yesterday."

"Same here. We'll see you in a few minutes."

"See who in a few minutes?" Andy asked once I hung up.

"Steph. She got a set, too."

"That makes this a whole new ballgame."

Fifteen minutes later, we were on our way to Glenwood Heights, a mix of elation and anxiety growing stronger in me the closer we got to Elm Circle. I was glad I'd see Steph again but didn't like the reason behind it. Someone clearly didn't think we should be meeting.

Steph was waiting at her door when Andy and I arrived. Ten minutes later, the three of us sat around her dining room table. While she wiped print ink off her fingertips, Andy got my pictures from the evidence bag. and laid them out. Then he matched Steph's photos with mine. "Now identify them. Tell me where they were taken and when."

Inside a half hour, Steph and I had nailed down the details. I jabbed a finger at the photos. "The last two were taken yesterday. So whoever shot them either develops his own film or has a digital camera and photo quality printer. It's the only way he could have gotten these printed so fast."

"You're sure of that?" Andy asked.

"Positive. No one in town does one-hour film processing, twenty-four hours is the minimum. With yesterday being a holiday, they wouldn't have gone out until today, and the customer wouldn't get them back until tomorrow afternoon at the earliest."

"How do you know that?" Steph asked.

"Photography's a hobby."

Her mildly surprised expression said this, like

dining often at Mitchell's, was not something she expected of me.

Andy slid the photos into evidence bags. "To be honest with you, this could be nothing more than some crackpot who thinks it's still eighteen-eighty, and it's improper for a married woman to be in the company of a single man. Or somebody who knows one or both of you is playing a nasty joke."

"'Stay away from her,' 'Stay away from him' doesn't sound like a joke, Andy."

"I'm not taking it lightly, Dan, I just want you both to be aware this could turn out to be nothing." He stowed the bags in his briefcase. "Either one of you know anyone who might disapprove of your friendship?"

Steph and I exchanged 'should we or shouldn't we' glances then she said, "I don't know if he disapproves of it, but Holland Carter has dropped some indirect hints he'd like to take Tom's place, should he die."

"What kind of hints?"

She explained Holland promoting himself as her guardian. When she finished, Andy asked me, "Have you seen any of that with him?"

I told him about Carter's visit to my office.

"I'll have our tech people process these, see what we can find. If nothing else, we can charge whoever took these with stalking." Andy stood. "I'll keep you posted. You coming?"

"Dan," Steph said, "can I talk to you for a minute?"

"Sure. I'll catch you tomorrow, Andy."

As soon as he left, Steph said, "Have you eaten dinner?"

"About an hour ago."

A glimmer of disappointment crossed her face. "Can I at least interest you in a cup of coffee?"

"Always." I followed her into the kitchen. Lots of windows, light yellow paint, and white oak cabinets and trim made it bright and cheery.

She waved me toward a bleached oak table in a breakfast nook then set up the brewer. "Do you think Holl did this?"

I shrugged. "You know him better than I do. Would he do something like this?"

"I want to say no. But I don't know. He might. He always seemed a little...controlling." She made a swirling motion with one hand, as if trying to stir up a better description. "Like he expects everything to go his way all the time and gets upset when it doesn't."

"How upset?"

"Judge Wintersteen slapped him with a contempt citation after he called the judge inept for overruling his objection during a trial. Tom went golfing with him one time. He had a fit every time his shot wasn't perfect. Tom never golfed with him again."

I thought for a moment. "He could be behind this if he expects everything to go his way. He could see our friendship as a stumbling block in his plans for a future with you."

"If it was Holl, how can we prove it?"

"Have you ever seen him with a camera—not one of those little point-and-shoot ones you can tuck in a pocket or your purse—a big one like a professional photographer might use?"

"I never saw him with any kind of a camera, not even a disposable one." She poured coffee and handed me a mug.

"If he's behind this, then someone took the pictures for him. Does Tom's firm have an investigator on staff?" I blew on the coffee then drank.

"They do. But he's not an employee. He's a private investigator they hire on an as needed basis, a retired state policeman, Ray something." She stirred sugar and cream into her coffee. "I think he has an office here in town. Do you think Holl asked him to take those photos?"

"Possibly."

She laid her spoon aside. "I can call Jeff and ask him."

I took another mouthful of coffee, savoring the flavor as I thought for a moment. Styles and Carter had double-teamed me on Steph. Could they be working together on something regarding her? If so, talking to one would be the same as talking to both. "How buddy-buddy are Jeff and Holl?"

"I can't say for sure. I think they get along okay, maybe not as close as Tom and Jeff were, but they're not at odds either." She lifted her mug and sipped.

"Then don't ask Jeff. For now, I think it best we don't let anyone know we suspect Holl's behind them."

She set her mug down with a clunk, and fire burned in her eyes. "I want to know who's spying on us! I don't care who it is!" She bolted from her chair and yanked open a drawer, slapped a phone book on the counter and thumbed through the pages. "Ray Elliot Investigations. Discreet. Professional. Thirty years' experience. Divorce. Custody. Theft. Background Checks. No enquiry too small. Fifteen-thirty-two Front Street." She snatched the phone from its base, jabbed in numbers.

I slid the phone from her hand and disconnected. "Don't."

She grabbed it back. "I won't have someone sneaking around taking photos and prying into my private life! What I do is none of their business!"

I took it from her again. "I agree, but confronting Ray Elliot may not be the best way to do it. He'll claim confidentiality and tell you nothing. Plus it has the same risk as asking Jeff. We can pass what we suspect on to Andy and let him talk to Ray. Chances are he'll be able to get more out of him than we would. And we won't tip our hand to Holl."

She huffed out a breath. After a moment, she said, "Yes, all right. You're right."

"We can't focus only on Holl and Ray either." I led her back to the table. "We have to consider other possibilities. You'd be embarrassed if you accused Ray, and he could prove he didn't do it."

She nodded then the fire flickered in her eyes for a second. "If he didn't take them, who did?"

"Holl could have hired anyone. A freelancer. A newspaper stringer. The kid down the block."

She stared at me, incredulous. "A kid?"

"Why not? A neighbor's boy, Jeremy Slater, is into photography big time. People hire him for weddings, baptisms, first communions, anything they want pictures of. Maybe Holl hired a kid like him."

"If he did, how do we find him?"

"I'll track down Jeremy. Maybe he can find out for me."

"I'll ask some of my neighbors, too. They may know someone."

I carried my empty cup to the sink and rinsed it.

"Time to hit the road."

She swallowed the last of her coffee. "Are you sure you won't stay for dinner? I'm not making anything fancy, just soup and a sandwich."

The plea in her eyes and voice told me she wanted me to stay. In spite of her earlier angry words, the photos had rattled her. I couldn't leave when she was so on edge. But being with her felt so comfortable, I needed to watch that I didn't get to liking it too much, or my resolve to be no more than her friend would collapse as it had last night. "Soup and a sandwich sound good."

Before I left a few minutes after seven, I wrapped her in a hug and promised, "We'll get to the bottom of this."

As I drove home, I hoped we could.

Chapter 17

07/08/2003 – Bad News

Tuesday morning, I was in the engine department with Chip Knox, my chief engine builder. Chip built motors for several NASCAR race teams until he burned out on the eighteen-hour day, seven-day work weeks and moved back to Pennsylvania six years ago. He eyed the disassembled 401 engine from a '62 Buick Wildcat convertible and shook his head. "It's bad. Block's got a crack in it and three scored cylinders. The crank journals, too. It was run dry at some point."

I checked my watch. A few minutes after nine a.m. "Where's Ronny, picking up parts?" Ronny Norton is Chip's accomplice in the engine shop.

"Hasn't shown yet."

At that moment, he did. "Sorry I'm late. I overslept. I'll make up the time, Dan." His voice was nasal, his eyes red-rimmed, his nose red. He sniffed then yanked a blue bandana from his back pocket and muffled a hearty sneeze.

"Got a cold?" Chip asked.

Ronny nodded, wiping his nose. "A dilly. Never heard my alarm go off. Cold pills I took last night knocked me on my ass."

Chip gave Ronny the raised eyebrows gaze. "Or the beers you had after bowling?"

"Or maybe the two together," I said. *Could something like that have happened to Tom Mercer?* I trotted to my office and called Andy. He answered on the second ring.

"Steph told me Tom never drove when he was tired. What if he wasn't tired? What if someone slipped him a Mickey at the Roadhouse that kicked in while he was on his way home?"

"Where'd that come from?"

"One of my guys mixed beer and cold medicine last night, slept right through his alarm this morning. Something similar might have happened to Tom."

"Similar how?"

"Someone tries to run him off the road, he's not going to say, 'Sure, go ahead, make me crash into this tree.' He's going to respond somehow, fight back or try to get away, unless something impairs his ability to react. What better way to do it than slip him some kind of dope in his drink?"

"Could be." Silence except for the soft sound of Andy's fingers doing slow drum rolls on his desk pad. "Mercer'd been drinking before he crashed. It could have been enough on its own to hamper his fight back ability. Hold on a sec."

The sound of pages ruffling came through the phone.

"His blood alcohol was point-oh-five-three at the hospital. Probably higher when he crashed, but not over point-oh-eight. He was at the Roadhouse for a little over two hours, had two light scotch and sodas, finished the second right before he left. That's confirmed by their server. His BAL wouldn't be high enough for the booze to take him totally out of the play." A pause.

"Maybe somebody did spike his drink."

"Would the hospital have checked his blood for anything other than alcohol?"

"Not without us or the ER doc telling the lab to. We wouldn't have, thinking it was a one car crash. And the doc was more interested in treating his injuries."

Nora entered my office. She was fifty-five and didn't hide the gray threading through her dark hair, called it her badge of honor for raising three sons. She laid a note on my desk.

"Hang on a sec, Andy." I skimmed the paper. Three more body shop owners had returned my calls. None of them had repaired damage to the right front and side of a dark red car in the weeks following Tom Mercer's crash. They didn't know anybody doing bodywork out of their garage, either.

"Thanks, Nora." I summarized the contents of her note for Andy. "How long after Mercer crashed before you got there?"

"Fifteen minutes, give or take. People with him at the Roadhouse said he left around eight-twenty. Doing the speed limit, it's five, six minutes to where he crashed. I got there twenty to nine, EMTs a minute or two later."

"Who reported the crash?"

"Guy driving by spotted Mercer's Caddy, called it in on his cell at eight-twenty-eight." Andy did another fingertip drum roll on his desk. "In light of what you said, I think I need to talk to the people with Mercer at the Roadhouse again."

I'd no sooner racked the phone than it rang again.

"Rick Williams from Henson's AutoHaus." Located outside Wilkes-Barre, a small city forty miles northeast of Schuylerton, the dealership sold every German make imported to the US. "You called a while back asking about red cars with right side damage we fixed last October. Sorry I didn't get back to you sooner. Be honest, it slipped my mind until last week. Anyway, I dug in our records and ran across one from down your way. Lady brought a '99 BMW 3-Series in on the seventh. Said she hit a light pole in a parking lot over the weekend."

The Monday after Tom's crash. "What shade of red?"

"Siena Red Metallic."

"You have the owner's name?"

"Yep. Mrs. Thomas Mercer. Name rings a bell." A pause. "Got it. Her husband was in a bad crash a couple days before then. I remember her 'cause she was waiting when we opened at eight, all worked up about her car."

"She said she hit a pole in a parking lot?"

"Unh-hunh. I tried to calm her down, told her it was an easy fix, and I'd have her car back to her in no time. Didn't seem to help. She kept going on about her husband's crash and now this, and she didn't know what she was going to do. She was so frazzled, I told her I'd bump her to the head of the line and put my best guys on it. I even said I'd handle all the paperwork, too."

"Thanks for letting me know." A sudden feeling of dread roiled in my gut. I had to ask questions I didn't want to. "Did the damage line up with what she said happened?"

"Nothing about it made me think, 'Yeah, lady, if you were doing sixty in the parking lot,' if that's what you're asking. Right corner light lens was busted out, fender crumpled, door scraped up pretty bad. Looked like she misjudged things and swiped the base of a light pole."

"That all the damage?"

"The headlight mount was cracked when my guy got the fender off."

Steph driving to Wilkes-Barre to get her BMW fixed made no sense when there were a dozen body shops in Schuylerton capable of doing the work and probably charging less. *Was she trying to hide something?* "Could the damage have come from her hitting something else, another car maybe?"

"Where did that come from? You thinking she ran her hubby off the road?"

"I don't know, but humor me for now, okay? Could the damage to her car have come from hitting another car?"

A moment's silence. "Yeah, could have."

The thud I felt was my gut taking a nosedive.

Chapter 18

07/09/2003 – The Assignment

I was on the shop floor Wednesday discussing the scarcity of authentic trim pieces for a '56 DeSoto Firedome with Mark Russo, the project manager, when Nora paged me to the showroom for a visitor. My heart beat a little quicker with the hope it was Steph. Or maybe it was because I was almost running to get there faster.

Reality dashed my hopes. Andy had a hip propped on Nora's desk, she had a go cup of Morning Mug tea in one hand and an éclair in the other. She raised the pastry an inch. "This is why I can't lose weight, Andy Cummings."

"You don't look a pound over one-oh-five."

"Oh, go on, you!"

I cleared my throat. "Bribing my people, Andy?"

"I didn't forget you." He hoisted a Morning Mug bag and a tray holding two coffees from Nora's desk. "You got a couple minutes?"

I aimed a finger at the goodies in his hands. "For that I do." I waved him toward my office.

He spread paper napkins from the bag on my desk and laid a pair of turnovers on them. "Cherry or apple?"

"You pick." I pried the cap off a coffee, dumped it into my D-J Auto Renewal mug, and downed a big hit.

"What's up?"

He bit into the cherry turnover, chewed, and swallowed. "Ms. Mercer ever mention any of their friends, say anything about them?"

"No friends I recall, just some people Tom worked with at his law firm."

"Next time you talk to her, you think maybe you could steer the conversation around to their friends, find out who the closest ones are?"

"I'll give it a shot. Why?" I let the tastes of cinnamon, apple, and pastry lay on my tongue.

"Now that I know Mercer's crash wasn't an accident, I need to look for motive. Close friends are often a good source. I thought you could find out who they are for me."

"You think one of them might have wrecked Mercer?"

"Or might know if Ms. Mercer had a reason to." He swigged coffee. "How well do you know her?"

"Not as well as I know you. But over the three months I've known her, I'd say I've gotten to know her fairly well."

"Tell me what you know about her."

Something in his tone hooked my attention. I set my mug down. "Why?"

"Call me curious." He offered an enigmatic smile saying that was all he would tell me for now.

I thought for a moment, organizing things I'd gleaned from our conversations, then laid it out for him. As I talked, he jotted notes in a small notebook. I left out she'd taken her Siena Red BMW to Wilkes-Barre for repairs the Monday after Tom's crash. When I finished, I leaned over my desk. "You want to tell me what this is about?"

"She ever say what she was doing the night Mercer crashed?"

"Nope."

"You think while you're talking to her about her friends, you could maybe steer the conversation around to that, too?"

"You think Steph ran Tom off the road?"

"Any time a hubby gets clobbered, the wife's always the prime suspect in the clobbering."

I thought Andy was unjustly suspecting a woman who'd gotten a shitty deal and didn't need any more crap dumped on her. And who roused feelings dormant in me since Amy died. "She didn't do it." But Rick Williams's phone call had stirred a doubt.

"You know this how?"

"I've heard the way she talks about Tom, heard the pain in her voice when she talks about all the things they planned to do but now never will. You haven't. She visits him every day, clinging to the hope one day he's going to wake from his coma, wanting to be there when he does. Does that sound like a woman who tried to kill her husband?"

He finished his pastry and wiped his fingers on a napkin. "No, it doesn't. But I still have to look at her. I'm not doing my job if I don't."

"Give me one—that's all I ask, Andy, one—good reason why she'd try to kill Tom."

He pursed his lips, holding the pose so long, I feared he was about to tell me Steph was a black widow. Or worse.

I set the turnover on my desk, my appetite suddenly gone. "What do you know that I don't?"

Andy flipped back several pages in his notebook. "The day Stephanie Lorraine Altman became Mrs. Thomas Leland Mercer, she received a half million-dollar trust fund from the Mercer family. She could tap the interest anytime she wanted but couldn't touch the principal until Tom died. If they divorced, the fund reverted to the Mercer family. That's called motive."

Turnover and coffee soured in my stomach. "Do me one favor. Please. Keep an open mind about her."

"I always do." His voice shifted to a wry tone. "Except when I see a car hugging a tree and assume it got there on its own."

"You get anything off those photos we got?"

"The lab guys say they're digital, printed on photo paper by a photo-quality printer, because under magnification, you can see the pixels. You come up with anything?"

I told him my ideas about who might have taken them.

"Ray's a pretty straight up guy. I don't see him doing it." He shrugged. "But I could be wrong. I'll see what he has to say. The high school kid angle has possibilities. I can see some teen jumping on a chance to make a pile of cash without wondering why some guy wants pictures of you and Mrs. Mercer. Especially if he's a little sketchy to begin with."

"I know the Photo Club advisor. He might be able to point me to a likely candidate."

Chapter 19

07/11/2003 – Things Go Wrong

Steph called me shortly after I got home two days later and asked if I had plans for dinner. When I said I didn't, she asked how burgers on the grill and fries sounded.

The microwaved chicken potpie I'd planned to have fell to fifth in a two-entree race, but I hesitated to accept, considering what happened on July fourth. The two of us with others around us was one thing, the two of us alone was something else. We might again unleash a beast best kept chained in the dark. Yet I could no more resist her than steel could resist a magnet. "Count me in."

I showered and shaved and got to her house at six on the dot. She greeted me at the door wearing a black safari dress. Seeing her sent a surge of elation zinging through me. "Thanks for inviting me."

"I'm glad you could come." The hug she gave me boosted the surge and its zing and revived memories of last week. She led me to the patio, where burgers sizzled on the grill, fries in oil crackled on a side burner, and the air carried the aroma of seasonings and toasting bread.

We ate at the wrought iron table again and talked about our day. Partway through my second burger, I decided it was time to fulfill Andy's request. "Can I ask you something?"

"About Tom?"

"Indirectly."

"Anything." She dipped a fry in ketchup and ate it.

"Who were some of your and Tom's closest friends last fall?"

She chewed and swallowed. "The same ones as now. Jeff and Lisa Styles, of course. Doug and Claire Shepton. Matt and Nicole Argenti. Will and Diedre Adler. Why are you asking?"

"Maybe one of them might know who ran Tom off the road and why."

"If someone was after him, he'd have told me about it, not one of them. And I would have told the police."

"He may not have said anything to you." I drank some Molson Ale. "Guys sometimes tell other guys things they don't tell their wives."

"Tom and I didn't keep secrets from each other."

"Maybe he did in this case because he didn't want to frighten you or was looking for advice from one of them on how to solve the problem."

"He still would have said something to me. I don't frighten easily, and he would have asked me what to do about any problem he had. It's the way we ar—were. But if you think talking to them will help, by all means talk to them."

"One more question. Did you own your Lexus last year?" I bit off more burger.

"No. I had the BMW we got the year after we moved into this house, so it would have been a ninety-nine. I don't remember which model. Tom bought it as my birthday present that year. I traded it in in November. It reminded me of him too much."

"What color was it?"

"Dark red."

Uh-oh! "Did you know Tom was going out for a drink after work the day of his accident?"

She nodded. "He left a message on our machine around two saying he was. He always let me know he was going to be doing something like that or working late so I didn't worry when he wasn't home at the normal time."

"Since he wasn't home, what did you do that evening?"

"Fixed myself dinner, read a bit, watched some—" Steph set down her burger. "What are you saying? Do you think I—"

"No, Steph, I don't. But Andy needs to know so he can definitely eliminate you as a suspect in Tom's accident."

"And instead of asking me himself face-to-face, he sent you to weasel it out of me."

Busted. "He didn't send me to weasel it out of you, but he did ask me to find out. He suggested I get it by steering one of our talks to it. I don't work that way, and I wasn't about to start with you, so I asked you directly."

"What else did Andy ask you to find out?" Coolness in her tone.

"That's all of it."

"I see." From cool to cold. "And did my answer eliminate me as a suspect?"

"I want to say 'yes' but I can't. Tom's Caddy was run off the road by a red car."

"And you think it was my red car." To polar. "You think instead of eating, reading, and watching TV, I was trying to kill my husband."

"You know I don't think that, but you took it to Henson's AutoHaus the Monday after Tom's accident to get it repaired. How did it get damaged, Steph?"

"I think you should go." She grabbed our plates and marched into the kitchen. "Go tell Andy I tried to kill Tom." The plates landed in the sink with a clatter.

I couldn't let it end this way. "Steph, just tell me how—"

"Go." She braced her hands on the counter and hung her head. Her voice sounded sad and disappointed. "Just…go!"

Chapter 20

07/12/2003 – Sorting Things Out

I woke later than usual the next morning, groggy and in a foul mood.

I had spent hours after I got home pacing my house. First, I'd cursed myself up, down, and sideways for the clumsy way I handled things with Steph. Then I'd ranted at Andy for using me to do his work for him then at myself for letting him. Then hardest of all, I'd lamented I'd probably driven a stake through the heart of my friendship with Steph.

I'd thrashed around in bed all night, unable to get comfortable, unable to clear my mind of the same thoughts I'd tried to pace out of my system earlier. When I did sleep, it was fragmented.

I dressed on autopilot. Picking my khaki slacks from where I'd dropped them last night, I reached in the pocket. My hand closing around my keys instantly recalled all the things I'd done wrong then. Yanking them out, I whipped them across the room, knocking over and cracking a domed display case holding my great-grandfather's pocket watch. I'm his namesake. Breaking it did nothing for my foul mood, but flinging my keys had felt damn good.

After Amy died, D-J Auto Renewal had been my refuge. I'd practically lived there for the next three years, working sixteen- to eighteen-hour days, often sleeping at my desk, and only going home when Nora dragged me there. If work could get me through the trauma of Amy's death, it could get me through losing Steph.

I laughed bitterly at that. She was never mine to lose. Still, any port in a storm.

Too restless and unfocused to cook breakfast or wait for coffee to brew, I swung by McDonald's. In my office, I wolfed down two sausage and egg McMuffins and guzzled a large coffee like a monk coming off a month-long fast then picked up the note Gene Parilli had left on my desk. *Paint chip from Caddy is Jeep Chili Pepper Red Metallic. The black smears on it look like low gloss black used on baseline Jeep bumpers.*

The knot of tension residing in my gut since Rick Williams's phone call unraveled. Gene's word was proof enough for me Steph didn't run Tom off the road. Whether it would be enough for Andy might be a different story. Curious about how close Jeep Chili Pepper Red and BMW Siena Red were, I opened a PPG paint chip binder and compared them. Twins, but fraternal, not identical.

I needed to get my hands dirty doing something on one of our project cars. A day's hard work would burn the anger out of my system. I strolled the shop floor, not sure what I wanted to do, but knowing I needed to do something. The stroll left me feeling as necessary as training wheels on a tricycle. My guys and gals are so good they rarely need my help. So my trip consisted of checking progress and leaving a few notes, knowing anything I did would only screw up their carefully planned out work.

When I entered the body shop, something I could do stared me in the face. A '62 Lincoln limousine once owned by a famous Hollywood producer had come out of the paint-baking booth Tuesday. Waxing it would occupy my hands while my mind mulled over what to do about Andy and Steph.

I washed the limo, dried it, and spread a thin coat of soft carnauba wax evenly on the body. I didn't reach any conclusions on what to do about Andy and Steph except to realize losing her friendship hurt.

We always let carnauba wax set up for at least an hour before buffing it out, so I made a quick run to Abe's Deli for a hoagie. I unwrapped it on Gene's desk in the body shop and grabbed his reference binder—a tome listing the components of every paint on the market—from a shelf. The difference between Jeep Chili Pepper Red and BMW Siena Red was minute.

As I grabbed a lamb's wool pad to put on a power buffer, the phone in Gene's office rang. I tried to ignore it, but the tenth ring broke me. I trotted to the office and picked up.

"You talk to Ms. Mercer yet?"

I almost hung up when I heard Andy's voice. Instead, I put a cold edge in my voice. "Yeah."

"You able to steer the conversation to the things we talked about?"

Another cold, "Yeah."

"Why didn't you call me?"

"I've been busy."

A pause on his end. "Did I catch you at a bad time or something?"

"No."

"So, what did Mrs. Mercer have to say?"

"Ask her yourself." I slammed the phone down and rose from Gene's desk.

The phone rang again as I reached the door. Figuring it was Andy again, and he'd let it ring until I answered, I picked up. He said, "What the hell's eating you?"

Like flinging my keys, hanging up on him had been pure snit. It sure felt good, but didn't accomplish anything. "Don't ask me to do your dirty work for you again."

"Ms. Mercer figured out you were asking for me, and now she's pissed at you."

"You got it."

"And you're pissed at me." Silence. "Look, I needed that information to clear her. I thought maybe if you asked her, it would sound less like an accusation and more like friendly curiosity."

"Well, she took it as an accusation."

"So, what did she have to say? Or are you gonna hang up on me again?"

"She was home alone the night Tom wrecked."

"So she says."

"She didn't run her husband off the road."

"How do you know?"

This could turn into a long conversation, so I plopped in Gene's chair. "Gene's sure the car that hit Tom's Caddy was a Chili Pepper Red Jeep. Steph had a Siena Red BMW back then."

"How do you know that?"

I'd walked right into it. Now I'd have to tell Andy about Steph's accident. "Rick Williams at Henson's Autohaus in Wilkes-Barre told me. She sideswiped a light pole in a parking lot the day after Tom wrecked and took it there to get it fixed."

"And just happened to get the same damage she would have if she'd hit Mercer's car?"

"Yep."

"What did Mrs. Mercer say happened?"

"She kicked me out when I asked."

"Probably because she punted hubby into the trees."

"She didn't. I told you Gene said the paint chip he found on Mercer's Caddy is Jeep Chili Pepper Red."

"And her car was Siena Red. I got that. Any chance Gene got it wrong, mistook one for the other?"

"Gene getting a paint wrong? That's like you getting a law wrong. Plus he found low-gloss black paint smears on Mercer's Caddy like from the bumper of a base model Jeep Cherokee. Even the cheapest BMW has body color bumpers and black rubber trim strips."

"Still doesn't put her fully in the clear."

"Come on, Andy. If you ran Sue off the road, where would you take your car for repairs? The dealer's body shop or a guy working out of his garage?"

"I'd go to the guy working out of his garage. Doesn't mean Mrs. Mercer would. Maybe she didn't know where to get it fixed on the Q-T. Maybe she paid someone with a red Jeep to nudge hubby off the road. Any of your friends in the business say they fixed one around then?"

"Not yet."

"How'd you do finding out who the Mercers' friends were back then?"

I decided to keep that info to myself for the time being. "She kicked me out before I could ask."

Andy was silent for a moment or two. "Whatever you've got going on with Ms. Mercer, I'm sorry if I messed it up, but I can't let it interfere with me doing my job."

I put cold back into my voice. "It's something called friendship, Andy. And you messed it up. Big time. You seem to have forgotten how friendship works. You don't have a friend do your dirty work for you."

"I said I was sorry. Now think about this: I could have done things by the book. I could have brought her in for questioning, made her wait for hours before I got to her, given her a hard time when I did. Would you have preferred I did that?"

I rested my head on my hand and sighed. "No."

"Here's something else to think about. Suppose she did try to kill hubby, and I give her a pass because of your feelings for her. And suppose he dies and you take his place and she goes after you and you end up dead. Then, not only would I *not* have done my job in the first place, I'd have lost a friend—you—because of it."

I had no answer for that.

"I'm on your side here. Okay? I don't think she tried to kill him. But I can't simply think it, I have to *know* it, have to prove it before I can rule her out."

"Why would she try to kill Tom?"

"A half a million bucks inches beyond her fingertips was too tempting to resist? He wanted a divorce and she didn't want to lose it? She wanted out and hubby wouldn't give her a divorce? He was abusing her? He had a lover and it pissed her off?"

"She said Tom never once raised his voice let alone a hand to her, and the few arguments they had were more like debates than fights. Frank Garrison told me she grew up in Sewickley, a wealthy suburb of Pittsburgh, with all the perks that go with living there. So I think you can rule out abuse and money. As for one of them having a lover, maybe. But, again based on the way she talked about the two of them, I don't see it."

Silence from Andy.

"Why does it have to be Steph who tried to kill Tom?" I paced as far as the phone cord let me. "Why couldn't it be someone he worked with? Or a client pissed at the work he did for them or the outcome of a case? Or a road rage incident? Or some dipshit at the Roadhouse thinking Tom eyed his old lady wrong and deciding to set him straight?"

"A guy like that would have gone after Mercer right then and there. I asked the Roadhouse staff. Nothing like that happened. Everything else you said is still on the table."

Chapter 21

07/14/2003 – Following A Lead

My phone rang shortly after I got to work next Monday morning.

"Dan? Hey, it's Paul Cole." Owner of Cole's Collision Repair.

"Hey, Paul. What can I do for you?"

"You called a while back asking about any jobs I had last fall fixing right side damage on red cars." His voice rasped from decades of inhaling sanding dust and cigars. "Finally got a chance to dig back through my records from then. I only had two with that kind of damage and neither one was red. Had a silver Mercury and a blue Chevy pick-up."

"Okay. Thanks for checking for me, Paul."

"My pleasure. Ran across something else though digging through those records, don't know if it will mean anything to you. Found an invoice from Ridley Auto Supply for a quart of Jeep Chili Pepper Red right around then. I didn't recall ordering it, so I checked with Ridley. I didn't. Guy working for me back then, Scott Harris, did."

I scribbled the name on a notepad. "He doesn't work for you anymore?"

"Nope. Fired his ass in December when I found out he was calling up folks I'd given estimates to, offering to do the job for less, then stealing my stuff to do the work. He was on his way out anyway. He was nothing but a mudslinger." A guy who hid sloppy metal straightening skills under a layer of plastic filler.

"He undercut you on a Jeep job?"

"I didn't write up any estimates on any Jeeps in the weeks before when you were asking me about. Had to be somebody he rounded up on his own."

"What's Harris doing now?"

"Last I heard, working for Hofnagle Ford in Branthorpe."

I told Nora I'd be out of the shops for a while and hit the road. I'm lucky. I have a great crew of talented people working for me. They give me their best every day without me hovering over them all day long. I reached Branthorpe ten minutes later.

Hofnagle Ford-Lincoln-Mercury occupied an entire block on the main drag a mile beyond Branthorpe's downtown area. I asked the service manager if I could talk to Scott Harris. He rolled his eyes. "If you take him with you when you're done." He called the body shop, and after a brief conversation, said Harris would meet me outside the building.

Strolling toward it, I eyeballed the lot. New cars don't do much for me. Old ones always catch my eye. A blue and white '84 Ford F-250 near the body shop caught it. Its ratty body eroded and holed by rust, it was too far gone to restore in my book.

Scott Harris leaned against the wall by a rollup door. He looked maybe thirty, about six feet tall and beefy, with a shaved head, dark eyes and a scruff of a beard on a round face. Crude blue-black tattoos covered his forearms, and white Bondo dust coated his blue shop overalls. He took a hard drag on his cigarette. "What do you want?"

Attitude galore. I handed him a D-J Auto Renewal card. "To ask you a few questions."

"You offering me a job?"

"No." I wouldn't even if my whole crew walked. Not after what Paul had said about him.

"Then I got no reason to talk to you." He dropped his cigarette on the paving, shredded it with his boot, and turned toward the body shop.

"Your boss here know Paul Cole fired you and why?"

He stiffened for a moment before facing me and sighing. "What do you want to know?"

"You ordered a quart of Jeep Chili Pepper Red paint from Ridley Auto Supply on Paul's dime a couple months before he fired you."

"How'd you know about that?"

"He spotted it going through his old records."

Harris lit a new Winston and shrugged. "So I ordered it? So what?"

"So, what was it for?"

"For a Jeep. What else would it be for?"

Could this be my first break in finding who ran Tom Mercer off the road? "Paul didn't have any Jeeps in for work at that time. So why did you order it?"

He sucked a long pull on his smoke. "I was doing cars in my garage on the side to get by. Paul didn't pay shit."

A lie if I ever heard one. Paul Cole paid his men a fair wage. If he didn't, they'd go to a shop that would. "So instead of going to work for someone else, you ripped him off until he canned you. You're lucky that's all he did. He could have had you arrested."

Harris offered up a smirk of a smile. "Yeah, I dodged a bullet there."

I wanted to punch him. "You wouldn't have with me. Back to the paint. Why specifically did you order a quart of Jeep Chili Pepper Red?"

Another long draw on his cigarette followed by twin plumes of smoke jetting from his nostrils. "Guy wanted me to fix his Cherokee."

"What year Cherokee?"

"Ninety-seven? Ninety-eight?" A shrug. "One of them."

"What was wrong with it?"

"Right front corner was crunched, side was all beat up. Guy said he had too much to drink the night before, sideswiped something driving home."

"If you didn't shanghai him from Paul, how'd he know to come to you?"

"Word was getting around I was in the business, doing good work for a good price."

"You write up an estimate?"

"Guy didn't want one. Just asked how much to fix it." A drag on the Salem. "Guy had money, so I pulled a number out of my ass, said seven hundred. Guy said fine but it had to be ready by Friday."

"How did you know he had money?"

"Guy with him when he dropped it off was driving a Lincoln. Same Lincoln brought him back to pick it up. Working stiffs like me and you don't drive Lincolns."

"When did all this happen?"

"Early October." A long drag on his cigarette. "Can't tell you what date. It was a Sunday."

Possibly the day after Tom's crash. "You

remember the guy's name?"

"Never asked it."

"What did he look like?"

"Skinny guy maybe tall as you."

"How about his hair color or eyes?"

He shrugged. "Couldn't tell you. Maybe brown for both."

Not much to go on, but it was a start. "What about the guy driving the Lincoln? What did he look like?"

"Never saw him. Only saw the Lincoln's front end out my garage door."

"What about the damage to the Cherokee? You remember what you had to repair?"

He dropped the butt, crushed it under his boot. "Replaced a busted headlight and mount. Fixed the front bumper. Pounded out the fender. Smoothed the side with Bondo. Painted everything. Pushed things a little and got it done Thursday. Guy gave me an extra hundred for getting it done so fast."

"You remember the plate number?"

He snorted. "No. That all you want? I gotta get back to work."

"One more thing. How'd you let him know it was done?"

He gave me a 'you're dumber than a bag of lint' stare. "Called him."

"You remember the number?"

"Nope."

"You write it down somewhere?"

"Tossed it all when I started working here. How come you're asking me about a car I fixed last year?"

"Doing a favor for a friend." I tapped my card. "You remember anything more about the guy, give me

117

a call."

    "Only if you got a job for me."

Chapter 22

07/14/2003 – Information Exchange

I stopped at the Schuylerton police station when I returned to town. Andy dismissed the patrolman who'd showed me into his office then waited until he'd gone before asking, "You come to bitch me out more, or are we square?"

"We're square."

"Good. So what's up?"

I told him what I'd learned from Scott Harris.

"Okay, so we've got red paint transfer on Mercer's Cadillac and Harris repairing a Chili Pepper Red Jeep about the same time."

"That's about the size of it."

"Harris say who the Jeep belonged to?"

"Said he never got a name. And he never wrote up an estimate, just quoted him a price."

"How convenient. Maybe PennDoT can give me a list of everyone in the area who owned red Jeeps last year. Worth a shot. Seven hundred out of line for a repair job like that?"

I did some quick calculating. "Six, six-fifty would be more in the ballpark. Jeep dealer might have charged more."

"Meaning this guy either didn't know what was average or didn't care. Only wanted his Jeep fixed and fast."

"And without leaving a paper trail. He didn't file an insurance claim or they'd have sent an appraiser to look the Jeep over then paid what they decided the repairs should run. And I doubt they would have paid a guy like Harris working out of his garage."

Andy finger-drummed the solo from "In-A-Gadda-Da-Vida" on his metal desk for a few seconds. "You think the extra hundred was for fast service like Harris claimed? Or was it to keep him quiet?"

"Could be either."

"What's your read on Harris?"

"Shady. He was stealing paint and supplies from Paul Cole for his own operation. He might have sensed Mr. Jeep was in a fix and socked it to him. Or maybe he lied to me, only charged the guy five."

"Either way, he needs talking to."

"Maybe he'll have a better memory for names if you're asking him."

Andy jotted some notes in his notebook. "Look, this still doesn't put Mrs. Mercer in the clear. Maybe Harris did fix the Jeep that hit Mercer. But maybe the guy who took it to him didn't drive it. Maybe she did."

"She didn't."

"How do you know?"

"She borrows someone's Jeep to run Tom off the road, tears up the right side doing it. The next day, she prangs her BMW the exact same way hitting a light pole. Sounds a little too much like a coincidence to me. You told me cops don't believe in coincidence."

"We don't." Andy rocked back in his chair. "Could be she hit the pole on purpose to throw us off, hoping we'd think if she ran Mercer off the road, she wouldn't call attention to herself by duplicating the accident in her own car."

Impasse. We could go round and round about this until hell froze over and thawed. "You dig any deeper into Steph's background?"

He nodded once. "Got nothing beyond what I told you before."

"How did you make out with the guy who spotted Mercer's Caddy?"

"Nothing new on the crash. He didn't see it happen, just saw Mercer's Caddy on its roof, and called it in. But he said a vehicle passed him coming toward Schuylerton a few minutes earlier. He couldn't give me a make, just that it was a dark colored, he thought brown or maybe black, medium sized SUV with a bad headlight on the passenger side."

"Bad how?"

"He said it was cockeyed—pointed down at the road—and flickering."

"Putting a lick on Mercer's Caddy could have easily knocked the headlight out of whack or broken the mount. Harris replaced the headlight mount on the Jeep he fixed."

Andy smiled. "Bingo. That's the car that hit Mercer. Now I just have to find it."

Chapter 23

07/18/2003 – Review To A Clue

My Friday morning flight from Florida left on time.

I'd been in the Sunshine State on a three-day business trip that had been good and bad. The good was I'd contracted to restore two cars. The bad was I hadn't enjoyed the trip because the way I'd screwed things up with Steph nagged me the whole time.

I got to D-J a little after two, and Nora followed me into my office, a stack of phone message slips in her hand. "Good trip?"

"Got us a '66 Plymouth Belvedere Hemi and a '68 Chevy Nova SS 396." I handed her a flash drive. "Here's the info."

Nora had worked for me for fifteen years and could read between my lines easily. "Did something happen that's bothering you?"

"Nah. It's…" I shrug. "It's nothing."

"You haven't been yourself all last week." She eyed me for a second. "Does it have something to do with the woman you showed around the shops last month, Stephanie?"

That Nora had figured it out didn't surprise me. But I wouldn't admit she had. "No."

She gave me the raised-eyebrow 'You expect me to

believe that?' stare mothers acquire right after their firstborn learns to speak. "If you say so."

"Anything happen I should know about?"

"She—Stephanie—called yesterday, asking to talk to you." She laid the slips on my desk. The top one was Steph's name and a number. "When I said you were out of town until today, she gave me that number and asked that you call when you got in."

I stared at the paper, lost in thought. A week had passed since the fiasco over hamburgers at Steph's home. I'd tossed our relationship on the 'lost friends' pile a few days later, sure she felt if she never saw me again it would be too soon. And I'd ached for my loss. She had stirred something in me that had been asleep since Amy died, something I'd feared would now crawl back in its dark cave to hibernate for the rest of my life.

Nora cleared her throat. When I shifted my gaze from the message slip to her, she waved the flash drive. "If you don't need anything else, I'll get started on this."

"I don't. Give the Plymouth to Mark, and let Neil have the Nova." Neil had proven himself over the last four years, his work defining meticulous. "He asked me several months ago about heading up a project. That'll be a good one to get his feet wet on. The car's in good shape overall, but the owner wants a complete teardown and rebuild with anything even slightly marginal replaced."

Nora smiled. "I love customers with deep pockets."

"So do I. See Neil gets the books, too, please."

The books—the two-volume factory shop manual, a restoration manual, and a binder of our notes on prior Nova projects—would be Neil's guide. He was staring at a foot-high pile of reading before the Nova arrived next month.

I picked up Steph's message slip again. Maybe our friendship wasn't kaput. I harbored a small hope that was the case and an equal unease the opposite was true as I dialed.

After five rings, her answering machine clicked on. "I can't take your call right now, so please leave your name and number and I'll call you back soon."

My heart raced at the sound of her voice. I had to take a second to slow it down and clench my jaw to force moisture into my mouth before I could speak. "Hi, Steph. It's Dan. What's up? Give me a call. I'll be at the shop until about five-thirty then home."

I set the phone down with my head spinning and my heart racing again with glee. Not only had Steph reached out to me, she'd done it with her phone number so I could reach out to her in the future. Finally. Then my glee turned to sadness. Maybe it had taken her this long to decide she never wanted contact with me again.

I couldn't do anything about it until I knew what she wanted, so I put my emotions away and focused on the paperwork that had climbed on my desk while I was away. Ninety minutes later, I pushed it aside, finished.

I kept all the information I had on Tom Mercer's accident in a file folder labeled with his name. But I'd never sat down and gone through it or put it in any sort of order. I buzzed Nora and asked, "Can you keep me off the radar for the rest of the afternoon?"

"Can a bear climb trees?"

"Thanks." While my laptop booted, I pulled the camera memory card holding photos of Tom's Caddy and the file folder from my desk drawer. When the laptop was running, I opened a New Project file—the same one I used to evaluate cars to be restored—connected the memory card through an adapter, and copied the pictures to the file. Using them for reference, I entered descriptions of the Caddy's damage then typed in my notes the same as I would for a restoration project.

In the middle of typing information in, my mind made a 'something doesn't add up' link between a *Sen-Trib* article I'd copied and one of the Caddy photos. I brought the pictures up on the laptop and cycled through them again. When I got to the shot of the Caddy's interior, my gaze went straight to the airbag drooping from the steering wheel's center. It was part of whatever didn't add up.

Time to do a little thinking. I leaned back in my chair. We didn't deal with airbags at D-J Auto Renewal. The cars we rebuild didn't have them—half didn't even have seatbelts—but I wasn't ignorant about them.

An airbag inflated in milliseconds, deflated almost as fast. The material had to be tough to withstand explosive inflation, thin to fold into the small space in the steering wheel hub, non-porous to hold the inflating air, and smooth enough not to deflesh a face hitting it. Nylon would fit the bill.

I called Paul Cole to confirm it. He did.

I leaned back in my chair again and thought. The thickness needed to withstand inflation and its non-porous nature would give the nylon a certain stiffness. I got the *Local Attorney In Coma After Crash* article from the folder and skimmed it, stopping at *Mercer was found with the airbag covering his face, possibly cutting off his air supply for several minutes.*

That was the 'doesn't add up' connection. The deflated airbag would be too stiff to mold to Tom's face tight enough to cut off his air—another thing Andy had missed the night Tom crashed.

Someone held it there.

Chapter 24

07/18/2003 – Apology Trade

I entered my home that evening to a ringing phone, saw Steph's number on the caller ID, but got only silence when I answered. I waited a few seconds and repeated, "Hello."

More silence then, "Dan, it's Steph. Please don't hang up."

"Okay."

Another moment of silence. "I'm sorry for what I said at dinner the other night. I...you shocked me so much with those questions about my car and what I was doing the night Tom had his accident. I thought you had turned on me, and I lashed out at you, and I shouldn't have. I am so sorry, Dan. Please forgive me?"

That evening, I'd gone about getting the information Andy wanted all wrong. I should have followed his suggestion, letting the conversation ease into the topic. The blame for the bitter way the evening ended rested as much on me as on her. "I'm sorry, too. I did wrong by you. I sounded like I *was* accusing you of wrecking Tom, and I've never thought that for an instant."

She vented a relieved sigh.

"I'm not the only one who thinks you're innocent. Andy thinks it, too. But he can't just think it, he has to prove it. That's why he had me ask those questions, not to convict you, but to clear you. He thought if I did it, you wouldn't feel like he suspected you." I inhaled a deep breath. "You thinking I suspected you hurt, Steph. It hurt bad."

"I know. And I'm sorry I did it. I really am. I took everything you said the wrong way that night. Can I treat you to dinner tomorrow night as an apology?"

"How about if I take you to dinner and you take me?"

"I'd like that."

We agreed on Red Mill Restaurant, a slightly upscale place in—as the name indicates—a former gristmill. I lowered my phone, smiling. My world had just gotten brighter. But I couldn't dwell on it. I needed to turn my attention to something darker. I called Andy.

"Hey, Dan. Nora said you were out of town for a couple days."

"Yeah. In Florida looking at some cars." I wedged the phone between my ear and shoulder and pulled on a pair of running shorts. "You got anything for me?"

"I was going to ask you the same thing."

"I do. An airbag is too stiff for Tom to suffocate merely by having it fall across his face." I explained how I reached that conclusion. "Someone held it over his mouth and nose."

"Making it attempted murder." Andy did a fingertip drumroll on his desk. "You got anything else?"

"Nope. What do you have for me?"

"The State Police Crime Lab finished going over Mercer's Caddy. They confirmed the paint on it is Jeep Chili Pepper Red, most likely from a ninety-eight to two thousand model. They had a crash reconstruction team out last week to go over his crash. Got the reports this afternoon. Given the time lapse, the best they could say was his crash most likely went down like you said."

Chapter 25

07/19/2003 – Repairing the Rift

Steph called the next afternoon as I stripped off my clothes prior to grabbing a shower.

"I don't feel like going to the Red Mill tonight."

My heart sank. Had she changed her mind about seeing me, decided she really didn't ever want to see me again? "Is something wrong?"

"I'd just rather stay home. Would you mind coming here instead? About six?"

My heart snapped back like a bungee cord diver. "Not at all." And I wouldn't have to wear a tie. I hate the damn things anyway.

"I'll make something simple for us for dinner, if that's okay with you."

"How about if I pick something up on the way? Do you like Italian?"

"I love it. And I've got the perfect wine to go with whatever you bring."

On my way to Glenwood Heights, I stopped at Flower Boutique for the planter I'd ordered earlier, then swung by Giancarlo's for our dinner. After I rang Steph's bell, I held the planter in front of my face. When she opened her door, I lowered it and gave her a sheepish grin over the blooms. "Forgive me?"

I wished my heart would quit the thumping race it

did every time I saw her. No, I didn't. Having that reaction to a woman again was wonderful, even if I couldn't act on it. Steph had on a black dress in the kind of light fabric that floated and swirled around her legs as she walked. A dress like that made a beautiful woman gorgeous. "If you will forgive me."

"Already done." I handed her the planter.

She touched the blooms, inhaled their scent, then set the planter on a table by the door. "Dan, I am so, so sorry about the other night, I—"

"We both made mistakes that night. Let's call it even. Okay?" I raised the bags in my hand. "Dinner."

Taking them from me, she led me into her kitchen, opened the larger bag and lifted out the lasagna. "This smells delicious." She opened the second bag. "And tiramisu!"

Minutes later, we sat at the bleached oak table and dug in. I told her about my Florida trip, and she told me she'd had a very good day at the clinic, making real progress with several of her patients, including a major breakthrough with one. I had expected awkwardness and tension as we took our first tentative steps to mending our rift. If there was any, it was too slight to sense.

She swallowed a small bite of lasagna and a sip of wine. "I should have told you about my accident as soon as you started looking into Tom's. I didn't because I didn't want you thinking I tried to kill him."

"I never did. But think how it might look to Andy once he knew Tom was run off the road. Days after it happened, you show up at a body shop with damage on your car matching what the car that hit Tom would have. It's going to raise any cop's eyebrows."

She seized my wrist in a grip so tight it hurt. "I did not try to kill Tom. Especially not for a stupid trust fund."

Time to play dumb. "What trust fund?"

She loosened her grip but didn't let go. "When Tom and I married, his family gave me a half-a-million-dollar trust fund. I could draw on the interest any time I wanted but not touch the principal until Tom died, and they removed that restriction two years ago. I didn't want it, but they insisted I accept it, said it was a tradition to give one to anyone marrying into the Mercer family. I haven't touched a penny of it. Ever." She tightened her grip again. "I married Tom because I loved him, not for his money. You have to believe me, Dan, you have to."

I took both her hands in mine. "I do. I always have. So what happened? How did your car get damaged?"

"I was coming home from the hospital the day after Tom's accident. The doctor had just told me all the tests indicated he was probably in a permanent coma, but I shouldn't give up hope because anything was possible." She shook her head. "The things you think of at a time like that. I remembered I needed shampoo. So I stopped at K-Mart. As I was leaving, it hit me that my whole world, my whole life had been turned upside down, and I was worrying about shampoo. I was so upset I wasn't paying attention, and I hit a light pole."

"The mind does funny things sometimes to cope."

"Have you heard anything from Andy about the pictures? I keep thinking about them and trying to imagine who would do something like that, and I can't come up with anyone."

"Nothing yet. I'm sure as soon as he knows

something, he'll tell us. We're following up on some other things." I swallowed some wine slowly. "I have one thing that's not such good news. I don't think the crash put Tom in a coma. I think after he crashed, whoever ran him off the road held the airbag over his face to suffocate him."

Steph paled and the hand holding her glass trembled. She set it down. "Oh, God."

I gathered her hands in mine. "I'm so sorry, Steph."

"Who could do something so cruel?"

I didn't have an answer for that. In a few moments, her color returned. She took a deep breath and a swallow of wine. In a strained voice, she asked, "Do you know anything else?"

"The state police have determined Tom was run off the road by a dark red Jeep Cherokee. Did any of your friends or neighbors own one when Tom crashed?"

"Do you think one of them—"

"I don't know." I cut another chunk of lasagna and shifted it to my plate. "Do you know anyone who owns a Jeep Cherokee?"

"I can't say. I really don't pay attention to cars. I'm not even sure I know what one looks like."

"They're SUVs, kind of boxy. Flat sides, roof, and hood. Vertical front and back end." I used my hands for emphasis. "This one would have been, like I said, dark red with black bumpers and possibly grill and roof rack, and maybe silver wheels."

"No, nothing like that." She squeezed my hands. "Will you promise me you won't stop trying to find out what really happened to Tom?"

I squeezed back. "I'll do everything I can. To do it,

I'm going to have to ask you a lot of questions. And Andy may ask them, too."

She nodded. "I'll answer them a hundred times if it will help."

I took a second to organize my thoughts. "Tell me everything you can remember about the day Tom crashed."

She sipped her wine. "He left for the office a little before eight. I left around quarter after for Safe Haven and got home a little after four. He'd left a message just before two that everybody was going to the Roadhouse around six-thirty for dinner."

"Did he say who all was going?"

"No, just that he'd be home by eight-thirty. When he wasn't home by nine, I thought he'd just lost track of time." She paused for a deep breath. "A few minutes later, a police officer came to the house to tell me he'd been in an accident and was on his way to the hospital."

I'd been in her shoes. Only the officer had been Andy, and he'd come to the shops to tell me Amy was dead.

"I drove to the hospital and spent the night there."

"What sort of mood was Tom in that day?"

"Tired. And a little down. He'd been working twelve, sometimes fourteen hours a day including every Saturday since Labor Day, and I think it was starting to wear on him." She gazed past my shoulder for a second. "But there was something else going on, too."

"How do you know?"

"I know my husband. He'd been...tense isn't the right word...distracted for about a month, like he had something weighty on his mind."

"What?"

"I asked, but he wouldn't tell me. He said it was something at work." She rotated her wine glass slowly on the table. "But I don't think it was. I'd never seen him like that about work before."

"Did he ever talk about his work? Cases, clients, anything like that?"

"Never about his cases or clients except to say something like 'I picked up a new client today.' He talked more about the people he worked with."

"Do you remember anything about the cases he was working on when he had his crash?"

"His field was civil law—estates, bankruptcy, partnerships, divorce, corporate matters, malpractice—so they all were something in that vein. That's all I can tell you."

"Did he say anything around that time about having a case or a client maybe making him uncomfortable?"

A pause while she pushed her empty plate aside. "Not that I recall."

I finished my second slab of lasagna. "If you do, or if you remember anything about cases he was working on when he crashed, would you let me know?"

"Absolutely. But why? Do you think Tom was run off the road over something to do with one of his cases or clients?"

"Maybe. I'm keeping my mind open. You said he talked more about the people he worked with. What did he say about them?"

"The usual things. Something funny one of them said or did, or if it was someone's birthday, that sort of thing. I'm sure you and Amy did it."

"We did." I smiled at the memory of Amy talking

about people at the hospital. For the first time ever, thinking about her didn't cause the ache I'd lived with since her death. "I'd still like to talk to your friends about Tom and his accident."

"Would you like me to call them and explain why you want to talk to them?"

"It might make them more willing to see me."

"I'll let you know when I've talked to them." She served us tiramisu and coffee. "Could we not talk about Tom any more tonight?"

We didn't. We rambled through the weather and music we liked and our favorite movies. A surprise to me, we had similar tastes, but hers in music were much more eclectic than mine. The conversation flowed between us so easily, it was almost eleven before I realized it. And we were back to where we'd been before the fiasco.

At the door, Steph gave me a long hug. "I really missed you these last two weeks."

"I missed you, too."

Then she kissed me. And no hesitation, I kissed her.

Driving home, I wished we'd shared a dozen.

Chapter 26

07/20/2003 – Visiting A Lawyer

I met with Jeff and Lisa Styles at their two-story brick home on Country Club Road a few minutes after seven Sunday evening. We sat at a round glass-topped table on a patio surrounding their pool. As Lisa poured lemonade, Jeff said, "Stephanie said you wanted to talk to us about Tom's accident. I thought the police had determined he crashed after falling asleep at the wheel."

Lisa set a tall glass decorated with daisies in front of me and indicated the plate of shortbread cookies on the table. "Please help yourself. Steph spoke fondly of you when she called."

That bit of news pleased me. "Thank you." I tried Lisa's lemonade. Wonderfully cold on the still, hot, humid night but tart enough to etch steel. "Stephanie, as you know, didn't believe Tom fell asleep. I looked at his car and found signs someone ran him off the road."

"Why were you looking at Tom's car?" Jeff's expression and tone said I was intruding on something that was none of my business.

"He's doing it for Steph," Lisa said. "That's good enough for us. Isn't it, Jeffrey?"

"Hmm?" Then a small nod. "Mmm, yeah, yeah. Yes, it is."

"After I told Andy, Chief Cummings, what I'd

found, he reopened the case and asked my help because I know cars. Feel free to call him. He'll confirm I'm on the up and up."

"You can tell a car had been run off the road by another car simply by looking at it?" A skeptical gaze matched Jeff's tone.

"I've been doing auto body repair for over twenty years, so, yeah, I can. But I'm not the only one. My head bodyman confirmed another car hit Tom's. The state police reconstructed Tom's crash and reached the same conclusion."

"Then why are you questioning us instead of the authorities?"

I braved another drink of Lisa's lemonade. "Call it satisfying my own curiosity."

"I see." His tone said that didn't satisfy him before it shifted to musing. "I have wondered from the start if there wasn't more to Tom's accident than him falling asleep and running off the road."

Which didn't line up with what he'd told Steph at the OSM Christmas party or me in my office. I didn't want to call him on it. I didn't want to let it slide either. "Because?"

He cleared his throat. "If he had felt the least bit drowsy at the Roadhouse, he would have asked one of us to drive him home or had Stephanie pick him up."

"Did you tell the police that?"

"My dealings with them have left me with the impression they are competent, thorough, and professional." He ran his hand down the front of his polo shirt like he was smoothing a tie, looking as uncomfortable as he had in Mitchell's and in my office. "So when they said Tom fell asleep at the wheel, I didn't question it."

"Did you tell Stephanie you thought something other than Tom falling asleep was behind his crash?"

"His accident upset her enough without me adding to it."

"Would you mind answering some questions about Tom?"

He washed a bite of cookie down with a quick sip of lemonade. "Not at all."

"How was Tom as a person?"

He nibbled more cookie. "Easy-going, polite, courteous to everyone. An outstanding lawyer."

"Did he have any enemies?"

"That sounds more like a police question than one from a curious friend."

"Just trying to learn more about Tom. So, did he have any enemies?"

"At the firm? No. I never heard anyone there speak a bad word about him."

I tried another mouthful of lemonade then checked my fillings for acid erosion. "How about clients? Any who maybe took offense for some reason?"

"If there were any, I never heard of them."

I decided to pass on any more of Lisa's lemonade. I liked my teeth too much. "He ever have a nasty run-in with someone outside work? A neighbor or someone in a store perhaps."

"None I'm aware of. If he found himself in such a situation, he'd do all he could to defuse it, not escalate it."

"Were you with Tom at the Roadhouse the night of his accident?"

"Only long enough to have one drink, twenty

minutes at most." He drained his glass and poured a refill. "We had plans to go away Sunday and wanted to get an early start in the morning."

"Why the Roadhouse? Why not some place closer to your offices?"

Jeff shrugged. "No real reason other than tradition. We always went there."

"Was it just you and Tom?"

"No. Holland was there. And Elizabeth Fremont, Jim Delany, and Patricia Monroe. The six of us who had worked that day."

"How did Tom seem that night?"

"Drained, like all of us, looking forward to having a day off to recharge his batteries. We'd been swamped by a flood of new clients and casework over the summer and fall, were working all kinds of crazy hours just to keep abreast of things."

"Steph said in the month before his accident, Tom seemed distracted by something. Any idea what it was?"

"No. To be honest, if he was distracted, I didn't notice it."

"Could he have been troubled by a case or client?"

"I doubt it." Jeff selected another cookie and chewed it slowly. "His field was civil law—wills, incorporations, and the like. All fairly straightforward work. He did get a new client last August. But every lawyer dreams of a client like that, one who generates lots of billable hours."

"Any chance another lawyer in your firm was jealous, maybe felt the client should have been his or hers?"

"Not jealous. Just wishing they had been the lucky

one to land the client. I don't know how much you know about lawyers, but billable hours are a lawyer's mother lode. They're how firms evaluate how productive their lawyers are. And they can put a lawyer on the inside track to a partnership. Plus, this particular client knew people who could open doors, help move Tom's career far beyond small town lawyer, maybe as far as the state supreme court."

Could that be behind Tom's accident? "How did Tom land this particular mother lode?"

"Art O'Reilly, a co-founder of the firm along with my father, was cutting back drastically on his workload and handed the client over to Tom."

"Do you know this client's name?"

"I do." He munched another cookie. "But I can't share it with you due to lawyer-client privilege."

"What happened to Tom's clients after his accident?"

"The most pressing cases were reassigned to other lawyers in the firm the following Monday, the others as the need arose."

"Who got this special client of Tom's?"

"I did."

"Did it put you on the inside track to partnership?"

"I made partner in January." Another uneasy look and stroke of his shirt front. "But I'd give it up in a second if it would bring Tom back."

Is he troubled by how he got his partnership or lying to me? "What make of cars did you both own at the time Tom had his accident?"

The topic shift had them gazing at me in confusion. Jeff recovered first. "Why do you need to know that?"

"Because we know the make and color of car that

ran Tom off the road."

"And you wish to eliminate us as possible suspects. I assure you neither Lisa nor I would do anything to harm Tom."

"Then you won't mind answering the question."

"The same ones we have now. A dark blue Lincoln Town Car and a beige Volvo wagon."

"Did we pass, Mr. Gallagher?" Lisa asked.

I didn't answer. "Were Tom and Steph getting along okay? Any problems in their marriage you knew of?"

The shift caught them off-guard again. A second passed before Lisa snapped, "Why on earth would you ask such an absurd question, Mr. Gallagher?"

A glare in Jeff's eyes. "If you think Stephanie had anything to do with Tom's accident, you're barking up the wrong tree."

"Tom and Steph were the most loving couple I ever knew," Lisa said. "They adored each other. She would never do anything to hurt him."

Confirmation I was right and Andy was wrong about their marriage. That covered everything I wanted to ask them. "I appreciate you both taking the time to talk to me." I laid two business cards on the table. "If you think of anything that might help find who tried to kill Tom, please call me or the police."

"We will. And if we can do anything to help, please let us know."

"Yes, by all means," Lisa added. "We'd do anything to help Steph."

"Can either of you think of anyone else I should talk to about Tom?"

"Roberta?" Lisa asked.

"Roberta Lynch?" Jeff asked her then turned to me. "Tom's secretary. You can talk to her, and I'll be happy to arrange it, but I doubt she'll be able to add anything."

Secretaries always know more than their bosses suspect. "I'd still like to talk to her. If you could set something up, I would appreciate it."

"I'll arrange it tomorrow. May I ask you a personal question, Dan? Do you golf by any chance?"

"No."

"Pity. Since Tom had his accident, I've been looking for a replacement for our Saturday afternoon foursome. How about tennis?"

"I played some in high school, but not since then. Why?"

"Stephanie plays very well. Since you've become friends with her, you should think about joining Pine Crest Country Club. I'm sure she'd be happy to sponsor you for membership. The pro there is phenomenal. He'll have you in top form again in no time."

Right. Pay two grand a month to hone my skills in a game I only took up in high school to catch the eye of a girl I wanted to date. "Thanks, but no thanks. Not my thing."

"How do you stay in such good shape?" Lisa asked, clearly puzzled why someone who didn't play tennis or golf wasn't a fat slob.

"My work mostly. There's a lot of physical activity involved in rebuilding cars. And I lift weights twice a week. Thanks again for your time."

As we made our way to the gate in the fence Jeff asked, "Has Holland ever approached you again?"

"Not since he came to my shops."

"What did Holland do?" Lisa asked.

"Questioned Dan regarding his friendship with Stephanie. Wanted to see proof of his financial stability, said he'd take Dan to court if he refused. If he tries again, Dan, let me know. I'll put a stop to it." He opened the gate.

"I took care of it," I said.

Lisa said, "You know why he did it, Jeffrey."

He gave her a surprised look. "I do?"

"Haven't you noticed how he looks at Stephanie? He's had his eyes on her since he met her. He even made a pass at her at the Christmas party their first year here. I wouldn't be surprised if Tom should die, Holland would pursue her."

"What? Why?"

"Really Jeffrey? You can't see it? He sees life as a competition he has to win—you know he does—and he measures winning by having more money, a bigger house, a more beautiful wife, a better everything than everyone around him. If he could get Steph to marry him, he'd have the beautiful wife."

"He has dozens of beautiful women to choose from, has one on his arm every time we see him. Why would he go after Stephanie when he could have any one of them?"

"Her looks are only part of her appeal to him. The biggest prize, the biggest win, in his book is money. Steph is a wealthy woman in her own right. If Tom would die, she'd be even richer." She clapped a hand over her mouth. "Oh, my God!"

"What, Leez?" Jeff asked.

"You don't think Holland ran Tom off the road so he could have Stephanie?"

Going by how Carter came after me for having

dinner with her, running Tom off the road wasn't beyond of the realm of possibility.

"He'd never do anything that crazy," Jeff said then paused. "Maybe he would. He's not long on patience. If he has his sights set on Stephanie, he may have decided to move things along."

Walking back to my car, I peeked into their garage. A beige Volvo and blue Lincoln filled it.

Chapter 27

07/22/2003 – The Secretary Talks

Roberta Lynch said she could spare me ten minutes Tuesday morning if I could meet her in the O'Reilly, Styles, and McNamara parking lot at ten-fifteen.

On the dot, a petite woman in a red dress came out the back door of their building. She headed toward me, lighting a cigarette on the way. Gray strands laced dark brown hair framing an oval face with cocoa brown eyes edged by laugh crinkles behind small gold framed glasses. "Mr. Styles said you wanted to talk to me about Mr. Mercer."

The rasp in her voice said she'd smoked a lot of cigarettes before this one. "That's right."

She blew smoke out in a thin cord. "What would you like to know?"

"Everything you can tell me."

She inhaled more smoke. "He was easy to work for. Always treated me with respect as a person and as a secretary. Never demanded the impossible. Always said please and thank you. Always remembered my birthday and wedding anniversary with a gift or flowers. Mr. Styles said you're looking into his accident."

"Tom was run off the road, and I'm trying to find out who did it. Do you know anyone who would want him dead?"

She went rigid for an instant. "I can't think of a single soul."

I nodded toward OSM's building. "Anybody here who might hate him enough to try it?"

She sucked in smoke and let it out as she answered. "No. Everyone liked him. Although he didn't get along well with Mr. Carter."

"Didn't get along how?"

"Every way. Like poles on a magnet." She lowered her voice. "To be honest, no one here likes Mr. Carter."

"Why?"

"He's everything Mr. Mercer wasn't. Rude, abrasive, demeaning, demanding, quick to remind you he is a lawyer and you aren't."

"What about Tom's clients? Any of them unhappy with his legal work on their behalf?"

"He had one or two over the years but none of them ever threatened him, just took their business to another firm. Mostly, when he had a problem with a client, it was a disagreement over what one of them said in a meeting. Mr. Mercer could always show them exactly what they both said. The firm's policy is to record then make a transcript of all client-attorney meetings." A puff on her cigarette. "Five years ago, Mr. Mercer started taping all his meetings after a file clerk accused him of...inappropriate behavior in his office."

Maybe Tom wasn't the paragon of virtue everyone portrayed him to be. "Did he?"

A woman in a business suit trotted across the parking lot, trading nods with Roberta as she passed. Roberta waited until she drove away in a silver Buick LeSabre. "Absolutely not. She was nothing but a troublemaking tramp. But he began taping all his conversations to protect himself from similar situations in the future."

Which ruled him out as the instigator. Sort of. "What happened to the woman?"

"She was fired, of course."

That might have angered her enough to go after Tom. But waiting five years to do it was unlikely. "Do you remember her name?"

"Truthfully, no. She'd only worked here six or seven months."

Which made it a dead end. "Did everyone here know Tom taped all his meetings?"

"He didn't formally announce it, if that's what you mean, but I'm sure word got around."

"And you typed a transcript of every meeting Tom had?"

Another drag. "Every one he gave me."

"What if it was, say, Jeff Styles stopping by to set up a golf date? Would he tape that?"

She laughed a raspy bark. "Good heavens, no. I'd have had twenty tapes a day to transcribe."

"What kind of tapes were they?"

"Microcassettes. Mr. Mercer had a pocket-sized recorder he carried everywhere."

"What happened to the transcripts you typed?"

"If they related to a case in any way, they went in the case file. Everything else went back to him until he had me shred it."

"Do any transcripts from before his accident still exist?"

A final puff on her cigarette then she dropped it on the paving and crushed it under a black pump. "Only the ones in case files."

"How did the two of you work the tapes?"

"He had two sets, A and B numbered one through ten. He alternated the sets daily and used them in order. One then two then three and so on. He'd put the tapes he used on my desk when he left for the day, and I would transcribe them the next day and return them to him when I finished." She got another cigarette from the pack in her purse, raised her lighter toward it, then lowered her hand. "Although, about a month before Mr. Mercer's accident, there were nine tapes on my desk when I came in that morning but the last one was number ten."

"Was skipping a tape odd?"

"It happened once or twice when the tape broke." She lit the cigarette and inhaled a hard drag. "The reason that morning sticks in my mind is because when I asked him about the missing tape, he snapped at me, said it was something personal. It was the first—the only—time he ever was rude to me."

The contents of the missing tape had to be something major for a man who always treated his secretary with respect to lash out at her. Could it also have gotten him run off the road? "This missing tape was from a scheduled meeting?"

"I would assume so."

"Can you remember who with? Or which tape was missing?"

Roberta delivered another raspy laugh. "My memory isn't that good. But I can go back through my day book from last year and find it."

"You can remember when it was?"

"Not the exact date. But I can use the day Mr. Mercer crashed as a starting point."

149

I handed her my card. "You'll let me know what you turn up?"

"Of course." She slipped my card into a side pocket of her purse.

"Can you think of any reason why Tom might snap at you like that?"

"No."

"I assume Tom had some personal items in his office. What happened to them after his accident?"

"I packed them up and someone delivered them to Mrs. Mercer."

"Do you remember what you sent to her?"

Another long drag on her cigarette before answering. "A Cross pen desk set, his nameplate, his tape recorder, a photograph of him and Mrs. Mercer, his diploma and license, several personal law books, and some other odds and ends."

"But no tapes?"

"I kept those because they contained work product." She glanced at her watch. "I have to get back to work. I'm sorry." She dropped her half-smoked cigarette and scuffed it out. "I hope you find whoever did this to Mr. Mercer. He was a wonderful man." She strode toward the building.

"One last question. Who do you work for now that Tom Mercer is gone?"

She glanced back without breaking stride. "Mr. Styles."

Chapter 28

07/22/2003 – The Task

I called Steph as soon as I got back to D-J and left a message for her to call me when she had a chance. She called that evening, and just hearing her alto voice raised a smile on my face.

"You said you had a question?"

"Yeah. Did you ever find any tapes among Tom's things?"

"You mean from his little recorder? There's an unopened pack of three and one still in the recorder in the desk."

"Do you know what's on that one?"

"Probably notes to himself. Make an appointment to get his car serviced. Pick up dry cleaning. Things like that. Instead of writing notes to himself, he dictated them. Why are you asking?"

"I talked to Roberta today." I told Steph about the missing tape from a month before Tom's accident. "Since he told her it was personal, he might have taken it home."

"Do you think it will tell us who ran him off the road?"

"Maybe. Other than the desk, if Tom wanted to keep something like a tape, where would he put it? Do you have a safe in the house?"

"No safe. Only a lockable box we keep all our important papers in. Something we could grab and run if the house ever caught fire."

"Maybe he put it in there." I strolled over for a glance out my office window.

"I've been in it probably ten times since his accident looking for things, and I've never seen one. But I'll look again to be sure."

Maybe Roberta had lied to me about no tapes being among the items she boxed up for return to Steph. "What about in the box of things from his office?"

"No. Just his work recorder and some," a hesitation, "personal things."

"Any other place else he might have put it?"

"I can't think of any."

I couldn't either. "Did you ever get Tom's things from his car?"

"The police returned them a few days after his crash. There was no tape."

I only had Roberta Lynch's word a tape *was* missing. Maybe she'd destroyed it because something on it could have been damaging to Tom. Or she could simply have erased it to make what was on it go away. Either way she wouldn't have said boo about it being missing. That stirred another thought. "How many of those little recorders did Tom have?"

"Two. One he kept at work and one he carried with him all the time."

"And you have them both?"

"Yes."

Copying information from one tape to another was as easy as plugging in a patch cord. "Before you look for another tape, did you ever play the tape in his recorder, listen to what's on it?"

"I haven't. But I will, and if there's nothing on it, I'll start looking for others. If I find one, is there a way to tell if it's the one Roberta said was missing?"

"She said he labeled his tapes A and B and one through ten but she can't remember which one was missing except it wasn't ten."

"I'll let you know if I find anything."

Chapter 29

07/22/2003 – Friends with Rumors

I met Doug and Claire Shepton that evening for drinks at Shenanigans on Market Boulevard. Doug was about my height with a wide receiver's build, Claire six inches shorter and cheerleader perky. Both were blond and blue-eyed, tan and extremely fit, and supported L. L. Bean. He was an investment advisor for First National Bank, and she taught fourth grade.

After our drinks arrived, I ran through the same questions I'd asked Jeff and Lisa Styles. Doug and Claire knew Tom and Steph socially and had gone skiing with them at Elk Mountain a few times. They knew nothing of Tom's professional life other than he was the lawyer who revised their wills after the births of their children. Neither owned a Jeep or BMW. Doug had a Chrysler sedan, Claire a Dodge minivan. They couldn't imagine anyone trying to kill Tom, the nicest guy anyone would ever meet. Both agreed his accident was a terrible tragedy, especially for Steph.

"It's cruel to say," Doug said after a swallow of his vodka Collins, "but I think it would have been better if Tom had died that night. Then Steph wouldn't be stuck for who knows how long in the limbo she's in now."

"I've often thought that, too," Claire said in her little girl voice. "It can't be easy for her, seeing him lying there, just…existing, day after day after day."

"How was their marriage?" I asked. "Any problems there you knew of?"

"Solid as a rock. Like ours." Doug hooked an arm across Claire's shoulders and gave her a hug and a smile. "Right, hon?"

She leaned away from him slightly. "I'm not so sure it was."

"Come on, Claire. They were like teens, always holding hands or touching each other some way."

"Maybe they weren't by the time Tom had his accident. Remember, the last time we saw them was last Labor Day."

Doug gazed at her, puzzled. "Do you know something I don't?"

Claire studied her gimlet for a second. "When you were at that seminar in Baltimore the next week, I ran into Terry Kendall at Contours, and she told me Tom was having an affair with a paralegal at his firm."

"Tom? Cheat on Steph?" He rolled his eyes. "Right."

"I didn't want to believe it either, but she works there part time and she saw the signs."

"Signs." Doug snorted. "What a bunch of shit!"

"It's not…garbage, Doug. Women notice these things. And watch your language."

Could Andy be right? Could an affair be behind Tom's accident? "Did Terry say who Tom was having an affair with?"

"It was something like Tiffany or Courtney, but it wasn't either of those." Claire thought through a sip of her drink. "Brittany. That's it. Brittany…Brittany Ferris."

Chapter 30

07/24/2003 – Feedback

Two mornings later, I told Andy what I'd learned from the Styleses and Sheptons. He said he'd been trying to talk to Scott Harris, but the guy had been ducking him.

My phone rang at ten after four that afternoon. "Mr. Gallagher? It's Roberta Lynch from O'Reilly, Styles, and McNamara."

"Yes, Mrs. Lynch."

"I found the date of the missing tape I told you about. It was Wednesday, September eighteenth. The next morning there were nine tapes on my desk and B-seven was missing."

"How do you know it was B-seven?"

"I made a note of it. I noted any unusual happenings every day to protect Mr. Mercer as well as myself should any questions ever arise over anything."

"Any idea which meeting he didn't give you a tape for?"

"Everything on his schedule was client-related—a review of a trust fund's provisions, a will signing, a filing with the court, similar matters—except for two. Mr. McNamara met with him at one to ask his opinion on a case, and Mr. Styles met with him at three. It must be that one."

"Why did Jeff want to meet with Tom?"

"I don't have a notation after his name, so he must not have said. Lawyers sometimes would ask to meet with Mr. Mercer but not give a reason. Usually, it was just to brainstorm a legal matter with him."

Probably all it was. But if that's all it was, why hide the tape? "Do you remember how long their meeting lasted?"

"My notes show him leaving at three-fifteen."

"Any idea why Tom would record a meeting then not give you the tape to type up a transcript? Why he would make the tape disappear?"

A long silence. "Mr. Mercer said it was personal when I asked him about it. That's all I can tell you."

"How did they both seem after the meeting? Happy? Sad?"

A short silence before she answered. "Mr. Styles seemed annoyed. He marched past my desk without even a glance in my direction. And Mr. Mercer seemed... troubled. Something was definitely on his mind afterward."

Odd emotions for best friends to have after a meeting. "Mrs. Lynch, do you have time to answer a few more questions?"

"As long as it won't take too long. I have a few things to finish before I leave today."

"I'll be as brief as I can. I've heard rumors Tom was having an affair with a paralegal at the firm at the time of his accident."

"Mr. Mercer was *not* having an affair. With anyone. Here or anywhere. He adored his wife, idolized her. Any man who loves his wife that much would never be unfaithful to her."

She had a point. Or was she covering for her former boss? "Does the name Brittany Ferris mean anything to you?"

She snorted. "That little piece of fluff? If you think Mr. Mercer would have anything to do with her, you're an idiot." She crashed the phone down.

Well, I guess she told me.

After supper, I met with Dr. William and Deidre Adler in the living room of their navy trimmed white colonial. They didn't add anything to what the Styleses or Sheptons had told me but dismissed rumors of Tom having an affair with a co-worker as ludicrous. Jeff and Lisa Styles had used the word preposterous when I'd asked them about it earlier.

Chapter 31

07/25/2003 – Dishing the Dirt

Minutes after I got back from lunch on Friday, Nicole Argenti, the last of Steph's friends I'd hoped to talk to, finally returned my call requesting we meet. She apologized, saying she forgot to call earlier. We arranged to meet at six at Bluebeard's Cove, a seafood restaurant in the Holiday Inn by the interstate.

I entered the bar area and scanned the crowd for a dark-haired man and woman at a table. An attractive woman at the bar turned and studied me. Wild curls of glossy black hair spilled past her shoulders, and she wore a tight red blouse, second-skin white slacks, and red stilettos. She gave me a small wave. I returned it and snaked through the tables to her.

"Dan? Hi. I'm Nicole." She held out her hand.

"Hi." Her handshake was firm, her hand lingering in mine as her dark bronze eyes raked me from brown hair to boot heels. Her perfume suggested moonlit tropical nights. The stool on either side of her was empty. "Where's Matt?"

"Away for the weekend." She dismissed it as nothing with a wave of her hand.

I sat next to her and asked the bartender for a Maker's Mark old fashioned. "I wish you'd told me that when you called. I really wanted to talk to both of you."

She sipped from something tall, red, and frothy. "I know everything Matt knows."

After the bartender delivered my drink, she said, "Why don't we get a booth?" and eased off her stool.

Every man in the bar tracked her sashay to the farthest corner of the room, and several got dagger-filled glares from the women with them. The moment we settled in the booth, she leaned toward me, flashing more than a hint of cleavage, and put her hand on my arm. "Steph didn't tell me I'd be talking to a hunk."

I held in a laugh. Hunk and Dan Gallagher don't match up on the page. I have all the normal parts in their proper places, but they're all ordinary. I slid my arm from under her hand. She sampled her drink, sat back, and pressed her shoulders against the cushion, tightening her blouse over her breasts. "What would you like to know about Tom and Steph?"

I asked her the same questions I'd asked the others. She used my name and touched my arm or hand often, each one lasting a second too long to be casual. After the third time, I slid my arm out of her reach so she shifted to leaning toward me. Her replies lined up with others I'd gotten until I asked about the rumor Tom was having an affair.

"Of course he was. Everybody does. It's no big deal."

"Some might disagree." I took in some old fashioned.

"Everybody, and I mean everybody, has at least one, Dan. Why should Tom be any different? And no woman in her right mind would have passed on a good time with him. I wouldn't have. He was a very handsome man."

"Any idea who the woman might have been?"

"I don't know." She covered my hand with hers again. "Does it matter?"

Did it? Would knowing her name change anything? I pulled my hand back. "If Steph found out Tom was having an affair, how would she react?"

"She wouldn't have dared raise a stink. The pot has no right calling the kettle black."

"She had an affair, too?"

"She spent a lot of time with the golf pro at Pine Crest last year." Nicole took a long draw on her drink. "And still is. Supposedly to improve her game."

"That's your proof of an affair?"

"What's good for the gander is good for the goose. Eric Greenwood was premium eye candy." Another sip of her drink. "And golf wasn't the only thing he was good at. With Tom in a coma, do you really think she's still working on her game with Eric?"

I didn't buy it, but it gave me pause. I had no more questions for Nicole so I downed the last of my drink. "Thanks for your time, Nicole. I appreciate you talking to me." I stood and dropped a twenty on the table.

"Walk me to my car?" She slid out of the booth.

Men again monitored her sashay as we left.

I followed her to a bright red Mustang convertible where she faced me. "Matt won't be home until Sunday night."

"So you said earlier."

She ran her hand slowly down my arm. "What I'm saying now is if you don't have any plans for the evening, we could have dinner." The sultry gaze in her eyes said we could do more than dine.

I passed.

Chapter 32

07/29/2003 – Death Arrives

A few minutes after nine Tuesday evening, I pulled into my driveway and almost rear-ended Steph's Lexus. My porch glider moving in the shadows caught my eye as I climbed the three steps. She came toward me. "Tom died this afternoon."

"Ah, jeez." I wanted to hug her but hesitated, not sure how she'd react if I did. "I'm sorry."

She held out her arms, signaling her need. I drew her close.

"A nurse went into his room to check on him and he was...gone. His doctor says it happens sometimes." Her eyes were sad but not inflamed and tension stiffened her body. She hadn't cried yet to release it. "I've been expecting this every day since his accident. Now that it's here, I can't quite accept it."

I steered her back to the glider and sat next to her with my arm looped around her shoulders. We rocked slowly, not speaking. After a minute, she said, "Last week one day, I squeezed his hand like I always do and he...he squeezed back, not strongly but I felt it. And other days, his eyelids fluttered like he was trying to wake up." Making losing him now that much harder.

She buried her face in the crook between my neck and shoulder and clutched my tee with both hands as sobs wracked her. I wrapped her tightly in my arms. I'd felt the pain she was feeling and wished I could do something to take hers away.

Between sobs, she said, "I didn't go see him today. If I had—"

"Don't say it. Don't even think it. As hard as it may be to accept right now, that wouldn't have changed anything."

She nodded against my neck. I held her until her sobs faded to an occasional hitch in her breathing. She sat up, dried her tears, and blew her nose. "I need a favor."

"Name it."

"May I stay here tonight? I don't think I can handle being alone right now."

"Sure." I stood. "Come on."

She picked up a small tan duffle bag as she rose, hoisted it waist high, and gave me a weak smile. "Presumptuous of me, wasn't it, assuming you'd let me stay?"

"Not one bit. You're more than welcome here. Any time." I held the door for her. "You want something to eat or drink? Or a nightcap?"

"No, nothing, thank you. I just want to go to sleep."

I led her into the bedroom and gave her a hug. "Anything you need, let me know. Good night. Sleep well."

Another weak smile. "I'll try."

"I'll be on the couch if you need me."

I grabbed a pair of gym shorts and a tee from a dresser drawer and changed in the bathroom then bedded down on my living room couch. I was tired from a long day at work yet I doubted I'd sleep much. A six-foot-four frame doesn't fit well on a six-foot sofa.

Tom's death nagged at my mind, too. Why, after almost ten months in a coma but now showing signs of coming out of it, had he suddenly died? It didn't seem logical. Since I knew almost nothing about the human body, maybe I was gnawing on a bone that didn't exist. Maybe it happened that way sometimes, like his doctor said. Would Steph's being there have prevented it? Those thoughts bothered me enough to keep me tossing and turning for a couple hours.

A sound woke me. I opened my eyes. The low moon and the streetlight across the way gave enough light for me to see Steph in a pale gray warm-up suit sitting in the rocker by the picture window, staring out at the night. I glanced at the clock on the bookshelf. Two-oh-seven. "Can't sleep?"

She started at my voice and gasped. "Did I wake you? I'm sorry. I didn't mean to."

"You didn't. So, can't sleep?"

She shook her head. "My mind just keeps swirling with everything I have to do and I don't see how I'm ever going to get it all done. I'm not even sure where to start."

I sat up. "So don't try to do it all yourself. Let me help."

"I feel like I'm always dumping my burden on you."

"That's what friends are for, to share the load when it gets too heavy for you to carry on your own." I patted the cushion next to me. "Come here."

She sat by my side and took my hand. "You *are* a friend. I don't know how I could have gotten through these last few months without you."

I slipped my arm around her, ran a hand along her shoulder. The muscles were as hard as rock. The other shoulder was equally taut. "You need a massage. Sit up."

She did and I stepped behind the couch. I rubbed from the base of her neck out to her arms and back for a few seconds to draw some heat into the muscles, then kneaded them, strongly at first then more gently as they relaxed. She rolled her head, sighed, and after another minute, put her hands over mine. "That feels heavenly. Thank you."

I sat again, and she nestled against me, resting her head on my shoulder. "Knowing you're here if I need you is enough. If I get overwhelmed, I will ask for help."

Five minutes later, her slow, gentle breathing said she'd drifted off to sleep.

I waited another minute then eased away from her and lowered her head to the pillow, lifted her legs onto the sofa and spread a blanket over her. My recliner had always been good for naps. It should do equally well for a night's sleep. I kicked back and closed my eyes.

I woke a few minutes before six-thirty. Steph had rolled onto her side on the couch and tucked her hands under her cheek. Chestnut hair partly veiled her face, free of the heartache and worry that had filled it last night.

I eased the recliner upright and stepped lightly toward the bathroom so I wouldn't disturb her. In the kitchen, I started coffee brewing then considered breakfast. French toast and bacon sounded good, so I got the bacon frying and mixed up the batter. The brewer was making its final gurgles when Steph padded into the kitchen, fingers raking her hair off her face. "Do I smell breakfast?"

"Yup." I snagged a mug from the cabinet, filled it, and handed it to her. "Morning."

She offered a weak smile. "Good morning." She doctored her coffee, sipped, and let out a long, "Mmm."

"How'd you sleep?"

"Better than I thought I would." She set her mug down with a thump. "I'm sorry about last night. I should have called first. I shouldn't have just shown up here." The words cascaded out. "I should have asked if it—"

"Shh." I wrapped her in my arms. "It's okay. Don't worry about it."

She held on to me for maybe a minute then looked at me as if she wanted to say something. A moment later, she backed out of my hug.

"How about some breakfast? French toast and bacon? Or I can fix you something else."

She smiled a better smile. "French toast is perfect."

I dipped bread slices in egg batter and laid them in the pan then spread the bacon on paper towels to drain.

"What can I do?"

"Nothing." I guided her to a chair at the table. "Sit and enjoy your coffee."

Another smile with more life in it. "You're going to spoil me."

"You deserve spoiling. Especially right now." I flipped the slices over. "Breakfast in two minutes."

When the coating on the French toast was golden brown, I dished everything up and served it. After I set her plate in front of her, she gripped my hand. "This all means more to me than you'll ever know. Thank you from the bottom of my heart."

I returned her gentle squeeze. "My pleasure."

We ate in silence for a bunch of seconds before I asked, "How are you feeling?"

"I don't know." She slid a bite of toast back and forth in a puddle of syrup. "Numb, I guess."

"Feel up to answering some questions?"

She put the bite into her mouth and made a small shrug. "I guess so."

"You said a nurse found Tom dead. Didn't they have him hooked up to a monitor so they could keep tabs on him at the nursing station?"

"They did his first month at Oakhurst but he was so stable, they disconnected it and only had the unit in his room. A nurse checked it about once an hour, and it had an alarm that would sound if anything went wrong."

"What time did they find him?"

"An Oakhurst nursing supervisor called me shortly after three to tell me he had died but didn't say when."

"And she didn't say anything about the alarm going off?"

"No. But I didn't think to ask either."

"Who visited him regularly besides you, friends, neighbors, anyone?"

She chewed a bite of bacon. "Jeff is the only one."

I finished my second slice of French toast before I said what I'd been thinking since I woke. "I think you should talk to Tom's doctor about having an autopsy done."

She halted the strip of bacon near her mouth then lowered it. "Do you think whoever ran him off the road went to Oakhurst yesterday and…and killed him?"

"I think we need to consider it."

She dropped the bacon, covered her mouth, and closed her eyes. A tear seeped from each one. After a moment, she nodded and lowered her hand. "I'll call him as soon as I get home."

Breakfast over, we parted company. I swung by the police station on my way to work to see Andy. "Tom Mercer died yesterday."

"I heard." He studied me for a moment. "Something about it bugging you?"

"He was hooked to a monitor in his room with an alarm that rang if anything went wrong. Otherwise, a nurse checked on him about once an hour. When a nurse checked on him yesterday afternoon, he was gone. If something did go wonky, the alarm should have gone off."

"You'd think so." Andy rocked back in his chair. "Where are you going with this?"

"Steph said he showed signs last week of coming out of the coma, squeezing back when she squeezed his hand, moving his eyelids like he was trying to open them. Seems kind of strange he'd show signs of waking up one week and die the next. Be interesting to know if he had any visitors yesterday."

"You think whoever tried to kill him on Millers Run Road finished the job?"

I shrugged. "I think it's possible."

Andy nodded. "Me, too."

Chapter 33

08/02/2003 – The Funeral

I arrived at Tom Mercer's viewing a little after seven Friday evening and joined the line of people waiting to pay their respects. Steph looked beautiful in her black dress, stirring thoughts I shouldn't be having about a new widow. I took her hand. "I am sorry for your loss."

"Thank you." She gave my hand a light squeeze. "Please stay." The plea in her eyes made refusing impossible.

Walking to the back of the room, I spotted Holland Carter giving me a venomous glare. I sat, feeling like a bit of an interloper, having only known Tom Mercer through what Steph and others had told me about him. About ten minutes later, Andy entered, spoke briefly to Steph, then sat next to me.

"What brings you here?"

"Paying my respects." He lowered his voice. "And to update you. Mercer's autopsy revealed petechiae—little blood spots, a sign of suffocation—in his eyes and cotton fibers in his mouth."

"Fibers. Like from a pillowcase?"

"Yep. The medical examiner ruled his death a homicide."

I glanced toward the front of the room. Steph was

talking to Jeff and Lisa Styles. The news would devastate her. "You tell Steph?"

Andy followed my gaze. "Thought I'd give her a day or two."

Jeff and Lisa took seats next to Carter. He said something that made Styles eye me coolly. I shifted my gaze back to Andy. "You get anything from the Oakhurst people?"

"After Mercer was taken out of his room," Andy said, "a nurse discovered the alarm on his monitor was switched off."

"By?"

"Could have been someone on staff. The button is easy to hit accidentally. Could have been his killer."

"Who visited him that day?"

"No way to tell. They don't make visitors sign in. And they were busy that afternoon—lots of visitors and three admissions—and shorthanded. Closest we could come was a nurse's aide remembered seeing a man and a woman in the hall near Mercer's room sometime before he was discovered dead."

"You show her Jeff Styles's picture?" I'd told him Jeff was Tom's only regular visitor.

"She couldn't ID him, said she didn't get a good look at them, only noticed them going into Tom's room."

"What about fingerprints on the monitor button?"

Andy shook his head. "By the time we got to it, it had been wiped down and in another patient's room for a day, and a half dozen people touched it. That's all I got." He headed for the door, pausing on the way to speak to Steph again.

Throughout the evening, every time our eyes met, a

touch of comfort filled hers. Carter and Styles, on the other hand, had a cold laser-gaze on me every time I glanced their way. The glares continued Saturday at Tom's funeral.

As servers at Pine Crest cleared away the after-funeral meal, a tall silver-haired man in black suit and a silver-blonde woman in a black dress, both in their late sixties, made their way toward me. The man leaned on a cane with each step. I stood as they approached and he offered his hand. "Leland Mercer. And my wife, Helen."

"Dan Gallagher." I shook his hand then hers. Clearly Tom's parents. "I'm sorry for your loss."

Grim tension stiffened them both for a second. "Thank you." Leland regarded me with a puzzled expression as we all sat. "Were you a friend of Thomas's?"

"This is Stephanie's friend," Helen said. "You remember her telling us about him."

Leland's brow creased for a moment then his brown eyes widened. "Oh, yes, that's right." He eased awkwardly onto a chair. "Forgive me, Mr. Gallagher. Since my stroke last year, I sometimes have trouble remembering things."

"No problem. And please call me Dan."

Helen said, "Stephanie's told us so much about you."

Leland gave a smile that sagged slightly on one side. "All of it good." He studied me, a finger pressed against his lips. "I heard your name somewhere before Stephanie ever mentioned it." His eyes took on the slightly unfocused look of someone dredging for a memory.

"We are so grateful she has had you to turn to over these last few months."

Leland said, "I remember now where I've heard your name. Henry Lowenthal, a friend, said you restored two cars for him."

"A pair of Thunderbirds. A '58 hardtop and a '59 convertible."

"You remember which automobiles you restored for someone?" Helen asked. "That's amazing."

"He had nothing but praise for your work," Leland said. "Praise from Henry is as rare as hen's teeth."

"Tell Mr. Lowenthal hello from me the next time you see him."

"We will."

"Stephanie told us yesterday Thomas's accident wasn't his fault." Helen touched my arm. "Is it true someone else caused it?" A flicker of hurt showed in both her and Leland's eyes.

"It appears so."

"Why couldn't the police see that?" Leland snapped. "Why didn't they believe Stephanie when she said Thomas wouldn't have fallen asleep and crashed?"

"The police deal in facts and evidence, and nothing they saw that night pointed to it being anything other than him running off the road and hitting a tree. Now that they have evidence it wasn't, they've reopened the investigation."

"Stephanie told us that," Helen said, "and that you are assisting them. Is there any way we can help?"

"By answering a few questions."

"Of course."

"Okay. Did Tom ever say anything to either of you about having trouble with anyone?"

"What kind of trouble?"

I muffled a sneeze. Bouquets on every table in Pine Crest Country Club's dining room perfumed the air, clogging my sinuses and brewing a headache around my eyes. "Any kind at all."

"I don't recall him saying anything along those lines," Leland said. "Do you, Helen?"

She pursed her lips for a second. "The only thing I remember is not long after he started at the firm, he said he didn't care for one of the lawyers there."

"You remember the lawyer's name?" Odds said it was Holland Carter.

"He never mentioned it. He merely said he didn't care for a fellow lawyer. And he never brought it up again."

Damn.

"He said something to me shortly before his accident." Leland furrowed his brow for a moment. "What was it? Something about not knowing who your friends were? No, that's not it." A brief shake of his head. "I hate it when I can't remember something."

"Calm down, Lee." Helen took his hand. "Dr. Holmberg said that is normal, and it would clear up in time."

"I know. But to have something here," he jabbed his forehead, "and not be able to recall it is so...frustrating." He sighed. "I am sorry for my outburst, Mr. Gallagher." He waved his hand. "Ask Helen your questions. Let me think. It will come to me."

"I understand you gave Stephanie a generous trust fund as a wedding present and that she could draw on the interest freely but not touch the principal until Tom died. Some people have hinted she wanted him dead so she could get her hands on the whole thing."

"That's rubbish!" Helen said. "When we gave it to her, she said she didn't want it, that she wasn't marrying Thomas to become rich, she was marrying him because she loved him, and we should donate the money to charity. She hasn't touched a penny of it the whole time she's had it. In two thousand and one, we amended the provisions of the trust, removing the clause prohibiting her from touching the principal. The money has all been hers since then."

"She knew that?"

"Oh, yes. We told her."

Removing any financial motive for Steph to try to kill Tom. But there could be another reason to want him dead. "Were Tom and Steph—"

"Pardon me for interrupting," Leland said, "But I remembered what Thomas said, and I have to tell you before it slips away. When we talked a few weeks before his accident, he said something about not being able to trust his friend. No, that's not quite right." He furrowed his brow again. "He said, 'Sometimes your friend turns on you.' That's it."

"Yes!" Helen said. "I remember him saying that. The way he said it, I had the feeling he was speaking of a close friend, not a casual one."

"That was my impression as well."

"But he didn't say who the friend was or how he had turned on Tom?" I asked.

"No. He sounded a little down on the phone that night, so I asked him what was wrong, and he said that. I pressed him for details, but he said, 'Nothing, Dad. Forget it,' and changed the subject."

"That was unusual for him," Helen said. "He never hesitated to come to us for advice when something was bothering him. Now, what were you asking, Mr. Gallagher?"

"Were Tom and Stephanie having any problems in their marriage?"

"Heavens no. I'm sure they had the little squabbles that arise in any marriage. But I never sensed anything more serious than that, and certainly nothing that could lead Stephanie to harm Thomas."

"I think that's all I have, at least for now. If I have more questions, may I call you?"

"Absolutely." Leland handed me a business card. "All our numbers are there."

I gave him one of my cards in return, asking them to call me if they thought of anything. He struggled to his feet with the help of a cane. "We have taken enough of your time. Thank you for speaking with us. It was a pleasure to meet you."

Helen and Leland took a few steps away then she whispered something to him. He nodded in reply, and she returned to me. "Mr. Gallagher, we love Stephanie as if she were our own child." She rested a hand on my arm. "You mean a great deal to her. Promise us you will always be her friend."

"I will." Although, to be completely honest, I wanted to be more than her friend.

Sitting down again, I chewed on what Leland Mercer had said. Tom had used the word friend, not friends, and I'd only heard one name mentioned with that word.

Jeff Styles.

I stifled another sneeze. I needed to clear the smell

of the flowers from my nostrils before my headache hit critical mass. Stepping onto the veranda outside the dining room, I inhaled deeply. The clean scent of pine and woods displaced the heavy aroma of flowers and quelled the incipient headache.

I was exhaling my third deep breath when the door behind me opened, and Holland Carter strode out. He eyed me as if he didn't think I would own a suit or know how to knot a tie and stopped close enough to hug me. "I know what you're doing, and you won't get away with it."

So, no hug. "Oh? What am I doing?"

"Worming your way into Stephanie Mercer's good graces so you can take her for everything she has." He stepped closer, crowding me.

I didn't step back. "What I'm doing right now is listening to an asshole falsely accuse me of something in an inappropriate place at an inappropriate time."

"I'm watching you, Gallagher. One wrong—"

"He's right, Holland." Jeff Styles crossed the veranda toward us. "This isn't the time or place."

Carter backed up a step and poked me in the chest. "Stay away from her." He stomped back inside.

"I apologize for Holland's behavior." Jeff stroked his tie into place. "He is...protective of Stephanie. He only wants what's best for her."

"Which includes himself, no doubt."

Jeff gazed down. "Yes. Probably."

"Threatening me isn't the way to accomplish it."

"I'm sure, while it may have sounded like a threat, that was not how he meant it."

"Unh-hunh." *You say po-tay-to, I say po-tah-to.* I stepped toward the door.

"A moment of your time, Dan?"

I propped my hands on my hips. "What's on your mind?"

"Tom's situation has been a prolonged strain on Stephanie. Now that he's gone, she needs time and space to grieve, to accept his passing, and to heal. Continuing your search for whoever was behind his accident will only be a constant reminder of losing him, delaying the process."

"Or expediting it. Until she has answers to what happened that night, she'll never be able to put Tom's death behind her." I turned away.

"She also doesn't need you using your friendship as an avenue to a closer relationship with her now that she is a widow."

I about-faced. "Your point?"

"It would be best if you distanced yourself from her completely."

First Carter, now Styles telling me to stay away from Steph. What was with these two? "Whatever she and I do is between us." I pivoted toward the door again.

"You'd be wise to follow my advice, Dan," Styles said to my retreating back.

His tone made that sound more of a threat than Carter's remark.

Chapter 34

08/12/2003 – Getting Away

"Can you meet me for a drink?"

Steph sounded as if her last nerve was fraying rapidly. "Sure."

A tingle of delight flickered in me when she entered Ye Olde London Pub on Pine Street a little after six and wound her way to my table. She easily outshone ever other woman in the place in a silver blouse, black suit, and heels. I told her that after she sat down and got a weak smile in return. A waitress in a renaissance maid's uniform and white mobcap parked a Rusty Nail in front of her a second later.

She picked up the glass. "How did you know I needed this?"

"You sounded like you might on the phone. What's up?"

"Give me a minute to unwind." She downed a swig then inhaled a breath deep and exhaled it slow. "It's been a frustrating day. A woman I've been seeing at the clinic for two years won't use any of the exercises I gave her to help her cope with her panic attacks. She wants a magic word that will make them instantly go away forever. And a regular at Safe Haven whose husband slaps her around all the time came in last night in tears, went back to him again this morning, and came back after lunch with a black eye. This is the fifth time it's happened this year." She drank again and let out a relieved sigh. "I really need this."

I worked on my Maker's Mark old fashioned and waited. Steph alternated sips of her drink with deep breaths, and the strained look faded. With the drink half gone, she leaned back in her chair and let out one more slow breath. "Okay."

"So what's on your mind?"

"I listened to that tape all the way through like you asked me. There was nothing on it but reminders to himself about all sorts of things. The yard, his car, a dentist appointment, a present for...for my birthday. And I checked every place I could think of for another tape, and I didn't find one. Did you talk to our friends yet? What did they tell you?"

I gave her a recap, skipping over any mention of extra-marital affairs for the time being. "Last week you said Tom was distracted for about a month before his accident. Jeff Styles told me Tom had taken on a new client last August. Could something about that client have been behind Tom's distraction?"

"I don't see how. He never said much about his clients but he did tell me this one could help him make partner and help his career in other ways, possibly even helping him gain a seat on the bench someday. It was always Tom's long-term dream to be a judge."

A long-held desire suddenly within reach could have been a distraction. But Steph had also said Tom was tense, which didn't go with a dream possibly coming true, even if not for some time. "Could the client have been pressuring him to jump into the political fray before he felt he was ready?"

"Possibly. But Tom would have said no." She downed the last of her drink. "He felt he needed to be at least forty-five before he'd have enough experience to be a good jurist. Beyond that, he never had a timetable in place. It was always, 'Someday, I'd like to be a judge.'"

I signaled the waitress for another round. "What else do you remember about this client?"

"It was a local company that had a steady stream of legal work. That's all I know."

"I want to ask you some questions." The last time I did, I'd been so clumsy I'd angered her. Maybe a little forewarning was needed. "They may hurt, but I'm not asking them to hurt you."

She gazed at her empty glass for a second. "Okay."

Her voice sounded as if I'd said I was going to torture her. In a way, maybe I was. "Were you and Tom having marital problems before his crash?"

"We had little glitches, like any marriage, but that's all. Nothing you could call even close to a problem."

"Some people I talked to said Tom was having an affair with a co-worker."

She glared at me. "He wasn't." Spoken sharply.

"How do you know?"

"I don't *know*. But without proof, I will never believe he was. Tom's father had an affair when he was eleven. It almost tore the family apart and the wounds took a long time to heal. Tom swore he would never put me through what his mother went through because of it. And I never saw any signs to make me suspect he was unfaithful."

Maybe someone had started the rumor, hoping to

stir up trouble between Tom and Steph. "Does the name Brittany Ferris mean anything to you?"

"Is that who they said Tom was seeing?" She rolled her eyes. "If he was going to have an affair, she'd be the last woman he would pick. Petite blondes were never his thing. And she's a sweet person but not a smart one."

"He liked tall, dark-haired, intelligent women. Like you."

She nodded, her face carrying a small, pleased smile.

The waitress delivered our refills. I waited until she carried our empties away. "One of the people I talked to said you had an affair, too."

"Nicole." There was acid in her voice. "Right?"

I nodded.

Steph sampled her fresh drink. "She cheats on Matt all the time and thinks everyone else does the same."

Judging by the way she'd come on to me, I could believe it.

"Let me guess. She said I was sleeping with Eric Greenwood."

"Mmm-hmm."

"I spent a lot of time with Eric, yes, but the only affair," she edged the word with air quotes, "I was having was with golf. Tom was great at it. I play poorly on my best days. We entered the Couples Tournament every summer but never survived the first cut because I play so bad. I signed up for lessons so I wouldn't let him down in the tournament last year." Defensive anger filled her voice and stiffened her posture. "That's *all* it was."

I'd riled her. "I'm sorry. I wasn't accusing you."

"And I shouldn't have taken offense. I should know better by now. It's just Nicole being Nicole."

"Are you still taking lessons from him?"

She nodded again. "It makes me feel closer to Tom. If that makes sense?"

"It does."

She swallowed another sip of Rusty Nail. "I've been thinking about what you said the night I lost it, about taking a day off once in a while. I'm going to do it. I'm taking this weekend for me. We have a cabin on Big Bear Lake. I'm going to drive up Friday and spend the weekend there."

"It'll do you a world of good, I promise." But something in her tone of voice told me she wasn't going there to unwind. "Just kick back, relax, and recharge your batteries."

She shook her head. "Now that Tom's...gone," her voice held the sadness of dreams lost, "I need to go through his things and decide what I want to keep and what to get rid of.

"That's not what I meant by taking a day off."

"I know. But it has to be done and if I don't do it now, I never will." She fell silent for several moments. "Could you—" She shook her head again. "I don't want to impose."

"Impose away."

She bought a few seconds with a swallow of her drink. "I know it's short notice, but could you come with me? I need to do this. I just don't know if I can face it by myself. I—I really could use your support."

I'd told her she could call on me any time for anything. But a weekend with her in a cabin far from home might hold too much of the wrong temptations.

Still, in for a penny, in for a pound. I'd just have to watch my step. "Sure. I'll help you."

Chapter 35

08/15/2003 – Friday Night at The Cabin

Pines, oaks, maples, and trees I couldn't name, all in their full summer glory, shaded Steph's cabin at the end of a gravel drive. Late afternoon sun tipped Big Bear Lake's gentle waves with gold, and the air was warm and rich with the smells of nature. Her cabin was rustic, cedar shingle siding weathered silver-gray, maroon trimmed windows and crossbuck door, and a porch all the way around. I parked my truck in front of a matching garage. The thick ground cover of leaves and needles made for soft walking on our way to the porch.

The interior was one big kitchen-living-dining room with a vaulted ceiling pierced by a skylight over the pine trestle kitchen table. Steph bustled around in dark blue jeans and a black tee opening curtains, letting in light to reflect off white walls and a shiny hardwood floor dotted with braided throw rugs, then showed me around. Three doors on the far wall led to bedrooms and a bath. A window wall pierced by French doors faced the lake. The living room furniture had open wood frames and thick cushions. The whole place said, 'Kick off your shoes, enjoy the view, and unwind.'

For a house that hadn't been used since before Tom's accident, it was immaculate. "Wow! This place is terrific."

"I had a cleaning service come in. I couldn't invite you to a place a hobo wouldn't sleep."

We'd picked up groceries and a take-out dinner in Buckleyville, the little town we'd passed through on the way. While Steph stowed the food and warmed the take-out, I carried in her overnight bag and my duffel and parked them in the bedrooms. After dinner, she poured two snifters of brandy and handed me one. "Come with me."

She led me through the French doors to the porch where we took Adirondack chairs facing the lake. Even though we were in the mountains, the evening air was warm. She took a swallow of her brandy and stared at the crescent moon for a second. "Tom and I loved to come here."

I let her reminisce without interrupting. The cabin had been a happy place for them. The clock didn't exist here. They did what they wanted when they wanted. Took long walks along the lake and midnight swims in it. Sat on the little pier and dangled their feet in the water. Hiked the woods. Sat on the porch and watched the sun rise in the morning and the moon come up at night. And planned their future.

As she talked, the wistful tone that had always been in her voice when she talked about Tom faded. She fell silent for several moments then stole a quick glance over her shoulder. "I think maybe I'll sell this place. There's no reason to keep it. I'll probably never come here again after this weekend."

"Don't rush into it. Think it through first and be sure it's the right move for you." I waved a dismissive hand. "Don't listen to me. Do what you think, what you feel is right."

"Always tell me what you think, Dan. Please?" She laid her hand on my arm. "I trust you, and I value your opinions."

The brandy was long gone and the night had cooled when I followed her inside. There, she put her arms around me. "Thank you for coming. And helping me. And listening. And for...everything."

She hesitated a moment then gave me a gentle, sweet kiss that was oh, so tempting. I resisted the desire to return it. And add several more.

Once I bedded down for the night, my mind mulled over what was happening between Steph and me. An attraction beyond friendship had been vibrating the air between us for the last few weeks. I was sure she had felt it as well and wondered if that was the real reason she'd invited me here. Not that I'd resisted her invitation all that hard. But I'd need to keep my guard up for the rest of the weekend so I didn't give into something we'd both regret.

My thoughts shifted to the photos someone had taken of us, and I worried whoever took them might be lurking in the woods, snapping more pictures. Or maybe planning something more sinister.

I didn't sleep well.

Chapter 36

08/16/2003 – Saturday at the Cabin

Dawn broke bright and clear, promising a glorious day ahead.

After a hearty breakfast, we began clearing Tom's belongings from the cabin. In black shorts and a gray tee, Steph stretched and bent with the fluid smoothness of a dancer as she pulled things from cabinets, closets, and shelves. I could have happily stood there all day, eying her and thinking increasingly lustful thoughts. She caught me watching her one time and gave me her full-on smile. It was the dazzler I'd predicted, turning my knees to mush.

As she filled each box, I stacked it on the porch. A time or two, I returned to find her staring at something in her hands while tears rolled down her cheeks. I let her keep those moments her own. Maybe they would help her come to terms with Tom's passing.

Over a soup-and-sandwich lunch, Steph said, "Would you mind cleaning out the garage this afternoon? Everything there is Tom's and I don't want any of it. Take anything there you want."

"That isn't necessary, Steph."

"Please. I want you to have it as a thank you for all your help. Everything else can go to Lucky Finds." A second-hand store in Buckleyville.

"That's very kind of you. Thank you."

The garage held the miscellany any homeowner acquired. I set the yard tools, lawn chairs, and almost everything else aside for Lucky Finds. Hand tools were a different story. Wrenches and screwdrivers, a ratchet-and-socket set, and a drill and bits never gather dust in an auto restoration shop. I tossed them in a toolbox I found on a shelf and stowed it in my truck bed along with a hose and extension cords. A box of assorted electrical supplies—junction boxes, switches, and outlets—would come in handy when I helped Gene Parilli wire the family room he was building.

Cleaning out a garage always takes longer than it looks like it will. I was still at it when the people from Lucky Finds came at four. I helped them load the donations into their Dodge van then went inside to see how Steph was making out. After I set two cartons of things she wanted to keep in the Toyota and snapped down the bedcover, we called it quits.

The day had been warm, and we'd both worked up a sweat. Steph asked if I would peel and slice some potatoes for home fries while she showered. I did and lit the gas grille on the porch. She came out of her bedroom in a pale blue summery-looking dress trimmed in white lace, heeled white sandals, and silver and sapphire jewelry. I'd never seen her in a color other than black, and my heart skipped several beats at how beautiful she looked. "Darn! I forgot to pack my tux."

She laughed. "That would be a bit much. Whatever you wear will be fine." She touched my arm, and I caught a whiff of softly tangy perfume. "It's the company that's important, not the clothes."

Even so, I was glad I'd added a pair of good slacks

and a polo shirt in my duffel at the last minute. I showered, dressed, and stepped out of my room as Steph brought the steaks in from the grill. At the table, I said, "Smells terrific," talking about both the food and her.

Over dinner, I commented on the tools and electrical supplies I'd found in the garage. "I'm guessing Tom was a handyman."

"He was. When we bought this place, it was in sad shape. We hired a contractor to do the major work and Tom and I did the rest on weekends. It had only one outlet on each wall, so Tom installed close to a dozen more." She pointed to the swag lights and ceiling fan in the living area. "He installed those, too. He called doing things like that his therapy."

After dinner, we again carried brandy snifters out to the Adirondack chairs. I sipped mine and waited. Steph would talk when she was ready. When she was, she asked, "What was growing up in Schuylerton like?"

"Norman Rockwell, The Movie."

We talked about our childhoods—hers one of wealth and privilege, mine blue-collar to the core—until the night was complete, the moon high in the sky, and a chill breeze off the lake nudged us inside. Something in her had changed since we'd arrived Friday. She was more at ease, as if she'd shed a heavy burden, and smiled her dazzler smile often. I was glad I was sitting down each time she did, or I'd have been picking myself up off the porch floor all night long.

At my bedroom door, she looped her arms around my neck and kissed me more seriously than the night before. Then a second time. Both put my vow to keep us just friends to the test. With the third one, I had my arms around her and was into kissing her back. Really into it. Several kisses later, she retreated from full body contact. "Well…good night."

Just in time to save me from doing something I shouldn't. I cleared my throat. "Yeah. Good night."

I settled into bed, my mind filled with the feel of her body against mine, the taste of her kisses, and the sensations both stirred in me. The lusting thoughts I'd had throughout the day played in my head synced to a slide show of her at the moment each one originally came to mind. An image of her in her bed ten feet away replaced them. I wondered what she slept in, and my thoughts turned to what any normal man would think about when a woman and a bed paired in his mind.

The click of the door latch interrupted my thoughts, the door opened, and Steph peered in. "Dan? Are you awake?"

"Yeah." I sat up against the headboard as she padded silently toward me. A band of moonlight revealed she had on a pale blue slip. "What's up?"

She sat on the edge of the mattress and kissed me even more intensely than she had outside my door then whispered, "Make love to me." Need filled her voice.

She kissed me again, the same need in the press of her lips against mine. Desire rose in me. Impossible not to with her kissing me like that and saying, "Make love to me," that way. I am a normal adult male and she was a beautiful woman, but I couldn't give in to wanting her. "We might regret thi—"

She put a finger against my lips and said, "No regrets," in the same soft voice. "Make love to me, Dan. Please."

The need in her tone demolished my resistance. I

raised the sheet, and she slipped into bed, nestled her body against mine, and kissed me with the same longing.

I realized this had to be about her. She needed to be loved physically now as much as she'd needed to be held other times and needed to vent her frustrations with the hand life had dealt her.

Her body was sleek and toned, her skin smooth and soft. I focused every touch, every kiss, every caress on giving her pleasure, made each one as gentle or intense as she desired. Only when she was ready for me to enter her did I unleash my desires and take my pleasure from her.

In some wee hour of the morning, muffled sobbing woke me. The mattress shifted as Steph got up. She picked up her slip and left the room, the latch making a soft snick as she closed the door behind her.

Everything had changed between us the moment I let her into my bed. I could lie to myself and say she'd seduced me. And I could say I'd never had a single lusting thought about her, but that was an even bigger lie. I'd had scores of them throughout the day. The bottom line was I'd let my lust run wild, and I shouldn't have.

I spent the rest of the night staring at the ceiling and feeling like a heel.

Chapter 37

08/17/2003 – Sunday at the Cabin

I didn't know what to expect from Steph when I entered the great room that morning. Anger at herself? At me? The cold shoulder? Name calling? Flying pots?

She turned at the sound of my steps. "Good morning."

No flying pots. Good. No smile on her face and lots of coolness in her voice. Not good. The big room hummed with the morning-after unease of two people who'd shared a bed the night before and shouldn't have. "Morning."

"Coffee's ready. I'll have bacon and eggs ready in a minute. Would you start the toast, please, and pour us some juice?"

"Sure."

Other than that brief exchange, breakfast was a silent affair. Evidently, we weren't going to talk about last night. I wasn't sure if that was a good thing or bad. I wanted to ask her why she'd left my bed, crying, in the middle of the night.

As we cleared the table, she said, "Do you have much more to do in the garage?"

She probably wanted to keep lots of space between us. "I'll need maybe an hour to finish up."

"I have a few things to do in here but I'd like to

leave for home as soon as we're done."

"No problem." I escaped to the garage.

As I packed up the last of the things, I mulled over last night. Had making love to Steph been the right choice or a terrible mistake? Should I have refused? Easy to say I should have in the light of day, impossible to do last night when she was kissing me and needing me. I had thoroughly enjoyed our lovemaking, but hoped it hadn't poisoned our friendship. That was far too high a price to pay for an hour of sexual pleasure.

I shook my head to clear the thoughts away. I couldn't undo what had happened. All I could do was live with the result. Still, I would miss her if she chose to end our meetings. I had come to enjoy them, look forward to them.

I loaded a final box with aerosol cans I'd dispose of at my shop and carried it to my truck. Steph stepped onto the porch as I pushed the last snap on the bedcover home. "Are you about done in the garage?"

Her tone said she was in a great hurry to leave. Running from memories of her and Tom? Or of last night?

"Just finished. Whenever you're ready, give me three seconds to grab my bag and I'm good to go."

"I'm ready now."

When I started down the drive, she turned in her seat to see the cabin until I pulled onto the road and the trees hid it from view. Then she let out a long sad sigh and faced front. We drove into Buckleyville in silence, left the last boxes on the porch at Lucky Finds, and I aimed my Toyota south toward the interstate.

Thirty miles down the highway, the silence was getting to both of us. We let it out as a string of shifts in our seats, throat clearings, and sighs. My odometer clicked off ten more miles before I couldn't take it any longer. "Steph, about last night—"

She waved her hand as if batting my words away and shook her head. Talking was clearly off limits, so we rolled silently through the August Sunday, not sharing our thoughts, the mood in my truck as gray as the overcast sky. I had the feeling once she was home, I'd never see her again. The possibility filled me with leaden sadness.

Five miles farther on, I glanced over at her. She was deep asleep, her head resting against the window. I wondered if, like me, she'd been awake the rest of the night after she left my bed.

She stirred when I slowed for the turn into Glenwood Heights then sat up when I stopped in her driveway. "I could not have gotten through this weekend without you. Thank you." For the first time all day, her voice held warmth.

"Glad I could help." I hauled her boxes into the house through a light drizzle and stacked them in the den's closet.

At her door on my way out, she stopped me with a hand on my arm. "I'm sorry I've been so distant all day."

I had it coming for yielding to my desires. "It's okay. I understand."

"No, you don't. Last night was the first time I've ever been with someone besides Tom."

I'd felt like a heel after she left my bed in tears. Now, I felt like King of the Heels for letting her in it. I turned away from her.

She tightened her grip on my arm a fraction. "Dan,

look at me."

I didn't want to, didn't want her to see the shame on my face, but her tone insisted, so I faced her.

"I'm not sorry last night happened."

Nor was I. That didn't make my rutting bull behavior acceptable. "But I shouldn't—"

"Don't." She squeezed my arm. "I needed you last night, needed what we shared. But it can never happen again, Dan. It just can't."

Maybe I'd never see her again, but I'd carry the memory of last night with me forever.

Chapter 38

08/18/2003 – A Bad Day

Shortly after nine Monday morning, Nora paged me to the showroom. Andy stood by a blue and cream '56 Chevy BelAir sedan when I entered. He shot me a quick glance then looked away.

"Hey, Andy, what's up?" With four white-on-navy Schuylerton PD cruisers in my parking lot, it couldn't be good.

His sour facial expression said he was suffering a major case of heartburn. Not meeting my gaze told me it wasn't from too much coffee. "Talk in your office?"

"Uh, yeah, sure." Once we were inside, I repeated my question.

He gazed past my shoulder for a few seconds then eyed me with a somber expression. "We need to search your shops."

"For what?"

Andy cycled through a deep breath. "Drugs. We—"

Talk about a blow to the gut! "Drugs? Here? Come on, Andy. You know—"

He cut me off with a wave of his hand. "We received a tip there was a large stash on the premises. I have to follow up on it. I hope you'll give me your permission to search, but I have a search warrant, if you insist on going that way."

"No, go ahead, search. But to protect myself and my people, I want to see the warrant."

Andy pulled papers from a pocket inside his sport coat and handed them to me. After I read them, he said, "Have all your people assemble in the break room right now. The sooner we get started, the sooner we finish and get out of your hair."

"First things first." I called Frank Morrison's office. He was with a client. I asked Betty to have him call me on my cell the moment he was free and told her why then disconnected. "I have some conditions, Andy."

"Long as they don't stop my guys from doing their job."

"One, some of the cars here are very rare and valuable, some of their parts one step short of irreplaceable. Any damage done to any of them, I'm holding the police department responsible."

"Calm down." He waved his hands in a placating gesture. "I brought guys who won't act like bulls in a china shop and gave them orders to be extra careful around the cars. Okay?"

I pointed to his waist. "Buckles scratch paint."

"I'll make sure they remove their duty belts. What else?"

"If Gene's painting a car, he can't stop in the middle. He'll have to finish it."

Andy weighed that for a second. "If he is, I'll post an officer there to keep an eye on him until he's done. Let's get started." His patience had gone thin.

I pressed the phone's intercom button. "Heads up, people. I need you all to stop what you're doing right now and gather in the break room." I racked the phone.

"Okay?"

"Yeah." Andy took a small radio from his blazer, and pressed the talk button. He ordered his officers to remove their duty belts then said, "Have at it." Tucking the radio away, he said, "Take me to Gene."

We stepped from my office onto the main shop floor. I willed myself to not eye the dozen cops trooping into my business. Andy asked, "You hire any new people lately, say within the last six months to a year?"

"No. Everybody's been here at least two years."

"Any of them here over the weekend?"

"Nope. Sometimes guys bring their own cars in to work on, but they have to clear it with me first. None of them did for this weekend."

"How do they get in if you're closed?"

"I'm here most Saturdays. If not, they get a loaner key they return Monday." The shop floor, usually alive with the clatter of tools, the blare of radios, the rumble of voices, and the throb of motors, had fallen silent, eerie for a weekday morning.

"Were you here Saturday?"

"No."

"Where were you?"

"Away." All he needed to know.

"Who all has keys to this place?"

"Nora. Gene. Me. That's it."

"Any chance one of your people has a key you don't know about?

"Maybe. But I doubt it."

"What about your old buddy, Jay?"

"I took his when I gave him the boot. Then I changed the locks anyway, just in case."

We stepped outside, and I reached back to swing the steel door shut. Andy snapped, "Stop! Look."

The door's brown paint was chipped, the door and jamb bent and gouged near the lock plate.

Andy radioed for a crime tech to process the door and jamb for evidence and an officer to search all my buildings for signs of a break-in then lowered the radio. "You notice any other signs of a break-in this morning, things out of place or missing?"

"No, but I didn't look, either. And none of my guys said anything."

"Anybody hanging around last week who shouldn't be here?"

"You mean like casing us?"

"Yeah."

"Nope."

"Maybe one of your guys saw something over the weekend or this morning. It's a long shot, but it's worth a try." He raised the radio again and called for a cop named Brown. When he responded, Andy said, "Ask all the employees if they happened to be near here over the weekend and noticed anything unusual." Stowing the radio, he asked, "Fire anybody in the last year?"

"Nope. Tell me about this supposed drug stash."

Andy weighed his next words for a moment. "Call came in yesterday afternoon. Male voice saying one of your employees was dealing pot out of here on a regular basis, kept his stash in the shops. Said he'd made several buys. Said others had, too."

I knew my people too well to believe one of them was selling drugs out of my shops. "He say who from?"

"No." Andy offered a wry grin. "He didn't identify himself either."

"He say where in my shops this stash was?"

"Says he meets the guy in the parking lot, does the deal there."

"Someone's setting me up, Andy. They broke in over the weekend and planted drugs then phoned the tip in to cause me trouble."

"I think you're right but I still have to treat the tip as valid."

The crime tech, toting a metal case, jogged up to us. Andy pointed to the damaged door, telling her to do a full workup. As we headed for the paint shop, he asked, "Any idea who's setting you up?"

"Whoever delivered those pictures Steph and I got."

"You think the two are related?"

"Somebody did that. Maybe they did this, too."

"Planting drugs in your shop is big step up from putting pictures in your mailbox."

We entered the paint shop. Gene, clad in a white coverall from corns to crown, his face masked by a respirator, was in the spray booth laying Plum Crazy—an intense purple—on a '70 Dodge Challenger. I pointed. "He's almost done. Another five minutes or so."

My cell rang. Frank Morrison returning my call. I explained what was going on and he asked to talk to Andy. After a few yeps and nopes, Andy read the search warrant to Frank, listened a moment, then said, "I agree...I don't believe it either," and handed me my phone.

"Comply with everything the police ask," Frank said, "but don't incriminate yourself or any of your employees. If they ask you anything you think might be incriminating, refuse to answer until you consult with me. And let me know immediately if they detain anyone."

"Will do."

Gene came out of the booth as I closed my cell, stripping off his coverall. Seeing Andy, he asked, "What's going on?"

I told him and sent him to the break room then pointed to the spray booth. "That's off limits until the paint dries. No one goes in until Gene gives the okay."

Andy nodded and posted an officer to guard the building.

Back in my office, I fumed silently while Andy searched my desk and file cabinets. When he closed the last drawer, he said, "I'm gonna need your financials for the last three years. And contact information for all your employees."

I got a new flash drive from my desk and plugged it into my computer.

"Wait. I have to watch you do this." Andy rounded my desk and peered over my shoulder.

Stabbing the keys on my computer, I opened my financial folder, showed him the file for each year, copied the last three onto the flash drive, then did the same for my employee file. "Anything else? A pint of my blood maybe?"

"Lighten up, Dan. It's nothing personal. I'm just following procedure and, no, that's all I need."

I jerked the drive free then jabbed it toward him. "Here. You making any progress on tracking down where those photos came from?"

"Nada. Sorry." He tucked the drive in a pocket. "You?"

"Talked to Jeremy Slater, my neighbor's kid. He said he'd ask around about anybody in the Visual Arts Club taking pictures. Hasn't gotten back to me yet."

The rest of the day was pure hell for me, waiting while Andy's officers poked through every inch of my shops and questioned my staff. At two-thirty, a cop stuck her head in my office door. "Chief, we found something."

"What?"

The cop swung her gaze from Andy to me and back, asking with her eyes if Andy really wanted her to say in front of me. Andy sighed and stood. "Sit tight, Dan,"

He left my office then returned a few minutes later, the expression on his face telegraphing I wouldn't like what he had to say. "What did you find?"

He sat facing me, inhaled hard, and exhaled slow. "Dime bags of pot. Looks like about two kilos total. In a box in your parts room."

I'd taken a few hard blows in my life, none harder than Amy's death. This one ran second without a doubt. There wasn't enough air in the room to fill my lungs, and my chest jumped with each heartbeat. "So what happens now?" My voice sounded scratchy.

"The dope goes to the county crime lab for confirmation it's marijuana and processing everything for prints. We're just about done searching so we'll be out of your hair soon."

"What about my people?"

"We've been sending them home after we questioned them."

Shortly after three, an officer poked his head in the door. "We're ready to roll, Chief."

you?"

"You'd have to ask him."

"Ask who? Who would do something like this to you?"

"When you find him, let me know."

Chapter 39

08/19/2003 – Musings

Tuesday was a lost day.

Andy's officers hadn't damaged any of the cars, but they'd gone through D-J like a tornado, leaving my guys one humongous mess to clean up. When we'd finished undoing the chaos a little after two, I'd sent them home, telling them to come in early Wednesday and plan on working Saturday morning.

With the shops empty and silent, I finally had time to think. I retreated to my office and did a ton of it. Overnight, I'd firmed up my conviction someone had planted the pot to set me up, the neatly packed box hidden in plain sight in my stock room sealing the deal. Which left only figuring out who had done it and why? Only one name came to mind. Holland Carter.

Yet I couldn't—or maybe didn't want to—believe a well-educated man like him would stoop to such a low trick. Then I remembered the cold stare in his eyes when I'd told him to get out of my shops. The only other time I had that cold a look laid on me was when I gave Jay Winters the boot.

Would Holland try to destroy me solely because, as Steph and Lisa had said, he considered me competition for Steph? Totally absurd. She and I were friends. At least I hoped we still were. Under different circumstances, I could have gone for being more than that, and I got the vibe she could, too. And, okay, yeah, Saturday night we'd gone so far beyond friendship, it was over the horizon, but that had been an aberration.

I'd called her Monday after ditching Les Hartman and left a message on her machine telling her about the drugs. She hadn't called me back. I didn't know what to make of that. Did she believe I was dealing? Or had my message scared her so much she'd run? Or, despite what she'd said Sunday evening, did she really regret Saturday night?

Or had she been part of it? Had she known the drugs were in my shops? Was she in part responsible for them being there? Was her invite to the cabin merely to get me away from D-J so they could be planted?

I kept seeing her as she'd been that Saturday night. So beautiful and so needing I couldn't resist her. Had she been sincere or acting? Had she really needed me or merely carried out a seduction she and Carter had planned? To what purpose? To keep me off balance or to blind me to the truth even if it was in front of me? I even began to doubt my feelings for her. Had they been totally my own, or had she carefully nurtured only the ones she'd wanted me to have?

I didn't have any answers.

Chapter 40

08/22/2003 – Another Clue

By Friday morning, things at D-J Auto Renewal were fully back to normal. At least as normal as they could be with the threat of losing my business doing the Sword of Damocles thing.

I was at Nora's desk in the showroom, touching base with her, when Ian McGruder entered the showroom wearing a black suit, white shirt, blue tie, and black wingtips. "Ah, Dan. Just the man I'm looking for. I wonder if you have a minute for me."

"Sure do, Ian."

"I stopped by to see how my car is progressing." The '62 Buick Wildcat convertible with the bad motor. Ian held up his hands. "Not to pressure you about getting it done. I simply wanted an update." With two restored Buicks in his garage, he knew how the process went.

"Come on in my office, and I'll fill you in." There, I fired up my computer terminal and called up his Buick.

"I heard of your troubles with the police, and I don't believe it for an instant. I contacted the chief, told him so, and vouched for your character."

"Thanks, Ian." Reading from the file, I told him the Buick's mechanicals, interior, and body were all on track. "The only snag we've hit is with the engine. It's bad, and Chip hasn't found a replacement up to his standards. We can repair the one from your car, if you want to go that way. It will be faster but it'll be expensive. Or we can keep looking. It's your call."

"What do you recommend?"

"Replace it. Over the long haul, it'll be more reliable."

"Then keep looking, please."

I called Chip Knox in the engine department to tell him. He said he had a lead on a good one. I hung up and passed that on to Ian. He thanked me then cleared his throat and ran a hand over his silver hair. "I wonder if I could ask you a business-related question?"

"Sure"

"Who does your legal work?"

"Frank Morrison." I checked my mug. Empty. I went to the brewer atop a file cabinet, held the pot toward Ian.

"No. Thank you. Are you happy with his work?"

I filled my mug and returned to my desk. "He's always done right by me. Why?"

"I'm dissatisfied with the lawyer we have on retainer. He isn't as...committed to my company as I feel he should be. Do you think Morrison would be interested in representing us?"

I swigged coffee. "I don't know. You can ask him." I jotted Frank's number on a scratch pad and handed the page to Ian. "If he's not, I'm sure he can refer you to one who is and will do a good job for you. Who are you using now?"

"O'Reilly, Styles, and McNamara. The last man we had there was terrific, came to us highly recommended, and backed it up with performance. This new man is," he paused for a second, "well, the most charitable I can be is adequate."

My ears perked up at that. "If you liked the first guy, why did you replace him?"

"We had no choice. The man we had—Tom Mercer—was in an auto accident that left him in a coma until he died last month. Now we're with Jeff Styles."

"Why did you go with him?"

"We didn't. He picked us. He called me minutes after I arrived at my office the Monday after Tom had his accident and told us he was taking over representing us."

Was Wilson-McGruder, Ian's company, the gonzo client that could have guaranteed Tom partnership in OSM? Could Ian have opened doors that could have led to a judicial position? Would Jeff try to kill his best friend for that? His grabbing Ian's company as a client the moment Tom was out of action seemed to say so.

Had I been focusing on the wrong guy? Was Jeff Styles, not Holland Carter, behind Tom's crash? I had kind of zeroed in on Carter, but was it because I didn't like him? Or because I did see us in competition for Steph's affections?

"Dan?"

"Mmm?" I realized Ian was still sitting across from me. "I'm sorry. What?"

"You went away somewhere for a minute there. I said I believe I will have some coffee, if you don't mind."

"Sorry." I shook my head to clear it then poured him a mug and passed it to him along with packets of creamer and sugar. "Why are you looking to replace

Styles now?"

He added one of each and stirred. "We have some complicated legal issues to resolve before the year is over, and I need a man committed to giving me the best service possible. I don't feel Styles is." A pause for some coffee. "When I consulted Tom on a matter, he got back to me no later than the next day and always with a firm answer. Styles usually takes a week or more, and everything is equivocation. It's always maybe, possibly, perhaps. I need to know whether I can or can't do something. 'It depends,' is not acceptable."

I knocked back a big slug of coffee. I needed to widen my focus. Only seeing one solution to a problem was never a good idea. There always might be a better way out there. I had to apply it here, or I could go far astray. "You mind if I ask you a question or two?"

"Fire away."

"If someone wanted to become a judge, do you have the connections to make it happen?"

A swallow from his mug before he answered. "Make it happen, no. But I know people who could. If you are referring to Tom, had he ever expressed a desire to be a judge, I would have introduced him to them in an instant." A pause. "That's another thing bothering me about Styles. He drops subtle little hints every time we meet he'd like me to introduce him to some of them."

Interesting. "How did he sound when he told you he was taking over for Tom?"

"I'll have to think back." He sipped several times from his mug. "His voice had the right tone telling me Tom had been in a bad accident. But when he said he was taking over our account, it changed to..." Ian paused, his brow furrowed and eyes pinched in thought. "well...I'd have to say happy. That's the word I'd use. Happy."

Chapter 41

08/22/2003 – Good News and Bad

I stopped at Lou's for dinner that evening. Seconds after Lou set my meal in front of me, Andy took the stool next to mine. "Got a minute, Dan? Coke with a twist, please, Lou."

My hunger vanished, replaced by nausea. "What's up?"

"Promised I'd update you on where things stand on the drug thing."

Meaning he probably wasn't here to arrest me. My hunger reappeared. "Let's hear it."

"As the saying goes, I've got good news and bad." He slipped a notebook from an inside blazer pocket and opened it. "The good news is none of your guys' fingerprints are on the box. The bad news is nobody's are."

"It was wiped clean?" I bit into my hot roast beef and cheddar on rye.

"Or whoever planted it wore gloves. Good news, round two: there are fingerprints on some of the baggies. Bad news: round two: We haven't matched them to anyone yet. Good news, round three: they don't match you or any of your guys. So you're all cleared." He leaned back as Lou delivered his soda. "You know where Jay is these days?"

"No. Why?"

"Maybe he planted the weed to get back at you for giving him the heave-ho."

I swallowed some hash browns. "Not Jay's style. He'd have taken a sledgehammer to my car the day I kicked him out."

Andy sipped his Coke. "Maybe it took him this long to figure out how to get back at you in a way that would hurt you the most and not point directly at him."

"Planning wasn't his thing. He'd jump into something with both feet then realize he landed in a quagmire and had no way out."

"I still want to talk to him." Another drink from his glass. "I've got some more good news for you, courtesy of one of your guys. Emmett Miller says he saw an eighties Ford pick-up parked in the U-Stor lot by the fence between your property and theirs around eleven-fifteen Saturday night. He said it was two-toned, white and dark blue or maybe black. Ring any bells with you?"

I chewed a bite of sandwich. "Blue and white was a popular color combo back then and there's a ton of them still around." I'd seen one not too long ago. At Hofnagle Ford in Branthrope. "But I don't know anybody who owns one."

Andy flipped a page in his notebook. "Caught up to Scott Harris last week. He told me pretty much the same story he told you, except he said the guy told him the Jeep belonged to a buddy, he was driving it while the guy was on vacation. He told Harris he wanted to get it fixed before his buddy came home, and was paying cash so the claim wouldn't show up on his or his buddy's insurance."

"Doesn't help us much."

"Nope." Andy tucked the notebook back into his blazer. "You ever think maybe one of Mercer's fellow lawyers ran him off the road?"

If Carter had his eyes on Stephanie, would he go that far so he could have her? It seemed a bit out there—like beyond Pluto out there. Could it be someone else at OSM? For some other reason? Possibly. "Tom took on a big client last year, one almost guaranteeing him partnership in the firm and could have maybe led to him becoming a judge somewhere down the road."

"Could be motive. With Mercer out of the picture, who got the client?"

"Jeff Styles. But I kind of ruled Tom's co-workers out for two reasons. First, Steph said everyone at his firm liked him. And second, killing Tom to get a client seems a bit over the top." *But maybe not to Styles?*

"People have killed for the last beer in a six pack." Another long swallow from his soda. "Talked to Ray Elliot last week. He doesn't shoot digital, only film. Says digital's too easy to manipulate to show what you want it to. And no one at OSM asked him to take the photos you and Mrs. Mercer got."

"He could have used his own digital to take the photos of us for a private client."

"He proved he was tied up elsewhere when most of them were taken and has an ironclad alibi for the Fourth of July. His wife tripped on something on their patio and broke her wrist and hit her head. He was at the hospital with her until suppertime."

After dinner, I showered then drove to the Northside Mall, outside Branthorpe, taking the LeMans instead of the Ventura. In JCPenney, I picked up two pairs of Wranglers, then snagged a couple CDs at Spinner Music, three books at Turn the Page Bookstore, and capped my trip off with a Cinnabon and coffee. Gene and his wife Donna were there, so we set a date for me to wire his family room.

Passing Mitchell's on the way home, I spotted a man and woman crossing their parking lot. I recognized the woman instantly. Steph. I recognized the man with her a second later.

Holland Carter.

Chapter 42

08/23/2003 – Sleepless in Schuylerton

I thrashed around in bed until almost two in the morning.

Giving up on sleep, I put on a tee and athletic shorts and wandered my house, trying to subdue the ache seeing Steph with Carter had caused, trying to sort out my feelings about her.

She hadn't been climbing all over Carter outside Mitchell's but she'd been a long way from slitting his throat. The initial spurt of chest-filling hurt I'd felt on seeing them together had given way to mind-filling doubts that hadn't gone away. Had Steph lied to me about disliking Carter? Had she been involved with him all along? Were they co-conspirators in Tom's crash? Had she been playing me from the get-go? That thought cut the deepest.

Fifteen minutes of that got me nowhere, so I decided to use those sleepless hours organizing what I knew about Tom's crash. In my den, I set up my laptop then went to the kitchen to make coffee but changed my mind. I wouldn't need caffeine to keep me awake. I filled a big glass with ice then water and returned to the den.

While my mind slogged through the morass of unanswered questions, a voice in its far back corner whispered *She's not that kind of person. Don't jump to conclusions. Give her a chance. Hear her side.*

It was more than that. Something in me had changed in the time I'd known her. There had been two women in my life since Amy died, but neither one for very long nor with the effect Steph had had on me. Images of her randomly popped into my head every day, and my heart did a little tap dance every time I saw her or just heard her voice on the phone. And I noticed little things—odors, sounds, colors, tastes, textures—that never really registered before. Like I'd come out of some sort of suspended animation since I met her.

Thoughts stampeded through my mind like patrons fleeing a burning club, tripping over each other, until they became nothing but a tumbling mass of gibberish. I held my head in my hands as if to keep my skull from shattering and my brain from exploding.

Slowly the chaos in my head subsided and I rocked forward. I picked up my glass to drink and got smacked in the nose by a lump of ice. I had drained it without being aware I had been sipping from it.

My laptop had gone into sleep mode. I goosed it awake, opened a new document, thought for moment then typed. Names. Facts. Guesses. Suspicions. Ideas. Whatever came to mind as it came to me. I wasted a lot of time scrolling up and down the pages as I put them in some logical order.

My thoughts shifted to Steph far too often and I mused over each one too long, weighed it, debated it, until I forced it away. And each time, the pro-Steph voice in my head spoke a little louder, the anti-Steph one a little quieter. Finally drained of thoughts, I closed my eyes for a moment.

When I opened them, the sky had changed from the black of night to the first gray of dawn. My neck ached from hours tipped to one side against the back of my chair, and my body was stiff. I wasn't as young as I used to be. Still, I felt fairly alert for only a couple hours sleep in a chair. I stood and stretched and bent most of the stiffness away. A hot shower would take care of the rest. I re-read what I'd written, added a few more thoughts, and headed for the bathroom.

Chapter 43

08/29/2003 – Pizza and More

I hopped in the shower as soon as I got home Friday.

A hot day and a rash of minor problems had kept me on the shop floor, working up a good sweat, most of the afternoon. The shop area was no sauna, but far from an igloo. Plus, I hadn't heard from Steph since the weekend at her cabin, and her silence had me on edge.

A little before six, I was pulling on clean jeans when my phone rang.

"Have you had dinner yet?"

Everything in me locked up for a second at hearing Steph's voice. It took me another second to unlock mine. "No."

"Can I treat you to a gourmet meal?"

I'd gladly skip the gourmet part, but I wasn't about to pass on time with Steph. I could get my doubts about her erased or proven. "Sure. Where and when?"

"Your kitchen in a minute. I'm pulling into your driveway right now."

That rattled me. "You're where?"

"In your driveway."

I jammed my feet into loafers and dashed to the living room. Steph stood on my porch when I opened the door. Royal blue silk blouse, white skirt, heeled white sandals, wavy chestnut hair spilling across her shoulders. Man, she looked beautiful. I recognized the logo on the box in her hand. "Romano's Pizza is a gourmet meal?"

She laughed, a delightful sound in my ears. "It is to some people."

Nearly everyone in Schuylerton. Romano's pizza was so good, the Pizza Hut went under.

I held the door for her. "I've been worried about you."

"I know. I got your messages." She planted a quick kiss on my cheek, catching me off guard. "They meant a lot to me. I'm sorry I didn't call back. I wasn't ignoring you. I needed some time alone to think through some things."

I'd done the same. But my time alone hadn't included dining at Mitchell's with someone who might have killed my spouse.

She stepped into my living room and stopped, her gaze fixed on four pictures—budding spring leaves on slender branches, the spectrum of summer sunset colors on clouds, fall leaves against a cobalt sky, and snow-crusted branches on a leaf-bare tree—on the back wall. "These weren't here the last time I was here, were they?"

"I got them back from the framer Tuesday."

"Dan, they're beautiful." She glanced at me over her shoulder. "You took them?"

"Unh-hunh."

"You could make a living as a photographer."

"Thanks, but I like cars too much." I followed her into my kitchen. "How're you doing?"

She let loose a sigh. "Better than I was." She set

the Romano's box on my kitchen table. "It's a medium with extra cheese. Is that okay?"

"Right on the money." I fetched plates. "Beer okay?"

She gave me her full-on smile. "Right on the money."

My knees did the jelly thing. "You want a glass?"

"With pizza? No way."

I took two Yuenglings from the fridge, popped the caps, and placed them on the table. No one bit into a Romano's pizza the second they got home. Unless they lived twenty miles away or were into blistered tongues. Steph separated the slices to speed cooling then swigged from her beer. "Is the mess at your shop straightened out?"

"Sort of. Andy cleared all my people. He thinks somebody planted the drugs to ruin me."

She grabbed my hand. "Who would do that?" A bit of a rasp in her voice. "And why?"

"No idea." Looking at her sitting across from me set my pain and doubts loose again. I freed my hand. "How was dinner with Holland Carter last Friday?"

She almost dropped her beer. "I—how did you know?"

"I saw you coming out of Mitchell's with him."

She read my thoughts in my tone or expression. "It's not what you think."

"No? What is it?" It sounded mean. And it shouldn't have.

"Not what you think!" She stormed from the kitchen.

I caught up to her at the front door. "Wait." I touched her shoulder. "I didn't mean that the way it sounded. When I saw you with Holland, it—" *made me jealous.* I couldn't tell her that. "It...threw me. Hard. I thought—" *you and he had stabbed me in the back.* I couldn't say that either. "I didn't know what to think."

She gave me an angry stare. "That I lied to you? That Holl and I have been friends all along? That I lured you to the cabin so he could plant drugs in your shop to destroy everything you've worked for? That you were a pawn in some sort of bizarre plot we'd hatched?"

"Yeah."

"Which?" She snapped the word out.

"All of the above." I knew it was the wrong thing to say the moment I said it.

The stare turned to a glare. "None of the above! I was trying to help you. I wanted to see if Holl knew anything about Tom's accident. That was the only reason I would ever have dinner with him."

I pinched the bridge of my nose. Why had I assumed the worst about Steph? I had no right to assume anything about her. "I'm sorry. Like I said, seeing you with him threw me hard, and I took it the wrong way."

She gave me a puzzled gaze that morphed to amused.

"I do want to find out what happened to Tom." I took her arm gently and turned her toward the kitchen. "Please. Come back and tell me what he said."

"Not until we clear the air on some things."

"Sounds serious."

She freed her arm from my grip, and the glare reappeared in her eyes. "It is. Very. Holland Carter will *never* be my friend. I have *never* lied to you about anything and *never* will." She clutched both my hands with hers. "And I would *never* do anything—*anything*—to endanger you or hurt you. If you can't believe me," she looked down, and shook her head, "I don't know how to convince you."

Something in the tone of her voice, the look in her eyes, or her fierce grip on my hands had done it for her. She hadn't lied to me, played me, or used me, and our friendship was real, not something she contrived for some ulterior motive. And she didn't run Tom off the road, someone else did. "You just did."

"I'm sorry, too. I should have told you I was having dinner with Holl and why."

"And I should have figured that out on my own."

We returned to the kitchen. Our pizza had cooled enough to spare our tongues. I took a bite then asked, "So what happened with Carter?"

She swallowed some beer. "After Tom's funeral, he asked me to have dinner with him."

"He ever do that before?"

"Every time we've crossed paths since Tom's accident, he's said we should get together sometime. But that was the first time he specifically asked me out."

"Maybe he thought you'd be more receptive to his...wooing now that Tom's gone."

"Possibly. The only way to find out was to have dinner with him. And I thought I could find out what he knew about Tom's accident at the same time. So I said yes."

"And what did he want?"

"From the time he picked me up—"

I stared at her, surprised, as fear iced my spine.

"You got in his car with him?"

"Why wouldn't I? He was taking me to dinner."

"Don't ever do it again."

"I won't, because I'm never having dinner with him again."

"Not just him. Anybody. Until we know who tried to kill Tom. Once someone has you in his car, you're trapped, at his mercy. He can do anything he wants to you."

Anger rose in her eyes. "Do you want to hear what I have to say or to tell me everything I did wrong?"

I took her hands. "I'm telling you because I don't want you ending up like Tom. Or worse. Whoever ran him off the road won't think twice about doing the same to you if they think you're onto them."

She looked down. "I didn't think of that." Her tone was subdued.

I raised my hand. "End of lecture. What happened with Carter?"

"He was extremely curious about you. The first thing he asked me after he picked me up was how we met. I told him you came to my rescue when I had car trouble. He wanted to know why I continued to see you if that was all you'd done. He said he wanted to make sure you weren't out to con me somehow."

"So he's still singing that song?"

She nodded. "He said I shouldn't trust you, that you'd want something in return for helping me. He even asked if you'd ever made any inappropriate advances—his words—to me."

She fell silent. I suspected she was remembering Saturday night at the cabin but couldn't tell if the memory held pleasure or regret. "While making them himself, no doubt."

"Mm-hmmm." She chewed rapidly then swallowed. "He suggested more than once the night shouldn't end with dinner." She shuddered. "Taking me home, he tried several times to get me to invite him in for a nightcap. It took five very firm noes before he got the message."

I picked up a second slice. "What did he tell you about Tom's accident?"

"Not much. He was more concerned with what I could tell him. He asked me a dozen different ways during dinner if the police had anything new, like he was cross-examining me. I said if he planned to interrogate me all evening, he could take me home that instant. Then I asked him what he could tell me about the night Tom crashed."

"And he said?"

She blotted sauce from the corner of her mouth. "After lunch, Jeff suggested they all go to the Roadhouse for dinner. When they got there, Tom said he was going to grab a quick bite and run because he wanted—" she swallowed hard, "to get home and spend...time with me."

I held her hand lightly while she composed herself. When she had calmed, I said, "Why did he stay then?"

"Holl said Jeff insisted on buying everyone a round after dinner. He said he finished his and left before Tom did so he doesn't know what happened after that."

Styles had told me he'd only stayed for one drink. Interesting. "Are you close enough to anyone else who was there to ask what happened after Carter left?"

"I am with Elizabeth Fremont. She said Holl left around quarter after eight. Tom and Jeff left about ten minutes later. She, Patty Monroe, and Jim Delaney had another round and left a little after nine."

"She's sure that's the sequence?"

"Positive." Steph studied me for a second. "Why?"

"Jeff told me he had one quick drink and left early because he and Lisa were going away Sunday and wanted to get an early start."

"Why would he say that?" She gazed at me quizzically. "Do you think he had something to do with Tom's accident? You do, don't you?"

"It crossed my mind." *Why else would he lie?*

A string of emotions washed across her face. "I also spoke to Art O'Reilly the same day I talked to Elizabeth. He said Tom would have definitely made partner this year."

"Because he took over Wilson-McGruder?"

She froze, a slice halfway between the box and her plate. "How did you know?"

"We're restoring a Buick for Ian McGruder, the head honcho."

She laid the slice on her plate. "Art said when word got around the office last August he was cutting back on his caseload, Jeff came to him and asked—almost pleaded—for the account. When the staff met the Monday after Tom's accident to distribute his cases to other lawyers, Jeff claimed it for himself the moment they sat down." She stared past my shoulder.

No need to guess what she was thinking. The same thing I was: Could wanting Wilson-McGruder be a reason to kill Tom?

She sighed out a long breath. "Could we not talk about this anymore?" She took a bite of pizza. "Do you like to read?"

It turned into a lively discussion. Unlike our similar taste in movies and music, we had more divergent ones in books. She read almost anything but sci-fi and fantasy. I stuck to mysteries and thrillers. After our 'gourmet dinner' was reduced to crumbs and empty bottles, I opened a pair of fresh brews and we settled next to each other on my living room couch to continue it.

When the conversation petered out, I set my empty bottle on the coffee table then planted a light friend-to-friend kiss on her cheek. I shouldn't have been hoping it would lead to something more but couldn't help it. "Thanks for dinner."

"My pleasure." Steph looped her arms around my neck and kissed me. Long and sensual, it left no doubt the same something more was on her mind.

I stared at her, surprised. "I thought you said this could never happen again."

"I'm a woman." She gave me a coy smile. "I'm allowed to change my mind." Her smile turned sultry followed by another lust-laden kiss.

Our lovemaking was gentle yet fiery, intense but unhurried, and lasted late into the night before we drifted off to sleep wrapped in each other's arms.

When I woke in the morning, she was asleep next to me.

Chapter 44

08/30/2003 – The Break-In

My phone rang fifteen minutes after Steph left for home the next morning. "He—"

"Someone broke into my house!" Steph.

"Are they still there?"

"No." A tremor in her voice.

Relief. "Are you okay?"

"Yes."

Huge relief. "Did you call the cops?"

"They're on their way."

"I'll be there in ten minutes." I sprinted for my Pontiac.

I made it a rule not to use my cell when I was driving. I'd had too many near misses from dingbats paying more attention to yakking than driving. This time merited an exception. I thumbed in Andy's number as I backed out of my driveway.

I turned my Pontiac into Glenwood Heights six minutes later. Andy took the corner right behind me. He'd made good time from the far side of town. But he'd had help from lights and siren. I only had a heavy foot.

We both skidded to a stop in front of Steph's house. A Schuylerton PD cruiser sat in her driveway. We sprinted across the lawn toward her front door. At the porch, Andy halted me with a glare that could burn holes in steel and pointed to the slate. "You stay here until I say you can come in."

"I want to make sure she's okay."

"I'll find out and let you know. Soon as I can let you in, you can see her." He poked his head out the door a moment later. "She's fine. Just rattled."

Minutes later, a Ford van stopped in Steph's driveway, two men took metal cases from the back, and strode to her door. Andy let them in, but I paced away another hour before he opened the door again. "Come on in, Dan."

Steph sat coiled into a ball at one end of the tan couch, still in last night's clothes, holding out her hand in a 'come here' gesture. I joined her on the couch and she clasped my hand in a gentle squeeze. Andy noticed as he settled in a chair on the other side of the coffee table.

I asked, "You okay?"

She nodded. "Just shaken." Her voice still carried a faint tremor.

"What happened?"

"Bad guy got in through the sliding door in the kitchen," Andy said, "tossed everything in the den like he was looking for something specific. Doesn't appear any other rooms in the house were searched."

I turned to Steph. "Was anything taken?"

"I don't think so but I won't know for sure until I get everything put back. The boxes from the cabin are dumped all over the floor."

"Do you or your husband have anything like a coin or stamp collection," Andy asked, "something with valuable pieces in it that might attract a thief?"

"No. Nothing like that. We're not collectors."

He leaned forward in his chair. "Anything from cases your husband was working on at the time of his accident still in the house?"

She shook her head. "He never brought work home with him."

"So there's no possibility something pertaining to one of his cases is here?"

"If there was," I said, "someone from OSM would have come for it long before this. And they wouldn't need to steal it. They just had to ask for it, and she would have given it to them."

She nodded, agreeing. "Absolutely."

Andy studied his notebook for a moment. "This could be just a random break-in. Nice houses in upscale neighborhoods are always prime targets. But the usual things burglars grab—TV, computers, jewelry—are still here. That tells me whoever broke in was after something specific and thought it would be in the den. Do you have any idea what it might be?"

She explained the tape missing from Tom's office.

Andy jutted his chin toward the den. "Was it here?"

"I don't think so. At least I never found it."

"Could this missing tape be tied to your husband's accident?"

"Seems likely," I said.

"If it does," Steph asked, "why would someone wait until now to come after it?"

"As long as everyone accepted the 'tragic accident' scenario, whoever did it may have felt he was safe," Andy said. "Now that we're taking a second look at things, he could be afraid it will lead us back to him."

"We have a cabin on Big Bear Lake. If whoever did this didn't find it here—"

"He may look there," Andy finished her thought. "I'll reach out to Buckley Township PD, ask them to keep an eye on your place." He jotted a note then closed his notebook. "I think that's all, Mrs. Mercer, but I may have more questions for you later. The crime scene people will be here for a little while yet finishing up. I'll keep you posted on what we find."

He stood. "Remember to get a board or dowel to fit in the track of your sliding door to prevent anyone else getting in that way."

"I'll take care of it," I said.

"Good. Dan." He motioned with his head for me to follow him outside then leaned against the fender of his cruiser. "Mrs. Mercer says she was with you all night. That true?"

"Yeah."

"Jeez, Dan! She just lost her husband after ten months in a coma. Or did you forget that?"

I shot him a glare. "I didn't forget."

"How long you two been spending nights together?"

"Two weeks ago was the first time. Last night was the second."

"Unh-hunh." His tone carried a ton and a half of doubt.

"Fine." I held up my hands. "Don't believe me. That's all it happened."

"You start stirring the pot on Mercer's accident hoping it'd get you bedroom privileges in return?"

"You asking as a cop or my friend?"

"A little of both."

"You know me better than that," I snapped. "I stirred the pot because she believed his accident wasn't his fault, and I wanted to find out if she was right or hanging on to false hope. We both know she was right."

Andy looked away and nodded once. "Yeah. Okay." He pushed off the cruiser. "Back to the mines. See you 'round."

"See ya." I stepped toward my car.

"Dan."

I faced him. "Yeah."

"What you and Mrs. Mercer do is none of my business. But, as a friend, I don't want to see it blow up in your face. She could be getting cozy with you, hoping to pull you into something that could come back to bite you in the ass.

"She's not."

"Wouldn't be the first time it happened. *Cherchez la femme* and all that."

Chapter 45

09/02/2003 – Incident at The Mall

"Dan, my car won't start," Steph said when I answered the phone Tuesday night.

"Where are you?"

"At the mall." Northside Mall, the only one in the area.

Nine-ten p.m. Steph must have shopped until closing time. "Won't start how?"

"I turn the key and nothing happens."

The back of my mind sorted through possible causes. "Do your headlights work? Did the warning lights on the dash come on when you turn the key?"

"Yes and yes. It just won't start."

Not a dead battery. "Was it okay earlier?"

"It started fine."

Maybe a dying one. "Turn your lights on then try to start it. Let me know if your lights dim."

Her seatbelt chime dinged clearly in my ear. "No," she said, "or maybe only a little."

I didn't hear the starter. Maybe it or the relay failed? Not common, but not unheard of. "Okay. I'm on my way. Where are you parked?"

"Near the Bon-Ton entrance."

I couldn't put my finger on why worry trickled along my spine. "Get in your car, lock the doors, and stay there. Don't open your door for anyone but me or the cops. I'll be there as soon as I can. Fifteen minutes at most."

I called Andy and told him what happened to Steph and the vague worry tingling my backbone. "Can you ask whoever patrols the Northside Mall to keep an eye on her until I get there? Tell them I'll be in my Ventura."

"On it."

I hit the road for the mall. At a red light, I called Bruno Jackson and told him to grab our rollback, I had a job for him. I reached the mall twelve minutes after leaving home, entered the lot, cut across it toward the Bon-Ton side of the building, and slammed on my brakes.

Black and tan Morton Township PD cars and a wrecker—light bars flashing blue, white, red, and yellow—clustered outside a ring of crime scene tape. I bailed from my Pontiac and sprinted toward it. Inside the tape, Steph's Lexus was crushed between a light pole and the dark blue and white mid-eighties Ford F-250 buried nose first in its right side. A yellow plastic sheet covered the Ford's cab. Memories of Amy's smashed car drilled pain into my gut and my lungs tried to check out.

Aluminum patches shaped the Ford's rear wheel well and rust had nibbled a ragged edge along the bottom of the fender. The truck looked familiar, but I was too anxious about Steph to dredge up where I'd seen it before. I grabbed the tape, lifted it, stooped to duck under. A Morton Township officer, sergeant stripes on his sleeves, blocked my path. "Stop right there."

I hadn't spotted Steph. I pointed to her Lexus. "The woman who owns that, where is she? Is she okay? Is she—"

"What's your name?"

"Dan Gallagher." I yanked my license from my wallet and held it up.

"Okay. And the person you're asking about?"

"Stephanie Mercer." I pointed again. "That's her car. She called me, said it wouldn't start, asked me to pick her up. What happened? Is she okay?"

A beige Honda CR-V stopped on the far side of the tape circle, and a stocky white-haired man carrying an old-fashioned doctor's bag got out. After a brief chat with another Morton Township officer, he ducked under the police tape, crossed to the Ford, and slipped behind the yellow tarp.

"What time did Ms. Mercer call you?"

"I'm not answering any questions until you tell me if she's okay."

The cop glared at me for a second. "She's being transported to Branthorpe General."

My heart jumped for the stratosphere. "How bad is she hurt?"

"I can't say. Now what time did Ms. Mercer call you?"

"Later." I turned toward my Pontiac.

"Now. Or I'll cite you for hindering a police investigation."

Telling him what he could do with his citation wouldn't get me anywhere. I took in a deep breath, let it out slow, and faced him. "She called me about ten after nine."

"What did she say when she called?"

"Just what I told you, that her car wouldn't start. Are we done here?"

"One more question. You know anyone who might have a grudge against Ms. Mercer?"

I had suspicions. I chose not to share them. "Are you saying this wasn't an accident?"

"Yet to be determined."

"Why's the yellow tarp over the cab of the pickup?"

"The driver was killed."

"Who is he?"

"I'm not at liberty to say."

Steph's car was definitely totaled, but I wanted to know why it wouldn't start. "Who's towing the wrecks?"

He pointed to the wrecker. "West End Towing."

I handed him a business card. "Any problem if my people take the Lexus?"

"I'll clear it with West End."

"Thanks. My rollback'll be here in a few minutes."

I dashed to my Pontiac, fired it up, and took off calmly. The moment the mall was out of my mirrors, I stood on the tall pedal and raced for Branthorpe General. An image of Steph bloodied and broken filled my head, and my heart thundered as loud as the Ventura's big motor.

I scampered from the parking lot to the ER, skidded to a stop at the registration window, and snapped, "Where's Stephanie Mercer?"

The woman behind the glass fixed me with a long cool stare. "Are you a relative?"

Like with the officer, blowing up at her would get me nowhere. Time for another deep breath. "No, just a friend. She was brought here after an accident, and I'm here to give her a ride home when she's released."

"She's still being treated. I'll notify you when they are finished. There's a waiting room across the hall."

"Can you tell me how she is? Is she hurt bad?"

A nurse slid a form from a rack on the wall behind the receptionist and left the room. The receptionist intoned, "I can't release any information to anyone not a family member," like a recording and turned her attention to her computer terminal.

I stalked to the waiting room and dropped into a thinly padded orange chair. Not a minute later, the nurse who'd picked up the form peered in. "Excuse me. Are you Dan Gallagher?"

"Yeah."

"You were asking about Stephanie Mercer? She's been asking for you."

"Is she all right? Is she—"

"She's fine, just minor injuries. The doctor is almost finished treating her, but a police officer's waiting to talk to her. As soon as he's done, I'll take you to her."

A dragging hour later, the nurse poked her head in the door and beckoned me to follow her. Inside the ER, she led me to Room Six. "She's in here."

"Thanks." I tapped on the door and opened it a crack. "Steph?"

"Dan? Come in."

She sat on the treatment bed in pale pink scrubs, and she smiled when I entered. A butterfly bandage spanned a small cut in the center of a purple lump above her right eye, and scrapes marked that cheek and her chin. Even battered, her beauty hit me with a visceral impact. A brace covered her left wrist, tape held a splint to a finger on that hand, and gauze pads covered the heels of both palms. "Are you okay?"

She nodded, wincing. "Sprained my wrist, dislocated a finger, hit my head, and scraped myself up pretty good when I got knocked down. The doctor says I'll be sore all over tomorrow."

For the first time since the cop had said she was on her way to the hospital, my heart and breathing subsided toward normal. And the knot in my gut loosened. "No concussion?"

She shook her head gently, wincing again. I lifted her off the bed in a hug and whirled her in a circle.

"Dan!" she shrieked. "Put me down!"

I did. "They're not keeping you overnight?"

"As soon as they do the paperwork, I'm free to go."

I bowed and made a sweeping gesture toward the door. "My carriage awaits you, milady."

"Thank you, kind sir." She offered a small curtsey and a big smile.

Fifteen minutes later, she came out of the room, still in the scrubs, a paper bag clutched in her hand, her purse hanging from her shoulder. As soon as we stepped outside, I slipped an arm around her, drew her close, and led her to my Pontiac. "What happened?"

"Right after I called you, this truck came racing across the parking lot and smashed into my car." She started to tremble. "If I hadn't gotten out—"

There would have been a yellow tarp draped over her car, too. No wonder she was trembling. I gathered her into my arms and whispered, "Thank God you did."

And thank God she hadn't listened to me. When

her trembling stopped, I said, "So the truck just plowed into you?"

"It went by once as I was walking to my car. I thought it was going around to the Penney's entrance until it came around again and came right at me."

"Could you see the driver? Did you get a look at him?"

"No. He had his high beams on. I couldn't see anything in the glare."

Nearing my car, she huffed out a hard breath. "I feel...wired, like I did when I won a race I shouldn't have at a swim meet. The rush never lasted this long though."

"Escaping with your life is a bigger win than any race."

A little shudder ran through her. "Don't I know it."

I got behind the wheel and started my Pontiac. Steph slid to the center of the bench seat, buckled her seat belt and, as I drove away, rested her head on my shoulder. "Thanks for coming for me. I didn't mess up your plans, did I?"

"Nah. I was keeping the evening open in case a damsel in distress needed a ride because her car wouldn't start."

She offered me a smile then returned her head to my shoulder. This felt so right, as natural as breathing, and so good it could be addictive. I hadn't felt that way driving with a woman since Amy died. I could easily get— "I'm sorry. What?"

She lifted her head off my shoulder. "I asked if you thought that man crashed into my car because we're looking into Tom's accident."

I didn't want to answer.

"Dan?"

"I think it's possible."

"Maybe he thought if he frightened me half to death, I'd beg you to stop looking."

Maybe frightening her half to death wasn't his goal. Maybe crushing her all the way there was. Either way, it had worked. I'd stop before I did anything that put her in harm's way.

She'd read my mind. "Dan, don't stop looking, please."

"I will if continuing means you might get hurt."

"Nothing could hurt me worse than what they did to Tom. And I can handle being scared. I can't handle not knowing the truth."

"What if the truth is something ugly? What if Tom was involved in something illegal?"

She was silent for a bunch of seconds. "Ugly or not, I'd rather know."

I put my arm around her. "You are one strong lady."

She smiled again and lowered her head to my shoulder. Yep, I could get used to this. We rode in silence until we reached Schuylerton, where she said, "I'll need to rent a car tomorrow."

"I have one you can use as long as you need."

"No, Dan. I can't take this one. This was your first renewal."

"I have another one sitting in my garage you're welcome to." Instead of turning onto the street that would take us to Glenwood Heights, I took the one leading to my Briar Avenue home. Three turns later, I pulled into my driveway, led Steph into my garage, switched on the lights, and showed her the LeMans in the last bay.

She let out a gasp. "Dan, it's beautiful!"

"Thanks." I opened the door. "Try it on. See how it fits."

She hesitated then settled in the tan interior and adjusted the driver's seat, ran a hand over the wood-rimmed steering wheel, and examined the interior. I leaned down. "It doesn't have the bells and whistles your Lexus does, but it's about the same size, so you shouldn't have any trouble driving it."

She slid out, closed the door, and studied the LeMans for a few seconds. "This was Amy's, wasn't it?"

"It was supposed to be. I hadn't finished it when she died."

She stepped back a pace. "Dan, I can't drive this. What if I get in an accident with it?"

"Then I'll fix it. It's a car, Steph, not a Ming vase."

"Well..." she looked the LeMans over again, "if you're sure."

"I am." I touched her arm. "Come on. I'll get the keys."

I plucked them from the key rack inside the back door and handed them to her.

"I'll be very careful with it and get it back to you as soon as I get a rental car tomorrow."

"Keep it for a while. It could use a stretch of daily use."

She eyed the keys on her open palm for a second then smiled wanly. "I guess I should be going."

I didn't want her to. "You hungry? Would you like something to eat?"

Her smile brightened. "Yes, I would." She dropped

the keys in her purse. "I'm glad a policeman grabbed this for me. I didn't even realize I didn't have it until he handed it to me."

"You were focused on something a little more important: escaping with your life. Now, what do you have a hankering for food-wise?"

"If I was home, I'd probably make myself some toast with jelly and a cup of tea."

"How about some scrambled eggs to go with that?"

"Oh, that sounds wonderful."

In the kitchen, I got the teakettle going then grabbed the eggs.

"What can I do to help?"

"Nothing. You got a bum wrist, scraped up palms, and a finger out of commission."

"Dan! I'm hurt, not bed-ridden."

I knew when to give in. I pointed. "Bread's in there." I tipped the whisked eggs into a pan and pointed to cabinets to the left of the sink. "Plates and cups are there. Silverware's in the drawer below."

Though my kitchen is small, we worked as smoothly as if we'd made hundreds of meals together. I shut off the burner and divvied the eggs between us. Steph ate a bite of egg then one of toast with Nora's homemade elderberry jelly. "Mmm. Comfort food."

"For sure." I assembled my eggs and toast into a sandwich and took a bite. "When I saw your car crushed like a tin can—"

"It reminded you of Amy?"

I nodded. "I was afraid you were in it when he hit it and were—" I couldn't say the rest.

"When he turned toward me and sped up, I knew he was going to hit me. I got out right before he did, but my car bumped me before I could get clear, and I went flying." She raised her hands. "I got these trying to break my fall." She touched her forehead. "And this. And I ruined the suit I had on, tore both knees in the pants, and ripped the jacket."

I swallowed my second bite. "Better your suit than you."

She sipped her tea. "What if he had nothing to do with Tom's accident? What if someone hired him to crash into me?"

"Why do you think that?"

"Right after he turned toward me, he slowed for a second, like he wasn't sure he could go through with it, before he came at me."

"He'd have to be one cold-hearted S.O.B. not to hesitate."

"Do you know what happened to him? Was he hurt?"

"Fatally."

Steph put her hand over her mouth for a second. "Do you know who he was?"

"The police wouldn't tell me." I took my empty plate and glass to the sink. "I'll call Andy tomorrow, see if he knows."

Steph huffed out a hard sigh as she set her plate and silverware next to mine.

I slipped my arm around her. "You okay?"

"I can't handle being scared as well as I thought. May I stay here tonight?"

I gave her a quick hug. "Sure." I squirted detergent and ran hot water into the sink, slid plates and glasses into it.

She reached for the sponge. "Let me do that,

please."

I grasped her hands. "With your hands in this state and a bunged-up wrist? Not a chance. It'll only take a minute."

"You loan me a car, you feed me, and give me a place to sleep. The least I can do is wash the dishes."

"Not tonight." I tugged a towel from the rack and draped it over her shoulder. "You can dry." I flashed her a smile. "But nothing else." I washed the first plate and passed it to her.

Washing dishes has always been far from my favorite task, not onerous, but low on the list. Doing them with Steph made it almost pleasant. A sure sign I was falling in love with her. And, damn, it felt good! But I couldn't let it continue.

I had let Amy down, and it had led to her death. I would never put another woman—especially Steph—in the same position. And I feared loving her then losing her as I'd lost Amy. I wouldn't put myself through that hurt again.

While Steph dried the last of the dishes, I hung a clean towel and washcloth in the bathroom and laid a new toothbrush on the counter by the sink. She came down the hall as I left the bathroom. Even in baggy scrubs, she looked chic. "Dishes are dried and put away."

"Thank you." I planted a quick kiss on her cheek and followed her into the bedroom. "Sorry I don't have any PJs you can wear."

She tugged at the scrubs. "These are fine."

I grabbed a tee and pair of jogging shorts from my dresser. "I'll be on the couch if you need me." I took a step toward the door.

She touched my arm, I turned to face her, and she stepped close to me. "I'm still a little on edge. Stay? And hold me?"

I did. In moments, she was asleep. Spooned against her back, my arms circling her, felt good and right. And as comforting to me as it was to her. The last vestiges of the knot that had lingered in my gut long after I knew she was okay unraveled completely.

Chapter 46

09/03/2003 – Things Get Hot

The phone jarred me awake at two a.m. Steph stirred behind me as I answered it.

"It's Andy. There's a fire at your shop."

Dread knotted my stomach. "Where?" If it was the main building and the twenty cars inside, I was in for a serious hit.

"Paint shop."

One of six ancillary buildings in my shop complex. Not as bad as the main building but not good by a long shot. "On my way." I dropped the phone and grabbed my jeans.

"Dan? What is it?" Steph's eyes were open, her head raised.

"Fire at my shops."

She tossed off the covers and rose. "I'm coming with you."

"It may take hours."

"I'm coming anyway."

The fire could be a ruse to lure me from my house, so leaving Steph here could endanger her. Was I overreacting? Why did I assume the fire had been set? It could have started a number of ways, most of them innocent. Still, better safe than sorry. And that she wanted to come touched me. "Thanks."

"How bad is it?"

"Andy didn't say." I tucked my tee into my jeans. "We'll find out when we get there."

She adjusted the scrub top. "Ready to go."

Five minutes later, I slowed to a halt a block from my shops, stopped by a Schuylerton PD cruiser blocking Covington Road, the cop by it pointing for me to turn left onto Fulton Avenue. By my shops, fire truck lights flicked red and white, firemen stowed gear in compartments, and dirty white smoke clogged the sky. Steph gasped. "Oh, my God!"

My thoughts exactly. I parked behind Andy's Dodge pick-up. "I'll be back as quick as I can."

"Take as long as you need. I'll wait here." Steph plucked at the scrubs. "I'm not really dressed to be seen in public."

I got out and started toward my shops. An acrid reek tainted the air. The cop intercepted me. "You can't go down there."

"Chief Cummings called me." I pointed. "That's my place."

He activated the mic clipped to his epaulette, mumbled "Owner's here," and listened to the reply. "Chief Cummings will be right up."

Andy in jeans and a tee and a blocky guy in turnout gear arrived a minute later, and Andy said, "You know Chief Bridges, Dan?"

"Yeah." We shook, and I asked, "So, what happened?"

"Officer Coyle on patrol spotted smoke a little before one," Andy said, "saw flames coming from your paint shop, called it in, tried to contain it with the extinguisher from his unit."

Bridges said, "Blaze was fully developed when we rolled up maybe ten minutes later. All we could do was keep it in check, stop it from spreading." He brushed a hand over a salt-and-pepper crewcut. "Building's a total loss. Sorry we couldn't save it."

"I appreciate everything you and your men did. Any of them hurt?"

"One guy turned an ankle. He'll be fine in a day or two."

"Glad to hear that's all. How bad is it?"

"Show you." He waved a 'follow me' hand. "C'mon." Walking toward my shops, he grabbed a big flashlight from the running board of his Chevy Blazer. Andy and I followed him across wet paving to a charred cinderblock shell ringed in FIRE SCENE tape. The stench in the air left a metallic taste on my tongue. Bridges clicked the light on. Glass shards from blown-out windows littered the paving, glittering in the beam. He played the light over the roofless building. "There you have it."

I fought down the urge to puke. "How did it start?"

"This way." Bridges led Andy and me to the side of the paint shop. There, he aimed the beam at the door. "One of my guys found this." The door hung open, the metal around the knob scarred, dented, and torn.

Andy leaned in for a closer look. "Used a crowbar."

"Had me a look inside once we got the fire out," Bridges said. "Looks like once he got in, he dumped a bunch of flammables on the floor, ran a trail to the door, and lit it. Got a call in to the fire marshal, gonna have him take a look, see if I got it right."

"Any of your guys working late tonight, Dan?"

"Gene maybe," I said. "If he was painting a car, he'd have to stay until he finished." A chill skittered the length of my spine. "You didn't find a body in there, did you, Chief?"

Bridges shook his head. "Nope."

I let out a big sigh. Losing any of my employees would hurt, but losing Gene would hurt more. Bodymen of his skill weren't found on every corner. "Was there a car in the paint booth?"

"Didn't see one."

I breathed another sigh of relief. Gene's crew spent hours making each body perfect before he laid flawless paint on it. Having the fire undo his hard work would have broken his heart. "Why this building? Why not the main one?"

"It's farthest away from the street," Andy said. "Less chance of being spotted in the act."

"And lots of flammables to speed things along," Bridges added. "I'll have a pumper and crew stand by overnight in case the thing flares up. And I'll let you know what the fire marshal says."

"Thanks, Chief. And thank your guys." Volunteer firemen are a special breed, leaving their beds in the wee hours of the night to fight a fire on a stranger's property then showing up at their day jobs on time the next morning.

"Appreciate it." Bridges lumbered away.

Andy said, "I'll have patrol swing by here more often, keep an eye on the place, too."

We stared silently at the burned-out building for another moment then he clapped me on the shoulder. "Let's go home."

We strolled toward the street. Andy asked, "What

happened with Ms. Mercer at the mall?"

I told him. Halfway through I recalled where I'd seen the pick-up that hit her Lexus—at Hofnagle Ford in Branthorpe—and added it. At my Pontiac, he said, "We'll talk tomorrow."

Steph stirred when I got in. "Sorry, I dozed off. How bad is it?"

"Paint shop's a total loss. I'll call around to other body shops tomorrow, see who can help us out."

"I'm sorry."

"For what? Nodding off? Hard not to in the middle of the night." I fired the engine and aimed my car toward home.

"No. For the fire."

"You didn't start it."

"But I feel—"

I took her hand. "The only thing you need to feel is glad no one got hurt. This is not your fault."

"It is. If I hadn't told you about Tom's accident, you wouldn't have looked into it and found out he was run off the road, and whoever did it wouldn't be trying to get back at you by planting drugs in your shops and trying to burn them down."

"This may not be connected to that. This could be an accident." I stopped for the blinking red light at Fulton and Front. "Could be kids looking for kicks, random vandalism."

"You know it isn't. You know this was because you're looking into Tom's accident."

"I don't know it. I suspect it, but I don't know it. Let's see what the fire marshal has to say tomorrow."

We rode the rest of the way home in silence. As we entered my bedroom, Steph let out a sigh as if the world rested on her shoulders. I turned her to face me. "What's wrong?"

"People breaking into my house, wrecking my car, trying to ruin your business, trying to burn it down." She leaned into me and put her arms around me. "I can't take it anymore. I want it to stop. Now!"

I rubbed her back lightly. "Hang on a little longer. We'll get through this. Together."

Chapter 47

09/04/2003 – Information

I woke late Thursday morning with Steph nestled in my arms. The more time I spent with her, the more I wanted to spend. I shoved the thought away before it could put down roots. She'd just lost Tom a month ago. Who was I kidding, anyway? She'd grown up in wealth and culture, was educated, had been to Europe several times. My dad delivered mail, and my mom was a waitress. I worked with my hands, and my only trip out of the U. S. had been to Niagara Falls with Amy on our honeymoon.

As soon as I got to the shops, I paged everyone to assemble in the break room where I shared the news about the fire. Gene said he'd already started calling other body shops, asking them to let us use their paint booth. I asked Bruno Jackson to come to my office and turned the rest loose to get back to work.

At six-foot-seven and three-fifty, if he was an ounce, Bruno Jackson made my six-four and two-forty-five seem puny. Shaved head, no neck, arms as thick as the cables on the Golden Gate Bridge jutting from a sleeveless shirt, eagle tatt on the left bicep. His basso profundo voice vibrated the pens on my desk when he asked, "What you want, boss?"

"Find out why the Lexus you picked up last night

wouldn't start. Lights and everything else worked, but it wouldn't start, wouldn't even turn over. Start by checking the starter motor."

"'Kay." Ten minutes later, he was back in my office. "Wouldn't start 'cause the battery cable was cut at the starter."

Leaving Steph trapped in an immobile car, a sitting duck for someone to smash into. "Thanks, Bruno." I should call Steph, decided not to. I'd tell her face to face later. I returned to reviewing the status of our projects. Two minutes later, my phone rang.

"Meet me at Pete's Perk in five." Andy hung up before I could say a word.

Once we settled in our booth with coffees and pastries, I asked, "So what's up?"

"Talked to Morton Township PD right before I called you. Driver of the pick-up that hit Ms. Mercer's car was your buddy, Scott Harris." The man who may have repaired the car that ran Tom Mercer off the road. "Doc Dryden, the coroner, says cause of death was severe head, neck, and chest trauma sustained in the crash. Harris had five one-hundred-dollar bills in his wallet. Morton PD checked with Hofnagle Ford. He nets around four-twenty-five a week, and payday is today."

"He got paid but not by Hofnagle." I forked spice coffee cake into my mouth.

"That's my thinking." Andy bit into his raspberry Danish.

"To destroy Steph's car and maybe her?"

"Be my take on it. Unless he walks around with a ton of cash in his wallet. You got any thoughts on who might have hired him or why?"

"The same person who torched my paint shop." I slugged back some coffee. "Remember me telling you last night Steph's car wouldn't start even though it was running fine earlier. The cable from the battery to the starter was cut."

"You think Harris did it?"

"It's not exactly rocket science. And it left Steph a sitting duck for him to hit her."

"Someone definitely sicced him on you and Ms. Mercer. Fingerprints we recovered at Ms. Mercer's break-in and on some baggies of weed in your shops are his." He took a bite of Danish, chewed it slowly, and washed it down with coffee. "Service manager at Hofnagle told Morton PD he was about to fire Harris. He's been stealing supplies there like he did at Paul Cole's. One thing they know he took was a gallon of enamel reducer. And the fire marshal says a field analysis of some of the evidence from your shop shows residue consistent with that."

"But Harris couldn't have done it because he was dead when the fire started."

"His brother Eddie wasn't. They're a real pair of winners. Both have priors for small stuff, B and E, criminal trespass." He downed a swallow of coffee. "Either one of them have a reason they'd come after you or Mrs. Mercer?"

"Target of opportunity?"

"Not the way they've been doing it. Scott and Eddie get tanked up and get in bar fights, break into a home by heaving a brick through a window. Stuff that's been happening to you and Ms. Mercer is beyond their brainpower. Someone put them up to it."

"Any chance Eddie's fingerprints are on the photos

Steph and I got?"

"Only yours and hers."

"But you're going to question Eddie about what's been going on?"

Andy drained his mug and set it down with a thump. "Soon as we find him."

Chapter 48

09/06/2003 – The Wiring Job

Saturday morning, I loaded a toolbox and the carton of electrical supplies from Steph's cabin in my truck and drove to Gene Parilli's home. Gene pointed to the carton as I set it on the floor of the unfinished family room he was building on the back of his house. "What you got there, Bossman?"

"Outlets, switches, junction boxes." I waved a hand around the room. "You want this place wired, right?" I can't cut a board straight to save my soul and bend probably half the nails I hammer, but I can wire up a storm.

Gene ran a hand through his black hair. "Yeah, but, jeez, I didn't mean for you to buy the stuff, too. I figured you'd tell me what you needed and I'd fetch it."

I nudged the box with my toe. "No reason to when I had these sitting in my garage. Unless you want more than I have here."

"Nah. Whatever you got should be plenty. Thanks. What do you want me to do?"

"Figure out where you want outlets and switches and mark the spots."

His wife, Donna, stepped onto the plywood subfloor of the sunroom holding a large thermal mug in each hand. "Freshly brewed." She handed me one.

"Thanks for doing this, Dan. Gene would probably set the house on fire if he tried it."

"For a fact." Gene took the other mug from her and downed a swallow.

I opened my toolbox and got out my drill, bits, and wiring tools then worked on my coffee. A few minutes later, Gene said, "Guess we're set. I marked the spots." He pointed to penciled Xs on some studs. "What do we do first?"

"Mount the outlet boxes eighteen inches from the floor." I handed him several. "You start here, I'll start at the other end, and we'll work toward each other." Taking the carton and my tools to the farthest X, I measured then screwed an outlet box to the stud. At the third X, when I reached into the carton, my hand grabbed something that definitely was no outlet box. I fished out a microcassette case with 'B7' on the label.

The missing tape from Tom Mercer's office had been within my reach all this time. I shook my head in amazement and disgust and stuffed it in my pocket.

I had to use all my willpower to see the wiring job through to the end and all my concentration to do it right. The tape in my pocket was like a gnat buzzing by my ear, distracting me from what I was doing. I double-checked every screw I tightened and every connection I made, and I let out a sigh of relief when Gene threw the breaker and sparks didn't shoot from every outlet.

I passed on Donna's invitation to supper and sped home far faster than I normally would have or should have. I wanted to hear that tape. Forty bucks plus tax at Radio Shack got me a microcassette recorder.

Jeremy Slater, my neighbor's son, in faded jeans, white tee, and multi-color sneaks was strolling toward my home when I turned onto my street. A waif of a girl dressed in black walked at his side, her head down. Each had a bulky camera bag hanging from one shoulder. Jeremy waved when he spotted my truck. After Steph and I had gotten the photos, I'd asked him to find out if anyone in the high school's Visual Arts Club had been paid to take our pictures. Evidently, he had.

They reached my truck as I got out, and Jeremy said, "Hey, Mr. Gallagher," then pointed to the girl. "This is Megan Clancy."

"Hello, Megan. Nice to meet you."

She glanced up, said a fast, "Hi," and looked down. A second later, she muttered, "I can't do this," and scampered down my driveway.

Jeremy sprinted after her. He caught up to her on the sidewalk, draped his arm across her shoulders, and whispered in her ear.

I wanted to get inside and listen to the tape but suspected what brought Jeremy and Megan to my door would be equally important. Still, the few minutes I waited until he led her back to me irritated like an itch I couldn't scratch.

They stopped in front of me, Jeremy's arm still around her shoulders, Megan's head still tipped down. After a second, Jeremy said, "Go on, Meg. Tell him. He's okay." He shot me a wink. "For a grownup."

She inhaled a deep breath, squared her shoulders, and raised her head. She was an attractive young woman with a round face and golden-brown eyes below short black hair. Inhaling again, she said in a soft voice, "I took the pictures of you and that lady."

As I'd suspected. I didn't want to frighten her, but I

did want to rattle her cage. "They upset us both and scared her badly."

"I'm-I'm sorry. Really sorry." She looked almost ready to cry. Then her eyes filled with worry. "Am-am I gonna get in trouble for taking them?"

"Not as long as you're honest with me. Why did you take them?"

"A guy asked me to."

"What guy?"

"Brian Fairchild."

I know a lot of people in Schuylerton, but his name didn't ring a bell. "What did he look like? Describe him."

"Big like you. Maybe a little bigger. You want to see his picture?"

This was too good to be true. "I sure do."

She took a Canon digital SLR camera and memory card from her bag. After swapping the card with the one in the camera, she scanned through the pictures on it for several seconds before reversing the camera so I could see the viewing screen. "Here."

The man had wavy light brown hair, dark brown eyes, a broad nose, and a square chin. Only his name wasn't Brian Fairchild.

It was Holland J. Carter III.

Chapter 49

09/06/2003 – The Tale on The Tape

"Listen to this," I told Andy, setting the tape recorder on the desk in his den and pressing PLAY.

Jeff: Thanks for fitting me in today, Tom.

(Door shuts)

Tom: No problem. What's on your mind?

(A chair creaks.)

Jeff: (Clears throat) You know you, Jim Delany, and I are being considered for partnership this year, and only two of us will get offers. There's talk upstairs you have a lock on one.

Tom: Talk isn't proof.

Jeff: Where there's smoke, there's at least a little fire. That leaves Jim and me chasing the other one.

Tom: You have as good a chance as he does.

Jeff: I wish. He brings in clients like flowers draw bees, and his billable hours are up more than mine. Dad told me if I don't step up my game, I'm going to lose out.

Tom: You have strengths. You're great at research, finding precedents where no one else would think to look, and nobody writes a better brief than you. You always cover all the bases yet they're lucid and to the point.

Jeff: Briefs and research aren't enough. I need to

boost my billable hours. I need to make partner this year.

Tom: Why? (Short silence) Jeff?

Jeff: (sighs) Lisa and I made some plans predicated on me making partner. We put earnest money on a summer place in the Poconos and on a condo in Stowe, both with a one-year option to buy. The year's up next June, and we won't be able to swing either place if I don't make partner this year. Plus, we lose our deposits.

Tom: Counting your chickens before they hatch. Not smart.

Jeff: I know. But when I didn't make partner last year, I figured I was a shoo-in this year so we jumped into both deals. You landed Wilson-McGruder, Jim's been going great guns all year, and I'm running fourth in a three-man race.

Tom: They aren't going to look only at the last six months, they're going to evaluate how you've been doing all year.

Jeff: I'm having a crappy one. My billable hours are down, and I lost that big liability case in April.

Tom: Your dad has one of the votes on partnership. That will count for something.

Jeff: (Snorts) Not when it comes to this place. I'm nothing but another lawyer to him. That I'm his son won't even enter his mind when the time comes. He'll vote what's best for the firm.

Tom: And you think I can do something to give you an edge over Jim?

Jeff: I need a deep pocket who comes back every month. I'm bringing in some clients, sure, but they're all bread-and-butter types, one shot deals. They don't come back next month needing more work. I need a

Wilson-McGruder. I had that, I'd have it made.

Tom: I wish I could help you.

Jeff: Are you taping?

Tom: Yes.

Jeff: Turn it off. Nobody can hear what I'm about to tell you.

Tom: Okay.

(Two clicks)

Jeff: It's off?

Tom: Yes.

(Someone shifts in a chair)

Jeff: Look, you didn't hear this from me, but Dad let it slip after dinner at his house last week they've already decided to make you a partner.

Tom: I'll believe it when I see it.

Jeff: I'm telling you, you're in. It's a done deal. Unless you do something monumentally stupid, like get disbarred between now and then, the vote will be a formality.

Tom: Why are you telling me this?

Jeff: I told you. I need a deep pocket like Wilson-McGruder to make partner.

Tom: You'll get one.

Jeff: When? Next year? The year after? I need one now so I can pull my fat out of the fire. Help me out. Let me have Wilson-McGruder.

Tom: No. Not so you can make partner.

Jeff: Look, I'll give you half of what I make off them. We can work something out. I don't care about the money, but I need that partnership.

Tom: (Hard exhale) It's not the money, Jeff. Your dad, Graham, and Art—especially Art—will know something fishy is going on if I suddenly turn Wilson-

McGruder over to you. They could fire us. Giving you the account so you can make partner also violates the canon of ethics. We could be disbarred.

Jeff: We can come up with a plausible reason for the transfer that will satisfy them and the bar. Will you at least think about letting me have Wilson-McGruder?

Tom: There's nothing to think about. I'm not going to change my mind.

Jeff: Then let me have a couple of your steady revenue producers. Or just one of them.

Tom: That's no different than giving you Wilson-McGruder.

Jeff: You owe me. Big. Four other people, all as good as you, were being considered for the position here. I went to bat for you, talked my old man's ear off to get him to give it to you because you were my friend.

Tom: I know, and I appreciate it.

Jeff: It's time you pay me back.

Tom: Not this way. If Wilson-McGruder is ever dissatisfied with my work and want a new lawyer or asks me to do something I won't do, I'll hand them over to you in a second. But I won't give them to you solely so you can make partner.

Jeff: Don't do this to me, Tom. I *need* to make partner or I'm screwed. Don't screw me.

Tom: I'm not screwing you. I'm trying to save you from making a mistake that could cost you your career.

Jeff: No, you're screwing me. It could come back to bite you in the ass.

Tom: If I didn't know you better, I'd say that sounds like a threat.

(Door opens)

Jeff: Call it a warning.

(Door slams)

(Click)

Andy stopped the tape. "It's damning, Dan, but it's not proof. There's no actual threat here, no 'Do this or I'll kill you.'"

I'd hustled over to Andy's the minute I finished listening to the tape at home. It disturbed me as much this time as it had then. Would Jeff Styles try to kill his best friend for a partnership? "No threat? 'Don't screw me, Tom. It could come back to bite you in the ass.' That sounds like a threat to me. Tom, too. He even says it does. Styles is telling him, 'If you don't give me Wilson-McGruder, I'll get you for it.' And he did. He ran Tom off the road."

"You don't know that." Andy leaned back in his chair. "How many times have you told someone, 'I could kill you.'? Probably a hundred. But you've never done it." He grinned. "Maybe you have, and I don't know about it." He held up his hands. "And I don't want to."

"Come on, Andy."

"Just kidding. I know you better." He rocked forward and rested his forearms on his desk. "But the point remains. Saying is not doing. A tape of Jeff Styles and another person plotting to run Mercer off Millers Run Road would be a different story. I could go after him based on that."

"Jeez, Andy. It's a one, two, three deal. One, Styles threatens Tom over Wilson-McGruder. Two, Tom wrecks. Three, Styles gets the partnership that would have gone to Tom."

He held up his hand again. "I'm not blowing this off, Dan. Styles standing to lose all that money he put down on vacation homes could be a motive for murder, and I'm going to look into it." He tapped the tape player. "Are you sure it's Jeff Styles's and Tom Mercer's voices on here?"

"Ninety-nine percent. I recognize Styles's, and he calls the other man Tom. And it matches the missing tape Roberta Lynch, Tom's secretary, told me about."

He tapped the player again. "Where'd you find this?"

"Last month, I helped Steph clean Tom's things out of their cabin. She said I could have anything in the garage I wanted. I found a carton of electrical supplies—outlets, switches, boxes—I put in my garage. This morning, I took the carton to Gene Parilli's house to wire the family room he's building. I reached into it for an outlet box and got the tape instead."

"You didn't look through the box at the cabin?"

"Nope. I opened it, saw it was full of electrical stuff, and put it in my truck."

"So the box was in the Mercers' garage at Big Bear Lake. It went from there to your truck to your garage then to Gene's, where you discovered the tape inside. Anybody know you had it?"

I shook my head. "Nope."

"Anybody been in your garage since you brought the box home?"

"Just me."

He popped the tape from the player. "Any idea how long this was at their cabin?"

"Steph said the last time they were there was the week before Tom's accident to close it up for the winter. So at least since then. Tom's secretary said it went missing the week before that."

"You think this was what the burglars were after at Ms. Mercer's home?"

"Makes sense."

"I agree. You play this for Ms. Mercer?"

"No. Jeff and Lisa Styles were their closest friends. Hearing Jeff threaten Tom might be hard for her to take."

"Play it anyway. Be interesting to see her reaction. Might jog a memory loose or, if she knows Styles that well, maybe she'll pick up on something we'd miss." He tapped the tape. "I'll make a copy you can play for her. Swing by the station tomorrow. I'll have it ready by then."

"Okay. If you think it will help."

"It might." He eyed me for a moment. "You're thinking something. What?"

"Tom had something two people wanted. Jeff wanted Wilson-McGruder. Holland Carter wanted Steph. Maybe the two of them got together to take Tom out so they could both have what they wanted."

"Could be, except nothing on here," he raised the tape a fraction of an inch, "indicates Carter was involved." He laid the tape on his desk. "And neither he nor Styles owned a late nineties red Jeep Cherokee last year. But a dozen other people in the county did."

"And?"

"Nobody reported theirs stolen or involved in unexplained accidents around the time Mercer crashed. They all say they know Styles but only by name and a few know Carter the same way." He flipped through a notebook he took from his desk and rattled off the Cherokee owner names. "Any of them mean anything to you?"

"Nope. Styles or Carter had to get the Jeep somewhere. Maybe one of them rented it."

Andy shook his head. "I checked. The national firms turn their vehicles over after two years or so many miles, so they wouldn't have had a late nineties Jeep in their fleet last year. None of the local rental places had any that old either."

"Maybe Carter or Styles owned it without leaving a paper trail."

"No way they could."

"They're lawyers. They're always looking for loopholes in the law. Maybe one of them found one. And I know someone who might know how to pull it off."

"And maybe they didn't. It could be a completely random thing. Some stranger tries to pass Mercer, sideswipes him, he crashes, the other guy panics, and takes off."

"I don't buy it, Andy. Styles and Carter are involved somehow."

"I believe you but without something solid to go on, I can't do anything about it."

"Maybe this will help. I know who took the pictures Steph and I got."

"What?" Andy sat upright in his chair. "Who?"

I told him about Jeremy Slater and Megan Clancy waiting in my driveway earlier.

"I want to talk to her."

"I thought you might. I set it up for tomorrow afternoon at her home."

Chapter 50

09/07/2003 – Teen Confession

Megan Clancy lived in a white-trimmed pale blue ranch-style home on First Avenue. When a forty-ish woman answered our knock, I asked, "Mrs. Clancy?"

She nodded. "Brenda."

I introduced myself then Andy and told her we were there to talk to Meg.

"She told me." Shifting her gaze to Andy, she paled. "Is she in trouble?"

"No, ma'am. We just need to talk to her for a few minutes. She may have information helpful to an investigation I'm conducting. May we come in?"

Brenda thought for a moment. "All right." She stepped back, swinging the door wide, then closed it behind us. The cool house was refreshing after the humidity outside. The living room was neat but not immaculate, the furniture older and well cared for.

Brenda's face took on a determined expression. "I intend to be with her while you talk to her." She called, "Meg! Mr. Gallagher's here!"

Meg appeared at the end of a hallway in black jeans and tee and pointed to Andy. "Who's he?"

"Chief Andrew Cummings, Schuylerton Police, Miss Clancy."

Meg glared at me. "You said I wouldn't get in

trouble!" She bolted back the hall.

Barbara marched after her with us in her wake. She tried a door at the end of the hall. It wouldn't budge. "Megan! Open this door!"

"No!"

"Meg," I said, "you're not in trouble. I promise. We just want to talk to you. That's all. Open the door please."

"Megan Catharine Marie Clancy," Barbara yelled, "Open this door! Now! Or you *will* be in trouble!"

"Okay! Okay!" Meg heaved a massive sigh as she opened her door. "Jeez!"

Her mother planted fisted hands on her hips. "What did you do that the police need to talk to you?"

"Nothing." Defiance filled Meg's eyes.

Anger filled Barbara's voice. "Don't lie to me!"

"I'm not. I didn't do anything!"

The two glared at each other like lionesses over a dead zebra.

"Mrs. Clancy, Megan," Andy said, "both of you, take a deep breath and calm down."

They held the glare for another moment then Barbara threw up her hands and shook her head, and Meg muttered, "Whatever."

"Let's move this somewhere we can all be comfortable."

"Yes. Of course. Where are my manners?" Barbara said. "Please come into the living room."

We'd barely settled onto a couch and chairs when she turned to Meg, sitting next to her on the couch. "I want to know what's going on right now!"

Andy raised his hand. "Let me handle this, Mrs. Clancy. Meg—or do you prefer Megan—you're not in any trouble." He took a notebook and pen from inside his blazer. "We just need you to tell us how you came to take pictures of Dan."

"You did what?" Brenda snapped.

"Mrs. Clancy," Andy raised his hand again, "please. Megan?"

"Meg's fine. I wasn't taking pictures of him. I was taking them of the woman with him."

Andy and I traded glances. He said, "Start at the beginning."

"Okay." She nodded several times. "Okay. I was taking pictures in Schuyler Park, and this guy comes up and asks if I like taking photos, and I'm like, 'Well, yeah!' Then he asks if I'd take some for him if he paid me for them. So I ask how much, and he says up to me. He was kinda creepy, so I say five hundred bucks, thinking it'd cool his jets." She hesitated. "Only he says okay."

Barbara's expression mixed incredulity with shock. "You took five—"

"Mrs. Clancy, please." Andy's patience with her was wearing thin. "When was this, Meg?"

"The Saturday before Memorial Day, whatever day that was."

Andy consulted a calendar taped to the inside of his notebook. "May twenty-fourth. And this guy was Brian Fairchild?"

Meg nodded. "Unh-hunh."

"Who's Brian Fairchild?" Barbara asked.

"A man who's part of the investigation I'm asking Meg about," Andy answered.

"You mean he's a criminal?"

"No, ma'am, nothing like that. Describe him for

me, Meg."

"I have the picture I showed him." She pointed to me. "You want to see it?" She scampered down the hall and returned a moment later with her camera bag. Taking out her camera, she turned it on, clicked through some images, and handed it to Andy. "Here."

Andy angled the viewer my way. I nodded, confirming it was the photo she'd shown me. He handed the camera back to Meg.

"Let me see." Brenda snatched the camera from her, looked at the photo, and shrugged. "I don't know him."

"How did he seem creepy to you, Meg?" Andy asked.

"I don't know." Another shrug. "Some guy I don't know coming up to me and asking me to take pictures for him? Like he couldn't do it himself? It's not that hard."

"If he seemed so creepy, why did you agree to do it?"

She shot an uneasy glance at her mother. "Be-because I wanted a better camera."

"And took money from some stranger so you could get it!" Barbara screeched.

"You said you and Dad couldn't afford it. And I want it so bad!"

"Mrs. Clancy, you can discuss Meg's behavior once we're done." Andy was no longer asking her to be quiet, he was ordering. "After you said you'd take pictures for him, Meg, what happened?"

"He gave me a picture of the woman and says he wants ones of her with men. Want to see it?" She opened a pocket on the side of the camera bag, pulled out a photo she handed to Andy.

He glanced at it then passed to me. Steph in a black evening dress and diamonds at some formal shindig. I'd been right in my July fourth assessment. Dressed to the nines, she was entrancing. I stared at the photo far longer than I needed to, captivated, my heart beating a little faster each second that ticked by.

Sliding it from my hand, Andy turned it over. Steph's work and home addresses were on the back in block print like the notes with the pictures she and I'd gotten. He handed the picture to Megan. Her mother plucked it from her hand. "She looks familiar. Who is she?"

"Again, someone who's part of my investigation," Andy replied. "Then what, Meg?"

"I ask him how many pictures he wants and he says as many as I can get. Then he gives me a hundred bucks and a paper with his number on it and says to call him when I have a bunch. I have that, too." She handed him a page from a scratch pad.

Andy jotted the number in his notebook. "Did you ask him why he wanted pictures of her with men?"

She shook her head. "I thought maybe she was like his wife or fiancé or something and was cheating on him and he wanted to catch her at it."

"How long did you follow her, taking pictures?"

She shrugged. "Like six weeks."

"How did you know where to find her?"

"I'd go to her home or work and follow her wherever she went."

"How did you follow her?"

Meg flicked a quick glance at her mother. "Had Chelsea drive me around."

"You roped your sister into helping you with this…this…*escapade*?"

Meg nodded. Her mother sighed in resignation.

"What you did, Meg," Andy said, "borders on stalking. Had the woman noticed you following her and filed a complaint, we would have had no choice but to charge you."

"You *are* in trou—"

Andy cut Mom off with a chop of his hand. "After you'd been following her for six weeks, Meg, what did you do?"

"I was starting to feel kind of skeevy about it so I called the guy and said I had like twenty pictures and did he want them. He said were they of her with men and I said yeah. They were all of her with him," she pointed to me, "he was the only one I ever saw her with, but I didn't tell him that. He said could I print them out and I said yeah, so he said make two sets and bring them to Schuyler Park."

"When was this?"

"I called him on the Fourth of July, and gave him the pictures on the fifth."

Andy took a manila envelope from inside his sportscoat and tipped out a stack of photos he set on the coffee table facing Meg. Atop the stack was the photo of Steph and me in her pool. "Are these the photos you took for him?"

She flipped through the pile in a few seconds then nodded. "Yeah." She looked up. "How'd you get them?"

"He gave those to Dan and the other set to the woman you followed. When you met Fairchild at the park, what happened?"

She shrugged. "I gave him the pictures, and he looked through them and said they were just what he was looking for and paid me the four hundred he owed me and left."

"When was this?"

"Like ten-thirty, eleven."

"Did he ever contact you again?"

"Unh-unh."

"One last question. Do you still have these photos in your camera memory or on some sort of storage device?"

She pulled a plastic gizmo holding six memory cards from her camera bag. After studying them for a moment, she selected one, inserted in her camera, and checked several images. "Yeah, I still have them."

"I'll need that memory card."

"No biggie." She ejected the card and handed it to Andy.

He tucked it into his pocket and closed his notebook. "I think that's all I need for now. But I may have more questions later. Thank you both for your time."

Walking to our cars, I asked him, "You going to talk to Carter?"

"Absolutely. You play the tape for Ms. Mercer yet?"

"My next stop."

Chapter 51

09/07/2003 – Questions and Answers

I was standing by my Pontiac in Steph's driveway when she came home around four-thirty that Sunday afternoon. I'd donned a light jacket because the weather had turned cool.

After she parked her new Audi A4 in her garage, she trotted toward me in a dark blue skirt and white blouse under a light blue topcoat. "Dan? Is something wrong?"

"No. Just some things I want to talk to you about."

"Well, come in." She hooked a hand around my elbow, led me to the kitchen, and started coffee brewing without asking if I wanted any. I always did. "What is it?"

I shed my jacket, hung it over a chair in the breakfast nook, and sat. "If you had to pick one person who might run Tom off the road, who would it be?"

Her eyes flinched and she hesitated a second. "I don't know."

"Someone came to mind the minute I asked the question. Who was it?"

"I don't want to—"

"Your subconscious made an instant connection between Tom's accident and who might have caused it. Who did it connect?"

She didn't answer until she'd taken two mugs from the dishwasher and set them by the brewer. "Holl. Holland Carter."

"Why him?"

"I don't know." She faced me and leaned against the counter. "Honestly. I have no idea."

"Think about it a minute. Something about him makes you suspect he ran Tom off the road. What is it?"

She shrugged. "Maybe it's just me projecting Tom's and my dislike of Holl into him making Tom crash."

"Brush that aside. What's still there?"

She was silent for several seconds. "Tom and Holl rubbed each other the wrong way from the moment they met."

"How?"

"Every way. Attitude. Personality. Even their view of the law. Tom felt the law should apply equally to all. Holl looked for loopholes to exploit for a client's advantage. Tom wouldn't let a client use the law to shaft someone. Holl reveled in doing it."

"Anything else?"

"Tom—I don't want to make him sound like a saint, he was human like everyone else—felt he had been incredibly fortunate in his life and tried to repay that. If a client didn't have a lot of money, he'd under-bill the hours he worked on their case. Holl was out for Holl. His main focus was how much money he could make from a case, and he'd bill the client for every single minute he worked on it."

"Was he jealous of Tom, too? Did Tom have something Carter might want so bad he would kill to get it?"

She gazed into the distance for a moment. "I can't think of anything."

I pointed a finger at her. "You?"

"Me? No, that's absurd."

"Is it? You said he has a real thing for you. Lisa Styles said it too, said he hit on you at OSM's Christmas Party the first year Tom was with the firm."

"He did." The brewer chirped it was done. Steph filled the mugs and brought them to the table. "But I told him if he ever did it again, I would report him to the senior partners. And he never did."

"Making you the unattainable goal, the one thing he craved but could never have. Unless Tom was out of the picture."

Steph covered her mouth. "He wouldn't—"

"He might. He's behind the pictures we got." I told her about him hiring Megan Clancy. "I'd say he's gone a bit beyond hoping you'd fall in love with him. He may have wrecked Tom, hoping to kill him, so he could have you to himself."

"No. I cannot see him going that far."

"Then maybe someone else at OSM wanted something Tom had so bad he or she was willing to kill him to get it?"

"Why are you asking about people Tom worked with?"

"Because Andy said after family members, friends and co-workers are most likely to kill someone."

Steph weighed that through several sips of coffee. "I can't think of anyone at OSM who would want to kill Tom."

"How about Jeff?"

"What? Jeff? No! Why would you even think he'd hurt Tom?"

"He wanted something Tom had. He wanted the partnership Tom was about to get. Maybe bad enough to run Tom off the road?"

"No. Not Jeff. I don't believe it. I *won't* believe it."

"You need to hear something." I took the tape player from my jacket pocket, set it on the table, and pressed PLAY.

Steph leaned forward more and more as the tape ran, her eyes widening toward the end. When the tape ended, she buried her face in her hands for quite a few seconds. When she raised her head, tears tracked her cheeks. "No. He wouldn't. He was Tom's best friend in the whole world. He would never let a partnership come between them."

Emotions washed across her face. Then it went blank and a touch pale. She brushed her tears away. "Maybe he would." Her voice held as much emotion as her face. "Jeff's always been competitive. Especially with Tom. If he had a tough case, Jeff claimed he had a tougher one. If Tom got a big settlement, he went after a bigger one. Lisa told me he was extremely unhappy when Art gave Wilson-McGruder to Tom, even accused Tom of stealing them."

Another batch of silence while she stared at the table. "I don't want to believe Jeff, for any reason, would do something to harm Tom. But I—" she shook her head then pointed to the tape player, "after hearing that, I just don't know."

Chapter 52

09/08/2003 – The Jeep

I stopped at Volpe Auto Sales, ten miles north of Schuylerton on the highway to Wilkes-Barre, mid-morning the next day. The 'HOME OF THE 30 DAY TEST DRIVE' banner hanging from the building started an idea forming in my brain. I got out of my truck and cast an eye over the forty or so cars on the lot. Only four of them were over three years old. Within a minute, a burly blond guy about my age came out, slipping on wraparound sunglasses as he hustled toward me. "Dan? That you? What can we do for you?"

"Hey, Bill. Long time, no see." Bill Prentiss, Andy, and I grew up together, went through school together, played football together. "I'm looking for information."

"Just information? Got an oh-one Bonneville SLE that's perfect for you. Midnight Blue, low miles, fully loaded, leather, sun—"

"Just information." I pointed to the banner. "How does that thirty-day test drive work?"

"It's like a one-month lease. You drive the car for thirty days, see if you like it. You do, we consider the lease money part of your down payment. You don't, you're only out a couple hundred bucks, not stuck paying off a five-year loan on a car you don't like." He called up a grin. "Unless you wreck it or something.

Then you're up the creek."

The idea firmed up a little more. "So if I had a car on the test drive, PennDoT wouldn't show me owning it until I actually bought it."

"More like a week, ten days after you buy it until the paperwork gets processed."

Giving me almost six weeks to run someone off the road with a vehicle no one could trace back to me. "Any chance you had a dark red late nineties Cherokee out on the program in October of last year?"

Bill thought for a moment. "Probably not. We don't usually hold onto anything over three years old unless it's cherry. I can check if you like."

"Please."

He waved me to follow him inside and to an alcove lined with file cabinets. "You said a red late nineties Cherokee?" He opened a drawer in one and fingered through the folders. "Hunh. I forgot about this ninety-eight." Pulling a folder out, he laid it atop the file cabinet and opened it. "Man, this thing really was cherry. Chili Pepper Red, low mileage, loaded for a base model. Regular maintenance. Never in an accident. No rust. No leaks." He showed me a photo of a dark red Cherokee four-door so pristine it could be mistaken for new.

"Was it out on a test drive last fall?"

Bill thumbed through several pages. "Yep. September twenty-first to October nineteenth."

"Can you tell me who had it?"

He closed the file and faced me. "Not until you tell me why you're asking."

"You remember Tom Mercer, the lawyer who crashed on Millers Run Road last October, landed in a coma? Someone ran him off the road using a red Jeep. I'm helping Andy track it down."

"And you think it was this one?"

"It might be."

"Since it's you and Andy." He opened the file again. "Alex Hopper. Got a Schuylerton address." Bill faced me. "But I can tell you he had nothing to do with it."

"How?"

"Our shop guys checked it over when he brought it back. It's a condition of the test drive in case there's any damage while in the lessee's possession. Not a scratch on it."

"Where's the Jeep now?"

"Hopper bought it."

I got the Jeep's VIN and Hopper's address from Bill and thanked him for his help, called Andy on my cell, and told him what I'd learned. He said he'd get back to me after he checked some things out. He was waiting in his unmarked cruiser when I pulled into my shop. "Feel like taking a road trip?" he asked.

"Where to?"

"Branthorpe. Hopper works maintenance at the U."

"Sure." I grabbed a flashlight and small magnet from my desk and got into his cruiser.

Fifteen minutes later, Andy parked next to Alex Hopper's Cherokee in Branthrope U's maintenance building parking lot. He nodded toward it. "Check it out while I fetch Hopper."

I took the magnet and flashlight to the Cherokee. The VIN at the base of the windshield matched the one Bill gave me. I squatted by the right front fender. I wasn't surprised it looked good. The mechanics at

Volpe Auto Sales would have spotted a bad repaint in May, but I picked out a barely there difference between the paint on the front fender and hood. Playing the light on the corner of the front bumper showed a wee variation in its black paint, too. If this Jeep ran Tom Mercer off the road, Scott Harris did a better job than I expected repairing it.

I got down on one knee and wormed a hand into the opening in front of the front wheel. Brushing my fingers over the backside of the fender, I felt the ripples of poorly straightened metal. I checked the passenger side body panels with the magnet, and it fell off each one, meaning there was Bondo under the paint. The oversize tires had faint scuff marks on their sidewalls.

Andy led a lean, neatly goateed man in brown work shirt and pants toward me. The expression on Andy's face asked the question. I nodded, and he frowned then introduced me to Hopper. Close-up, I pegged his age as early thirties. He asked, "What's going on here?"

Andy said, "He's looking for damage to your vehicle."

"Then he needs his eyes checked, Chief. There's nothing wrong with it."

"Not now," I said, "but there was. It was in an accident."

"That's bullshit!" Hopper snapped. "The guy at Volpe's said it was never in an accident and I sure as hell never had one."

"I can show you where it's been damaged."

"You'd better. Otherwise, I'm outta here."

I placed the magnet against the passenger front fender. It fell away again. "It does that on every panel on this side. That means—"

"I know what it means. I tested all the way around that way the day I brought it home to make sure Volpe wasn't feeding me a line, and it didn't fall off once."

"Where were you the night of October fifth of last year?" Andy asked.

"What? Why do you want to know?"

"Answer the question, please.

"Not till you tell me why."

"Someone in a red Jeep ran a car off Millers Run Road that night, causing injuries to the driver that left him in a coma."

"Wait! Whoa!" Hopper raised quivering hands, palms out. "It wasn't me! I wasn't even in town back then. I was in Florida."

"Where in Florida?"

"Disneyworld," Hopper answered instantly. "The kids had been begging us to go for years, we thought they were finally old enough to really get something out of it, and they had off fair week." Schools in the county closed the first full week in October for the Branthrope Fair.

"When did you leave?"

"That morning, the fifth. Our flight took off at ten to seven, landed a little after one. We got to the hotel around three, checked in, got settled in the room, went over to Magic Kingdom, got back around eight, put the kids to bed. Deb and me sat out on the balcony 'till midnight then turned in."

I didn't know what Andy thought, but I read Hopper volunteering detailed information as a good indication he hadn't run Tom Mercer off the road.

"Pretty accurate memory, Mr. Hopper," Andy said.

He shrugged. "Once in a lifetime adventure for us."

"You flew out of Avoca?" An airport an hour northeast of Schuylerton.

Hopper shook a Marlboro from the pack in his shirt pocket and lit it. "Yeah."

"How'd you get there?"

"My brother drove us up."

"How long were you in Florida?"

"All week. We came home on the twelfth."

"You have any proof you were there? Plane tickets, hotel bill, receipts of any kind?"

"All of that. Deb kept track of every dime we spent. We'll show you the receipts, if you want."

I pointed to the Cherokee. "Did this drive different after you got back from Florida? Shimmy, pull to one side, anything like that?"

Hopper took a slow drag on his cigarette. "Yeah, it had a shimmy that wasn't there before. Had Mason Tires check it. They said the big tires put a strain on the front end, make it go out of alignment real easy. Pissed me off Volpe didn't tell me that."

Andy asked, "Where was this while you were in Florida?"

"Locked in my garage."

"And where were the keys?"

"Where I usually keep them, on my dresser."

"Anybody have access to your house while you were away?"

"Deb's cousin. She stopped by a few times to water the plants and check everything was okay."

"Why her? Why not your brother or his wife?"

"He's not married, and he works out of town."

"What's Deb's cousin's name?"

"Lisa Styles." He took a final drag on his cigarette then crushed it under his shoe.

Andy and I exchanged a glance before he said, "Did you give anyone permission to drive your Jeep while you were away?"

"Nope. I had it on that test drive program Volpe has. They said me and Deb were the only ones who could drive it." Hopper flicked a glance from Andy to me and back. "You think Lisa ran that guy off the road? That's nuts! She's not that kind of person."

"Somebody did. Would you mind if I dusted some areas of the interior for prints?"

Hopper shrugged. "I guess not."

"Thanks." Andy took the metal case he'd brought into my home to fingerprint me from the trunk of his cruiser. "Would you open your car for me, Mr. Hopper?"

After he unlocked the Jeep, Andy climbed in and asked, "Was the rearview mirror out of position when you got back from Florida?"

"Yeah, but I was always fiddling with it back then, couldn't seem to get it set the way I wanted it. Still have to adjust it sometimes."

"What about the driver's seat? Was it out of position?"

He lit a fresh cigarette. "Not that I noticed."

Andy spent five minutes dusting the Jeep's interior for prints, thanked Hopper for his cooperation, then motioned for me to get in his cruiser. Driving away, I asked, "Get anything?"

"A couple clear lifts off the back of the mirror and the seat adjustment lever. I'll have my fingerprint guy compare them to Styles's and Carter's. Lawyers get fingerprinted when they're admitted to the county bar."

We rode toward Schuylerton in silence for several minutes before Andy asked, "What are you thinking?"

"How this could all play out."

"I'm listening."

"Some of this is conjecture, some of it we know. Sometime October fifth, Styles goes to Hopper's, grabs the Cherokee, and stashes it somewhere to pick up later and drive to the Roadhouse."

Andy glanced my way. "Probably had help. Somebody drives him to Hopper's, follows him to where he parks the Jeep, drives him back to wherever. Smart thing to do would be take it right to the Roadhouse, leave it there."

"Makes sense. The other lawyers there said Carter left about ten minutes before Styles and Mercer that night. He gets in the Jeep and waits. Styles and Mercer come out, get in their cars, and drive off. Carter waits a minute, follows Mercer, wrecks him on Millers Run Road, stows the Jeep somewhere, and heads for home."

"You thinking Carter did it?"

"Everything points to him." I recapped all we knew about his relationship with Tom.

"Where's Styles in all this?"

"Maybe waiting for him where they stashed the Jeep overnight."

Andy stopped for the light at the Walmart plaza. "If he was smart, he hauled ass straight home from the Roadhouse, giving himself an alibi for when Mercer was wrecked. Okay, go on. What did they do next?"

"Saturday morning, he and Carter take the Jeep to Scott Harris to be fixed. The following Thursday, they pick it up and return it to Hopper's home, and he's none the wiser it's been used to run Tom Mercer off the road."

Andy smiled. "I like it. I need to talk to Hopper's neighbors, see if any of them remember seeing anyone go into their house."

Chapter 53

09/10/2003 – Atonement

"Come down to the station," Andy ordered when I answered my phone mid-morning on Wednesday.

"Why? What's up?"

"That phone number the Clancy girl gave us belongs to Holland Carter. I called him and he agreed to come in for an interview. Says he'll answer any questions I have about the attacks on you and Ms. Mercer. Wants you to hear what he has to say, too."

I wondered what Carter's game was. "Leaving now." I hung up.

The moment I entered the police station, Andy waved me into his office. Holland Carter, in a light gray suit, blue shirt, red tie, and black loafers, sat in a chair facing his desk. He offered a mild smile. "Hello, Dan."

I didn't return it. "Carter." I took the chair next to his.

Andy settled in his chair, grabbed a pen, and flicked open a notebook. "What do you know about the attacks on Ms. Mercer and Dan, Mr. Carter?"

Carter cleared his throat. "Let me begin by saying I love Stephanie. I have since I met her." Contrition filled his face.

As if that made what he'd done okay. "So much that you tried to get her to cheat on Tom with you minutes later," I said.

Andy glared at me.

Carter asked, "You know about that?" At my nod, he looked down and shook his head. "That was stupid. I never should have done it, and I never tried again, but I never stopped wanting her, though I knew it was futile because she would never leave Tom for me."

"So you tried to kill him by running him off the road."

"Dan," Andy said, an edge in his voice, "be quiet."

"Chief, let me answer him. I would never do anything to cause Stephanie pain, Dan. Just the opposite. I vowed if anything ever happened to Tom, I would be there for her, someone she could lean on in her hour of need, and hope it would lead to her falling in love with me."

"And when you got tired of waiting, you tried to kill him!" I snapped.

"Dan." Andy pinned a stern gaze on me.

I raised my hands in surrender. "Sorry."

Andy shifted his gaze to Carter. "What do you know about the photos Ms. Mercer and Dan received?"

"I sent them."

"I know you did. I want to know why."

"You do?" Carter's gaze darted between Andy and me. "How?"

"We tracked Megan Clancy down, and she told us everything."

"Was that her name? I never asked it, just made the deal with her. I'd seen her taking pictures around town several times and thought she'd jump at the chance to make some money doing it."

"Now tell us why you did it."

"That will take a little explaining." Carter blew out a hard breath. "I hoped when Stephanie reached an emotional nadir—a grief counselor I consulted said it would happen between six months and a year after Tom's accident—she would turn to me for support and solace. Instead, she turned to Dan. When Jeff said he'd seen them having dinner at Mitchell's, I went a little crazy."

"A lot crazy," I said. "You threatened legal action if I didn't cease all contact with her."

"Dan," Andy said, his voice cold, "drop it."

"He deserves an answer, Chief. I thought it would make you back off, Dan. Only you called my bluff."

"So you paid Megan Clancy five hundred dollars to take photos of Ms. Mercer and Dan." An edge in Andy's voice. "Why did you want them?"

"I felt like Dan was invading my turf, and I had to do something to stop him." He offered a weak grin. "Juvenile, right?"

"More like pathetic," I said.

Carter nodded. "I had that coming."

"Why'd you call yourself Brian Fairchild?"

Carter took a second. "I doubted Megan—you said that was her name, right?—knew me, but I thought using a fallacious name would negate any chance she might recognize me."

"After you hired Miss Clancy, what happened?" Andy asked.

"When she had twenty photos, I had her print out two sets, then I drew a red X across Dan's face on each one, added a note telling them to stay away from each other, and gave them each a set. I hoped warning them to stop seeing each other might scare him away."

"How did they get to Dan and Ms. Mercer?"

"I delivered them myself. I knew you'd check them for fingerprints and that mine were on file, so I wore gloves whenever I touched them." He swallowed. "Could I have something to drink? Coffee or a soda?"

"Either one."

"I think soda."

Andy buzzed the front desk and told the officer who answered to fetch three sodas from the break room. "What do you know about the attacks on Ms. Mercer and Dan? The break-in at her home, the drugs and fire at his shops, the attempt to kill her at the mall?"

Carter raised his hand. "I swear I had nothing to do with them."

"If you believe that, Andy," I said, "I've got ocean-front property in Nebraska for sale."

"Dan," Andy fixed me with a hard glare, "shut up! Or get out!"

I raised my hands once more. "It won't happen again."

"No, Chief, he's right. He has every reason to doubt me. But I give you my word as an officer of the court that I'm speaking the truth." A pause for a deep breath. "After I delivered the photos, I came to my senses. I realized I was becoming obsessed with Stephanie and had to get it under control before it consumed me." Another pause. "If I really loved her as much as I told myself I did, I wouldn't do things that would hurt her," he looked at me, "or her friends."

A young cop entered Andy's office, set three Cokes on the corner of his desk, and left. Andy passed them around then popped the tab on his and took a swig. "If you didn't attack Ms. Mercer and Dan, who did?"

Carter gulped a big swallow of soda. "I have no proof, but I suspect Jeff Styles was behind it."

Andy jotted a note. "Behind it how?"

Carter looked at me. "After he talked to you at your business, he had our investigator do a background check on you, hoping I think, to find something he could use as leverage to force you to stop looking into Tom's crash."

"Why wouldn't Styles want Dan looking into Mercer's accident?" Andy asked.

Carter was silent for a long moment. "I think he ran Tom off the road."

I almost choked on a swallow of Coke, and Andy and I traded surprised looks. *Jeff Styles tried to kill his best friend?* Andy asked, "Why would he do that?"

"In July last year, the senior OSM partners announced they would promote two lawyers to partners at the end of the year. Art O'Reilly giving Tom one of his major clients a week later was tantamount to declaring he would be one, leaving Jim Delaney and Jeff to battle for the other slot. Jim had been doing great for a couple years, Jeff hadn't—he is at best only an average lawyer—so it looked like he was going to miss out and he wasn't happy about it. Tom's accident handed him a partnership on a silver platter."

Andy noted something on his pad. "He ran his best friend off the road for a partnership?"

"It's not *just* a partnership. It's bonuses and a big jump in salary that go with it. Jeff needed both. He put big deposits down on two vacation properties last spring, positive he'd make partner. Without it, he wouldn't have the funds to close either deal and would have lost his deposits as well."

Carter paused for another slug of soda. "The client Art passed to Tom also had connections that could open doors for him if he ever wanted to run for elected office. Jeff had dreams of being a senator some day and wanted that 'in' as much as he needed the money."

"Where do Scott and Eddie Harris fit into the picture?"

"When Dan's background check came up clean, I think Jeff hired them to scare him off."

"Why would they do that for Styles?"

"One word. Money."

Andy and I exchanged a glance, remembering the five hundred dollars in Scott's wallet. "You're saying Jeff Styles hired the Harrises to attack Ms. Mercer and Dan to stop him from looking into Mercer's crash?"

"Essentially," Carter said. "Although I think the break-in was done for a different reason. I don't know if you know Tom taped all his meetings. This is speculation on my part, but he may have taped one where Jeff said something the police might consider motive for killing Tom. I think Jeff believed it was in Tom's home and sent one of the Harrises to retrieve it."

Carter had guessed right. He just had some specifics wrong.

"Why didn't you come to us with your suspicions about Styles when drugs were found in Dan's shops?"

"I had no proof, only a suspicion." He faced me. "And I was at the time still resentful of your friendship with Stephanie, so I hoped it might ruin you."

"Why are you telling us now?" Andy asked.

"I'm not justifying what I did, but threatening photos are one thing. Arson, burglary, planting drugs, and attempted murder are something else."

"Let's back up to the night of Mercer's accident. What can you tell us about that?"

"Six of us were at the office that day, and we decided to go to the Roadhouse for dinner." He then told us the same story Steph had told me.

Andy added more notes. "Anything unusual about that night stand out in your mind?"

"Like what?"

"Like friction between Mercer and anyone else at the Roadhouse?"

"Not that I noticed."

"What did Mercer have to eat and drink?"

"I can't say for sure." Carter ran a hand over his hair. "Maybe a sandwich of some kind and a baked potato. Definitely a scotch and water. That was his drink."

"Did he leave them unattended at any time?"

"Do you think someone tampered with them?"

"We're considering it." Andy took in some soda. "So did Mercer leave the table at any time?"

"After he finished eating. He said he was going to use the men's room then go home. As soon as he left the table, Jeff ordered another round for everyone including him. I didn't see anyone doctor that drink. But I wasn't watching it all the time."

"What happened when Mercer returned from the john?"

"He said he didn't want the drink, wanted to get home, but Jeff talked him into staying. I don't know what happened after that. I finished my drink around eight-fifteen and went to my car. Jeff and Tom came out five or maybe ten minutes later."

"Why were you still in the parking lot?

"I was on the phone with a lady friend making plans for the rest of the evening."

"I'll need her name," Andy said, "so we can confirm your story."

Carter hesitated a second. "Brittany Ferris."

"What happened when Styles and Mercer came out?"

"I can't tell you." Carter drained his soda and set the empty can on Andy's desk with a tinny clunk. "I wasn't paying attention to them. I was focused on talking to Brittany."

"Anything else you can tell us about that night?"

"No." Carter rubbed his palms together for several seconds. "But around eight Sunday morning, Jeff called me and asked if I knew anyone who could repair Lisa's car fast for cash. I gave him Scott Harris's address."

"Why Harris?"

"I knew from representing him numerous times he did auto body repair. A few years ago, he told me if anyone ever needed their car repaired fast for a good price to send them his way."

"Did you ask Styles why he needed her car repaired?"

"He said Lisa had a minor accident. He wanted to get it fixed in a hurry because she was upset, and he didn't want to file a claim because she's had so many accidents, this one would have put her in the high-risk category, sending their rates through the roof."

And creating a paper trail that could lead back to him. I asked, "Do you believe Jeff?"

He shrugged. "Lisa's had so many fender-benders, he calls her Crashy Cathy."

Andy pinned Carter with a hard stare. "Why didn't you come to us with this then?" he asked, his tone sharp.

"As with the other things I told you, I had no proof Jeff had anything to do with Tom's accident, only suspicions. But it seemed funny he'd call me the next day, wanting to know somebody who could fix Lisa's car fast for cash."

Andy leaned forward. "You should have come to us with this then. We would have investigated it whether you had proof or not." He glowered at Carter. "Now we're playing catch-up because you sat on your hands for the past eleven months."

Carter nodded, silently accepting Andy's rebuke.

"Get out of here before I charge you with hindering a police investigation."

When he was gone, Andy asked, "You buy his story?"

"It fits with what we know. You gonna look at Jeff Styles?"

"Oh, yeah."

Chapter 54

09/11/2003 – Walking Can Kill

Steph rang my doorbell minutes after seven Thursday evening. She looked terrific in jeans and a white tee. "Feel like taking a walk?"

With you? Oh, yeah! "Let me get my sneaks."

We stepped out of the house, and she took my hand. Loving the way hers fit in mine, I smiled, and she smiled back. The evening was perfect for strolling, mild with the cloudless navy sky fading to indigo. Walking with Steph made it nicer yet. As we started along the sidewalk, she said, "I had lunch with Lisa Styles today. After what Jeff said on that tape, I wanted to find out what she knew about Tom's accident."

"You didn't tell her about the tape, did you?"

"No, I said I just wanted to know what she remembered about that night."

"What did she say?"

"The same thing Jeff told you, that he was at the Roadhouse only long enough for one drink because they were going away Sunday and wanted to leave early in the morning." A pause. "She lied to me."

"How do you know?"

"Because she always goes on the offensive after telling one. She said instead of asking her about Jeff, I should ask you what you were doing the day Tom died.

298

Then she asked me how long before he died did I start sleeping with you and said you probably killed Tom so you could have me for yourself."

We both laughed over that for a second or two. "You set her straight, I take it?"

"In no uncertain terms." She shook her head. "I doubt she'll want to have lunch with me again soon."

Streetlights flickered on as the sky continued to darken. "Don't do it even if she begs you to."

"What? Why?"

I took in a breath and let it out slowly. "Andy and I have reason to believe Jeff is behind Tom's accident." I told her about our meeting with Carter.

She looked at me in shock for a second. "No, I don't believe it." She looked down, shaking her head slowly, assimilating what I'd told her. "Yes, I can." After a few steps, she asked, "What do we do now?"

"What we've been doing all along: ask questions, seek answers. Did Tom usually take Millers Run Road home from The Roadhouse?"

"Always. It was longer distance-wise than going through town but shorter time-wise because you miss all the stoplights and several stop signs."

Guys talk about things like that, so it was no stretch to imagine Styles knew it as well. Sparsely populated with long stretches of woods lining it, Millers Run Road was the perfect place to ambush someone. "Andy and I found the Jeep Cherokee we think ran him off the road. It belongs to Lisa's cousin-in-law, Alex Hopper."

"You mean *he* ran Tom—"

"He couldn't. He was in Florida that night. That leaves Jeff or Lisa. She had keys to the Hopper's home—she's his wife's cousin—so she could make sure everything was okay. And could get to his Jeep, too."

Her hand gripped mine a little tighter. "I thought it odd they didn't come to the hospital as soon as they saw the news about Tom. It was the lead item in the *Sentinel-Tribune* that day and they read the paper at breakfast every morning, but it was after ten when they arrived."

We paused for a car coming down Willow Lane. "Did they say why?"

"Lisa said they overslept." She shook her head. "They wouldn't have done that if they were going away."

"Probably not." Crossing Willow, we turned toward Maple Lane. "Someone who could be Jeff took a Jeep we think was Hopper's to a guy named Scott Harris to get it repaired the morning after Tom's crash." Pieces were starting to fall into place but some were still missing. Could Lisa be one of them? Could she have had a hand in Tom's accident? Maybe. "What do you know about Lisa?"

"She's from here originally, like Jeff. They started dating his junior and her sophomore year in high school. They got married when he was a senior at Penn State because she was pregnant with Brian. He's fourteen now and attends Lowell Seminary." A private school in Wilkes-Barre. "They also have a daughter, Allison, who's nine."

"What else?"

"Well, let's see. She was studying English literature at Penn State but never went back after Brian was born. She told me once all she ever wanted to be was a wife and mother. I think she was only going to college to fill time until Jeff graduated and they could get married."

"What kind of person is she?"

"She always seemed a bit...shallow to me. She can tell you where hemlines will be next spring and who's dating who in Hollywood, but can't name our mayor. I'm not condemning her. It's just the way she is." A brief pause. "She's also very insecure. About everything. Her looks. Growing old. If her children are in the right activities to help them get into a good college. If her home measures up to others. They put their pool in the year after a neighbor down the street got one. And the minute she heard we bought a cabin, she started pressing Jeff about getting one."

"A 'keep up with the Joneses' type?"

"Very much so."

"If she knew Tom was going to make partner, would she get on Jeff's case about making partner, too?"

"Definitely."

"What about Jeff? Would he want to make partner as much as she wanted him to?"

Steph nodded. "Because it would alleviate some of Lisa's insecurity. At least for a time." She covered her mouth for a second. "Oh, God, that sounds terribly shrinky, doesn't it?"

"It does," I said with a smile as we turned from Maple onto Holbrook Drive.

"He'd do it anyway to win his father's approval. He said one time no matter what he achieved, it was never enough to please Lawrence. He always demanded more from Jeff, better. Lawrence didn't let it slip," she scribed air quotes around those words with her free hand, "Tom was going to make partner. He said it explicitly to rub it in Jeff's face that Tom was and he wasn't."

Near mid-block on Holbrook, a white Honda Accord with a wheel well-to-wheel well crease on the passenger side pulled alongside us and slowed to our pace. The passenger window went down as if the driver wanted to ask us directions. Streetlight glinted off the barrel of a gun pointed at us. I shoved Steph hard, sending her sprawling on the grass.

Three loud booms fractured the twilight, and she screamed. Something whacked my left shoulder, sprawling me on the grass next to her. Metal pinged against metal. A car alarm blared harsh beeps. Someone in the house behind us shouted, "What the hell?"

An engine roared and tires chittered. I scrambled to my knees. The Honda sped away, tires squealing as it slued around the corner onto Park Drive. Steph turned to me, her startled-wide eyes easy to see in the fading light. "Somebody just shot at us!" Her voice was as stunned as her eyes.

I drew her into a hug. "You okay?"

She returned the hug, nodding, then drew back, looked at her hand, and let out a short, sharp shriek. "Dan, you're bleeding."

A sting like a line of acid crossed my shoulder, a warm wetness lay on my skin, and my shirt stuck to my back.

The car alarm stopped bleating. Somewhere behind us a door squeaked open. "You folks okay?" A balding man, his gut straining his tee and the waist of his slacks, waddled toward us.

Steph pointed at me. "He's hurt. Call an

ambulance, please."

"Madge!" he barked. "Call the amb-lance!"

Steph and I flinched at his bellow.

He knelt behind me with a grunt. "How bad is it, buddy?"

"Stings like hell."

He tugged my shirt up. "Damn, buddy, you been hit. Madge!" he yelled. "Get the first aid kit! And a flashlight!"

Ten minutes later, I sat in the back of an ambulance, Baldy's bandage covering my wound. Andy stood with one foot on the back bumper. "Tell me what happened."

I did. When I finished, he said, "You get a look at the driver?"

"Never saw him, just the gun. Saw it, shoved Steph out of the way, and ducked. Just not fast enough."

"How old was the Accord?"

"Ten, maybe twelve years."

"You get the plate number?"

"By the time I looked, he was too far away, hanging a left onto Park."

"Anything distinctive about it?"

I shifted on the gurney and inhaled hard through my nose as pain stomped cleats into my shoulder. "A deep crease wheel to wheel, passenger side."

"We need to roll now, Chief," the EMT said.

"Okay." Andy closed his notebook and stepped back. "We'll talk more tomorrow, Dan."

Four hours later, the ER staff set me free with fresh bandages, wound care instructions, pain medicine and antibiotics, a scrub top, and a sling. My left shoulder had that same 'there but not part of me' feeling as a jaw full of Novocain. Steph rose from a chair in the waiting area. "Are you ready to go?"

Joy filled me at seeing her. "Yep. You been waiting here all this time?"

"Mm-hmm. I heard there was a handsome man here needing a ride home after he was discharged."

"He's still being treated. He'll be out in a few minutes."

"Stop it, Dan. I was talking about you." As we stepped outside, she slipped her arm through mine. "Are you okay?"

"Yeah."

At her Audi, she gave me a gentle hug. Another hour of that, and I'd be completely healed.

She ended it a minute later. Damn. We got into her Audi, and she asked, "How bad is it?"

"Dr. Adler said the bullet hit the bottom edge of my shoulder blade, travelled along it under the skin, came out at the top of my shoulder."

"I called Will as soon as the ambulance drove away. I wanted the best taking care of you. Why are you wearing a sling?"

"He says immobilizing it for a couple days will help it heal faster in the long run."

"Chief Cummings said you—" she took in a breath, "you could have been seriously wounded. Or killed." Fear edged her words.

Damn Andy for telling her. I remembered the fear chilling me when I saw the gun. I groped for her hand, clasped it, an awkward move with my arm in a sling. "So could you."

"If you hadn't pushed me down." She squeezed my hand. "Thank you."

Several blocks from the hospital, a sharp pang in my left shoulder made me stiffen and suck in air. She jerked her car to the curb. "Dan? What's wrong? Do you need to go back to the hospital?"

I shook my head. "Just a twinge." Delivered by a cattle prod. "I'm okay."

She drove away and a few blocks later, my cell rang. Andy. "How you doing?"

"Not as bad as I could be, not as good as I should be."

"Don't bitch. Slug that hit you was a nine-millimeter. It tags you at a different angle, and you're still in surgery getting your shoulder put back together. Or in the morgue waiting for a hearse."

"I heard."

"So take it easy for a couple days. Okay?"

"Will do." I closed my phone.

"Andy?" Steph asked.

I smiled at her change from 'Chief Cummings' to 'Andy.' "Yeah." I sensed she had something on her mind.

A block later, she said, "He thinks we should go away for a few days."

"Because someone shot at us?"

"And broke into my house and wrecked my car and planted drugs in your shops and tried to burn them down."

"You should. Definitely." I would feel infinitely better if she was far out of harm's way. "I can't. I have a business to run."

"A business you say practically runs itself."

She had me there. "It does for the most part but—" I took a breath. "The thing is I don't give up on a restoration when it's half done. I'm not giving up on this."

"But you're not giving up. You're letting someone better equipped to handle it do the rest." She glanced at me. "Gene is your best painter, right?"

"Yeah."

"He doesn't build engines or reupholster interiors or anything else. People who are better at those things do them. He does what he does best, they do what they do best. You did a phenomenal job finding proof Tom was run off the road and figuring out who might have done it. Now let Andy track them down and arrest them."

"I want to see this through, Steph, to the end."

"If you're not going, neither am I."

"Okay. We'll go." If it took that to make her safe. "Where did you have in mind?"

"Our cabin."

"Bad idea."

"Why? It's far enough away from here that we should be safe."

"Jeff and Lisa know you have it. If they can't find us in town, that will be the next place they look."

"No, they won't. No one knows where it is. It was Tom's and my—" She stopped for a deep breath. "Our private place. We never invited any friends, not even Jeff and Lisa, there, never told anyone where it was. Not even our families. All we ever said was we had it."

"You're absolutely sure?"

"Yes."

"That could work then."

Minutes later, she pulled into my driveway, got out with me, grabbed her tan duffle bag from the back seat, and locked her doors. I questioned her via raised eyebrows.

She shrugged. "I made a quick stop at home before I came to the hospital." She offered a sultry smile. "You shouldn't be alone tonight."

I walked around the car, hooked my good arm around her, and pulled her close. "I agree."

Chapter 55

09/12/2003 – Hiking the Trail

Steph left after breakfast Friday morning to pack a bag for our stay at her cabin.

I was packing my own bag when my phone rang. Andy was on the other end. "We picked up Eddie Harris a couple hours ago." He sounded drained. "Guess what we found wedged under the seat of his ninety-two Honda Civic."

"A nine-millimeter of some sort."

"Bingo. He claims it isn't his, he never saw before, has no idea how it got in his car, blah, blah, blah. His fingerprints all over it blew that line of bull out of the water. The lab matched the three slugs we recovered near where you were shot to it as well. We laid all that on him, said we were charging him with assault, assault with a deadly weapon, attempted murder, and a ton of other felonies, and he turned into Chief Blabs Many Words."

"And what words did he blab?"

"The best kind. Owned up to him and Scott doing everything that happened to you and Ms. Mercer. But he confirmed Carter's claim he didn't put them up to it, someone else did."

"Who?"

"Said he didn't know, said Scott always met with

the guy. He paid them five hundred to plant drugs in your shop and another five to break into Ms. Mercer's house and steal some tape—I'm guessing the one you found at their cabin—then wanted his money back when they didn't get it. Scott was going to tell the guy to hit the road next time he called, but five hundred each to torch your business and cream Ms. Mercer's car was too good to pass up. Eddie thought Scott getting killed meant the end of the money train. Then the guy offered him five hundred to take potshots at you."

"Wait. If Eddie never met with the guy, how did he know it was the same guy?"

"He thinks the same guy came up to him in Costello's last week." A bar on Canal Street favored by our town's shadier citizens. "Wanted to know if he was interested in making some money. Harris says doing what. The guy says take some shots at you. Harris says he's no killer. The guy says he doesn't want you dead, just scared off. Harris says okay, the guy hands him your address and two C-notes upfront money and says he'll get the other three when the job's done."

"Eddie ask him why he wanted him to shoot at me?"

"He's not exactly the inquisitive type. Five Cs answered the only question he had."

"He say what this guy looked like?"

"Tall, thin, dark hair under a ball cap, shades, dark clothes was all he could tell me. Costello's doesn't waste money on lighting." The reason it was the favorite watering hole of the town's sketchy denizens. "Sound like Jeff Styles to you?"

"It could be. You gonna pick him up?"

"I don't have enough yet, and he's not some dumb

punk like Eddie, so I have to go about it a little differently. Soon as I get some ducks in a row, I'll give him the choice of coming in for a chat or me visiting him at OSM. I'll let you know how it goes."

I finished packing, dropping the sling in my bag last. My shoulder felt fine but I wanted it with me in case the injury flared up at the cabin. I stowed my bag in my Pontiac, picked up Steph, and we hit the road for Big Bear Lake minutes after nine. A gorgeous September day, a beautiful woman beside me, a powerful car under me, and Bob Seger's greatest hits on the stereo. Steph and I sang along, my raspy baritone clashing with her smooth alto. We laughed when one of us flubbed a lyric then shouted at Seger, "Learn the words."

I couldn't imagine life getting any better.

Autumn wouldn't arrive for ten more days, but some trees in the mountains had started showing their fall colors. We hauled food into the cabin and opened the windows to clear out the stuffy air. When I went out to grab our bags from my Pontiac, I heard a car approaching. A moment later, a beige Volvo wagon nosed into the end of the driveway. Sun glare on the windows blocked my view of the interior. I stepped toward it, and the driver backed out and raced away. *Was it Jeff?* I'd be foolish to assume otherwise. But I'd keep it to myself. No point worrying Steph over a maybe.

I carried our bags inside and stowed them. We'd grabbed hoagies at Sub King in Buckleyville and had just sat down to eat when raps sounded on the door. I glanced out the window, expecting the Volvo had returned. Instead, two gold lettered dark green Buckley

Township cop cars sat behind my Pontiac.

Steph opened the door to two officers in green-piped tan uniforms. One touched the brim of his ball cap in a salute. "Afternoon, Mrs. Mercer."

"Chief...Boston, is it?"

"Yes, ma'am. And Officer Knowles. May we come in?"

"Please." Steph stepped back.

The cops shed their caps and entered, their gazes sweeping the cabin. Boston's landed on me. "And you are?"

"Dan Gallagher."

"We heard about your husband's passing, Mrs. Mercer. Our condolences on your loss."

"Thank you, Chief. In some ways, it was a blessing."

Boston nodded. "The reason we stopped by, Mrs. Mercer, is we had a request from Schuylerton PD a while back to keep an eye on your place. I noticed the strange car in the driveway and—"

"And wanted to make sure we weren't robbers cleaning the place out?"

A small smile. "Yes, ma'am. Something like that. I need a word with you in private." He pointed toward the porch.

Boston reminded me of Andy. Not physically. He was stocky and dark to Andy's lean and fair. But he had the same competent aura as Andy, the same shrewd look in his eyes. He may have been a rural cop, but I'd bet not much got past him, and if it did, it didn't make it a second time. He nodded in my direction. "Knowles."

The big-boned, sandy-haired cop said, "May I see some ID, sir."

I got my license from my wallet as Boston led Steph outside. Knowles compared me to my photo then stepped away and muttered something into the mic clipped to his lapel. After a static-laden response, he came back to me and returned my license. "Sir, what is your relationship to Mrs. Mercer?"

"We're friends."

He gave me the 'just friends?' gaze. "And how long have you known her?"

"Six months, give or take."

On the porch, Steph laughed at something Boston said.

Knowles asked, "And the purpose of your visit here?"

"A weekend away from everything." *Including people trying to kill us.*

Boston and Steph came back inside and Boston motioned for Knowles to join him by the door. I asked Steph, "What did Boston say to make you laugh?"

She snickered. "He asked me if you had coerced me into coming here. I told him the only coercion was me forcing you to hike around the lake. You did bring hiking boots, didn't you?"

Not exactly, but the well broken-in lug-soled work boots I'd packed should fill the bill. "Yep."

At the door, Boston said, "Thank you for your co-operation, Mrs. Mercer, Mr. Gallagher. Sorry to have bothered you folks."

"No, Chief. I'm glad you did. Better to be safe than sorry."

"Yes, ma'am. You have any problems, don't hesitate to call us." He touched his cap brim again. "Have a nice day now."

"Chief, before you go," I said, "have you seen any other strange cars in the driveway since Schuylerton PD made the request?"

"I haven't. How about you, Knowles?"

"Not on the property. Maybe a month ago, one was parked across the road. I approached and asked the driver what he was doing. He said he was in the area looking for a place to buy, got turned around, and wasn't sure where he was. I got him oriented, and he drove away."

"You get an ID on him? Or run the plate?"

"No, sir. Nothing about him tripped my alarms. He was just lost."

I asked, "What kind of car was he driving, Officer Knowles?"

"That okay, Chief?"

"Yeah. Why not?"

"A dark blue Lincoln Town Car, PA tag, a year old, two at most."

"How about the driver?" I asked.

"Mid- to late-thirties, brown over brown, average build. No visible identifying scars or tattoos."

"Chief Boston, if your men see a blue Lincoln Town Car or tan Volvo wagon near here, have them check the driver out, please."

He shook his head. "We can't stop people because they're driving a certain make of car, not without a good reason."

"A man close in appearance to the one Officer Knowles helped has been harassing Stephanie. We came here to get away from him. And a tan Volvo pulled into the driveway shortly after we arrived but backed out and took off when I approached it."

"That changes things. This man's name?"

"Jeffrey Styles. He owns those two cars, but he could be driving anything."

Boston nodded. "We'll keep an eye out for him but, to be honest, it's a big township, and I only have eight sworn officers to cover it all. We'll do our best. And I'll see if the State Police can give us an assist."

"Thank you, Chief."

We returned to our lunch. After my second bite of hoagie, I asked, "Steph, are you positive none of your friends know you have this cabin?"

"Absolutely. Tom and I decided even before we started looking that we wouldn't share any place we bought with anyone, that it would strictly be *our* place." She wiped a dot of mayo from the corner of her mouth. "Why are you asking?"

"Jeff Styles owns a blue Lincoln Town Car like the one Officer Knowles saw out front. And Lisa has a tan Volvo like the one that poked its nose in your driveway while I was getting our bags."

She set her hoagie down. "They know we have this cabin."

I swallowed some Dr. Pepper. "Looks like it. That's why I asked Boston to have his men keep an eye out for their cars."

"Do we need to change our plans?"

"I don't see any reason to. We'll just have to stay on our toes a little more than we hoped."

Lunch over, we changed for our hike. The day had warmed enough for tees and shorts. Steph okayed my work boots but said I should get a proper pair of hiking boots for the future. Knowing there would be more hikes with her stirred glee in my chest. She handed me a quart water bottle, saying I'd need it on the hike. At the edge of the trail, she took my hand and off we went. Nature isn't really my thing, but I'd slog through a gator-infested swamp with her if that's what she loved to do.

A breeze carried the smells of fresh water and forest. The air was cool in the shade, the sun hot in the open. Each felt wonderful as it followed the other. The trail was well worn and easy to hike. Only a few spots on it approached steep, and those were short enough to take in a step or two. We could walk side by side on most of the trail. Where it narrowed to single file, I let Steph go first. Watching her was much more appealing than the flora and fauna around me.

Unseen critters rustled the underbrush, and a woodpecker rat-tat-tatted a tree. Steph pointed out animal trails and birds, shrubs and trees, and a hawk's nest high in a pine, identifying each one as easily as I could identify parts of a car. At one point, a doe and fawn ambled onto the path twenty feet away, paused to study us, then strolled into the woods with stately grace.

About halfway around the lake, after going up a gentle rise, the path curved onto a rocky plateau abutting the lake for a hundred yards or so maybe thirty feet above the water. Steph stopped there and leaned on the railing secured to the rock. "This is my favorite spot."

"I can see why." The high ground gave a picture postcard view of the roughly oval lake. A motorboat drew an arcing wake across water glittered by sunlight, and fishermen cast lines in the shadows. Along the far shore, boats bobbed at piers, and cabins squatted in the shade of trees whose tops etched a jagged horizon on the blue sky.

I sensed a change come over Steph as we stood there. Her brow furrowed and she had a far-away look in her eyes. Remembering past hikes with Tom probably. I let her reminisce in peace until the mood passed.

We encountered other people often throughout our hike. Some marched past as if racing to a deadline. Others, like us, strolled along at an easy pace. Trail etiquette called for at least a friendly wave each time but often included a cheery "Hi," or "Nice day, isn't it?"

It was almost five when we returned to the cabin. Once we were inside, Steph turned to me. "What did you think? Did you like it?"

"Very much." On my own, I wouldn't have thought it anything special, but she was so thrilled by it all, I found myself caught up in her excitement.

She hooked her arms across my shoulders. "I'm glad." Then she kissed me.

It was more than a peck on the lips and it caught me off guard for a second. But only a second. We spent the next several minutes trading equally serious kisses.

Clouds had started gathering overhead toward the end of our hike and, by the time we took the barbecue chicken, baked potatoes, and corn on the cob off the grill, a misty drizzle was falling. After dinner, Steph poured brandies and, as we did last time, we carried them out to the porch. A light but steady rain pattered on the roof, bigger drops plopped leaf to leaf through the trees, and the air had the ozone-y smell rain brings.

Steph stood at the railing and stared into the darkness. Her expression said she had something on her mind but wasn't ready to share it. After a bit, she took the first sip from her snifter then glanced at me. "There's something I've wanted to tell you for several months."

She fell silent again. My heart thumped harder against my ribs with each passing second. My lungs had gone on sabbatical as well, and my mouth had turned Saharan.

Finally, she faced me, uncertainty filling her eyes. "I love you, Dan."

A smile grew on my face, driven by joy welling up from the deepest part of my soul, where it had hidden since Amy died. I set my snifter on a table and touched her cheek. "I love you, too."

Another hesitation before she laced her fingers through mine. "I don't mean as a friend."

"Neither do I. And I've wanted to tell you for just as long."

"Why didn't you?"

"You were married. It wouldn't have been right."

"And now it is?"

"And now it is." I kissed her gently.

"What about Amy?"

"She will always be a part of me, of my past." I set her snifter next to mine and wrapped her in my arms. "You are my now and my future."

She nestled against me. "And you are mine."

We made love to the soft thrum of light rain on the roof. Sometime in the night, the roaring drone of a heavy downpour woke me. I snuggled closer to Steph, looped my arms around her, and went back to sleep.

Chapter 56

09/13/2003 – Dangerous Hike

We slept until almost nine, made love again, and cuddled through the afterglow then whipped up a brunch of eggs, sausages, and pancakes. Last night's rain had moved on, and morning sun streamed through the cabin's windows. As we carried dishes and pans to the sink, Steph said, "Feel up to hiking the trail again? It's a totally different world after a storm."

I hooked an arm around her waist. "I'd hike it again in a blizzard as long as I'm hiking it with you."

Dishwashing got delayed by ten minutes of intense kissing we ended before it led to a return to bed for an encore. Steph insisted on doing the few dishes herself, so I poured the last of the coffee into my mug and stepped outside. Last night's steady rain had left the ground muddy and strewn with fallen leaves. The air had a nip to it, meaning the radio probably had it right saying the high would be in the low fifties. Not a day for shorts and tees.

My cell rang as I took the first drink from my mug. The moment I said my name, Andy crowed, "We got them!"

"Them?"

"Jeff and Lisa Styles."

"How?"

He chuckled. "Miss Henrietta Rutherford, retired sixth grade teacher—you remember her, right?—five-foot-nothing, the Invisible Man couldn't sneak past her."

"Only too well."

"She's the Nosey Nellie on Alex Hopper's block. Yesterday, she told me Lisa Styles drove up to Hopper's home in a tan wagon at ten after one the day the Hoppers left for Florida and—"

"Wait." I paced the porch. "How did she know it was Lisa?"

"She recognized her from seeing her at the Hoppers' other times and remembers teaching her. She said Lisa left an hour later driving Hopper's red truck, and the tan wagon was still there the next morning but disappeared sometime later that day. And the fingerprints I lifted from Hopper's Jeep come back to Lisa Styles."

A sip of coffee. "All that proves is that she took his Jeep."

"I have more. Last night, one of Styles's neighbors said about nine the morning after Mercer crashed, he saw them drive off, Jeff in a red Jeep Cherokee with the passenger side all beat to hell, Lisa in their Lincoln. And last but not least, the Thursday after Mercer's accident, Henrietta saw the Styleses return Hopper's Jeep to his garage. It's enough for us to bring them in. Soon as I get the warrants, I'm on their doorstep."

I stopped on the lake side of the house, looked out at the placid water. "Are you sure they're home?"

"Why wouldn't they be?"

"Because yesterday, shortly after we got here, a Volvo like theirs showed up in the driveway here then took off when I went toward it."

"Where is here?"

"Steph's cabin near Buckleyville."

"Was it Styles?" An edge of worry in Andy's voice.

"Couldn't tell. Glare on the windows wouldn't let me see."

"Damn. I'll send a car to their place pronto. Keep your head down. I'll clue the chief up there in on things."

"He knows. We talked to him yesterday."

"Good." He hung up.

I tucked my phone away, went inside, and told Steph about Andy's call. When I finished, she said, "I am not letting them run my life. Let's go."

After refilling our water bottles, we set out wearing sweaters and jeans. Steph was right. The trail was a different world after the rain. The air smelled fresher, everything looked brighter and cleaner, and crisp paw and hoof prints dappled the muddy spots. Unlike the day before, we didn't meet anyone on the trail.

I willed my cell to ring with every step I took, wanting it to be Andy telling me Jeff and Lisa were at the police station answering questions but dreading it would be him telling me they'd flown the coop. When impatience got the better of me, I checked for messages. If Andy sent one, I didn't get it. Because I had no signal. Great.

The heavy rain had made the trail slick in places. Steph and I both almost landed on our butts going down a steep spot a several yards past the rocky outcrop. A hundred feet later, Holland Carter stepped out of the woods to block our path. The big black automatic he pointed at us guaranteed we'd stop. He said "Hello, Stephanie," as if her name had mystical powers.

"What are you doing here?"

"We're going for a walk." He pointed the gun up the path then gripped her arm. "That way. You stay by me." He jabbed the gun at my chest. "You lead the way."

Going for a walk didn't sound good. The gun in his hand said Carter's only interest in nature was how woods like these were a good place to hide a dead body. Or two. Steph was thinking the same way. "No," she said, "we're not moving."

"C'mon!" Carter tugged her arm but she'd planted her feet firmly and wide apart and hooked her other arm around a tree, and he wasn't budging her an inch. I admired her courage to resist him but feared it might make him snap and do something deadly.

"Why are you doing this?"

He slipped his arm around her, nestled against her side. "Because I love you. I have since I met you. Now I can show you. Like I tried to show you after Tom died."

Steph eyes widened, and she pushed his arm down and twisted free. "You killed Tom to show me you love me!" She turned pale and shaky, like she was going to puke. "You make me sick."

"I didn't do anything to Tom." Carter pulled her close again. "I'd never hurt you like that. I love you. More than Tom ever could." He poked the gun into my chest. "Move!"

"Do that again, Carter, and I'll make you eat that goddamn gun."

He stuffed the nasty end under my nose. "Will

you?"

The hole in the muzzle looked big enough to climb into. "Yeah," I said with a courage and confidence I didn't feel.

Carter cocked the pistol. "Will you?"

"Dan. Please," Steph pleaded, "do what he says."

I turned.

"Good choice." A jab in the back. "Now move."

We started toward the rocky outcrop. I needed a way to get us out of this. I needed to buy time to think, to figure out a way to save us. I shortened my stride and slowed. Carter almost bumped into me. "What the hell are you doing? Get moving."

"I can't go any faster. I've got bad ankles. They're starting to hurt."

"They won't much longer."

His cold tone put fear in Steph's voice. "What are you going to do?"

"A better job than Jeff did with Tom." Another prod from his gun. "Move."

Solid proof Jeff caused Tom's accident but I had to get it to Andy. If Carter carried through on his plan to kill me that wouldn't happen. He'd have to kill Steph too. He couldn't let her live after he murdered me. I needed to get us out of this mess. Fast.

Steph stopped walking, grabbed Carter's arm. "Don't kill him, Holl. Please!" Fear quivered her voice. "I'll do anything you ask. Marry you. Be your mistress. Whatever you want. Just don't kill him. Please!"

"Too late. He should have stayed away from you. I need to make sure he does."

Everything Carter had done and said so far was scary, but now he sounded truly around-the-bend crazy.

"So all that talk about having your obsession under control was bullshit," I said. "Or did it take you over again?"

"Shut up!" A hard poke of the pistol into my back. "Move!"

"If you love me as much as you say, Holl, you won't do this." Steph was trying everything to stop him. I doubted it would do any good.

Could I do something where we'd almost fallen earlier? No ideas. I'd have to improvise. Whatever I did had to be perfect. I wouldn't get a do-over.

"I have to. He could take you from me. I can't have that."

"Then you'll have to kill me, too, Holl. Or I'm going straight to the police and tell them you murdered him."

"No! No, I'd never—I'm doing this for us, Stephanie. Can't you see that?" His tone was almost pleading. "I have to get rid of him. So we can be together."

One yard to the slick spot. I took a short step, and Carter closed up on my back again. Now or never. I planted my right foot on the slope and pushed off with my left leg. I 'slipped' my right foot, pitched forward, and shot both legs back hard, hoping to nail one of Carter's shins. I scored. He landed on top of me with a hard grunt, bringing Steph with him. His gun skittered across wet leaves, beyond reach.

"Steph! Run!"

She scrambled into a sprint. Carter squirmed off my back, going for the gun. I grabbed an ankle. He kicked, landing a hard blow on my injured shoulder. Spots danced before my eyes. I climbed atop him, pressed his face into the muck, stretched my hand toward the gun. He bucked me off, I pounced on him, and we brawled, punching, clawing, and grabbing at each other. We rolled off the trail, down a slope covered in slimy forest debris, separated, and I crashed into a tree. My shoulder took the brunt of the impact and I groaned in pain. Carter lunged at me, I slammed a hard right into his jaw, and he went down. I jumped on his back as he pushed himself up, hooked my right arm around his neck in a chokehold, and squeezed. He bucked, rolling us over, and clawed at my arm. I kept the pressure on until his grabs faded to feeble swipes then stopped, and he sagged atop me. I held it a little longer to be sure he was out.

I shoved him off me and checked for a pulse. He had a steady one. Even out cold, I didn't trust him. I picked up a fallen branch and bashed him twice, splitting open the skin on his forehead. Dragging him to a tree, I pulled his arms to the far side, crossed his wrists, and lashed them together with his belt, drawing it as tight as I could. Pain scalded my shoulder with every move, and blood wet my back. My left eye had closed down to a slit, and blood trickled from my nose and lip and dripped off my chin. I sucked in deep breaths for several more seconds then crawled up to the trail and picked up Carter's automatic.

"Neatly done." Jeff Styles stood on the path, a walking ad for J. Crew, his arm around Steph's waist. She had a trapped rabbit look in her eyes and a pistol pressed to her side.

Jeff jabbed it harder into her ribs. "Now drop the gun, Dan."

Chapter 57

09/13/2003 – Another Surprise

I straightened slowly, pointing my gun at him. "Not gonna happen." My mouth had gone bone dry.

"Do it," he lifted his pistol to her temple, "or she dies."

"Okay, okay." I raised my left hand in surrender. "Just...please...let her go." I lowered the gun and eased into a slow squat. "Do what you want with me but let her go."

"Dan! Don't." Steph twisted in his arm, trying to wrench free of his grasp.

"I can't. You both know too much. You have to go." Jeff aimed his gun on me.

Steph stomped his sneakered foot with her heavy hiking boot. Pain froze him for a moment. She twisted left, raising her right arm, whipped right, smashing her elbow into his nose. His head snapped back, his gun fired, and a bullet zinged past my ear. Steph broke from his grip and bolted up the trail. Jeff shouted, "No!" and swung his pistol toward her.

I jerked my gun up and fired, hoping to startle him into missing. My bullet drilled his thigh as he fired.

Steph let out a short cry.

Jeff dropped. His pistol flew from his hand, landing a yard beyond his fingertips. He gripped his right leg above the wound, a glower on his face. "You shot me!"

"You're lucky I didn't kill you." I tucked his and Carter's guns into my belt at my back. "Steph!"

"Here." Her voice quivered.

Thirty feet up the trail, she sat on the ground against a tree to the right of the path, pale and shivering, cradling her left arm against her stomach. Red stained the sleeve and front of her sweater and right hand. I dropped to my knees beside her. "Your arm?"

She nodded, tears in her eyes.

"Let me take a look." I gently pried her hand away. She bit her lip when I lifted her arm. Jeff's bullet had torn two ragged holes in the wool.

She whimpered as I pushed the sleeve up. "Where is he? Where's Jeff?"

I nodded over my shoulder. "Back there. Out of the game."

Jeff's bullet had pierced her forearm. Blood leaked from both holes but was starting to clot around the edges. The give under my fingers and her sharp inhale when I touched her arm by her wound told me her ulna was broken.

"And Holl?"

"The same."

She touched my face. "Did he do this to you?"

I smiled and felt dried blood around my mouth crack. "He wanted his gun back. I need your T-shirt to make a bandage."

I helped her shed her sweater and long-sleeved tee, hating the pain every move of her arm caused, then folded her tee into a pad I wrapped around her wound and tied in place by the sleeves.

She gasped when I turned to look for something to use as a splint. "Dan! Your shoulder's bleeding."

"Tore a stitch. Also thanks to Carter." I grabbed a long thin branch a few feet away and broke off two pieces I eyeballed to the right length. Peeling off my sweater and tee, I splinted Steph's arm with the tee and wood, and converted my belt into a sling. "You hurt anywhere else?"

"I stepped on a rock wrong and fell right as—" Her eyes widened. "Oh, God!"

The chill icing my blood had nothing to do with the cool air. If she hadn't fallen, Jeff's bullet might have hit her body instead of her arm. "We need to get back to the cabin, let Chief Boston know what happened."

"I turned my ankle on the rock. I don't know how bad. Help me up."

I lifted her to her feet. With my arm around her waist and hers over my shoulder for support, she took a few tentative steps along the trail then slid her arm from my shoulder and took a few more on her own, limping heavily on her right ankle. "It's okay. Just tender. I can make it if we go slow."

She clasped my hand, and we hiked back to Styles. He sat against a tree, his right leg angling to the side above his knee. Blood stained his slacks dark and soaked the ground underneath. He gripped his thigh above his wound, grimacing as a burst of pain signaled things were bad wrong below his hands. "Help me. Please." He drew in a ragged breath. "Don't let me die."

Steph gave him a cold blue-eyed stare and spit out, "I hope you do."

Tears welled in his eyes. "I'm sorry, Stephanie. So very, very sorry. I never meant for things to go this far. They...they just got out of hand."

"Out of hand?" Steph shouted. "Out of hand is a fistfight, Jeffery." Venom filled her voice saying his name.

"All I wanted was partnership in the firm. That's all."

"A partnership?" she shrieked. "You killed him for a partnership?" She glared at him for a second, turned her back on him, and limped a few steps away.

I waved a pistol in his face. "Take off your belt."

He fumbled the buckle open, tugged it free, and offered it to me with a shaking hand.

"Hands behind the tree. Now."

I pulled them together, backs touching, wrapped his belt tightly around his wrists, and buckled it, pain flaring in my shoulder with every move. I squatted facing him. "Tell me something. Was a partnership worth this?" I slapped his injured leg, and he jerked and howled in pain. "You'll never walk normal again. And that's the least of your worries. You're facing major jail time. Something to think about while you're waiting."

Despair filled his eyes, from pain, frustration, or the realization his old life was over. I didn't really give a damn which. "Where's Lisa?"

"I don't—home, I guess." He groaned as pain flared in his shattered leg then panted hard as it abated. "Not, not here, if that's what you're asking. She had nothing to do with this."

I didn't believe him but had no way to prove him wrong. I stood, took Steph's hand, and we strolled away while Jeff called, "Wait! Don't leave me here! Help me! Please!"

I shifted one pistol from the small of my back to my front pocket, wanting it handy in case we met any more surprises on the trail. We hiked as fast as Steph could comfortably go, ranting with her every step about Jeff and Lisa's betrayal. I checked my phone every few yards, hoping for a signal. After the fifth time, I muttered, "Shit."

"Reception has always been unreliable up here. The only place we can always get a signal is at the cabin."

"What about your neighbors' places?"

"Not really. Our place seems to be the sweet spot."

"Do any of the cabins have regular phones?"

"A few, but it won't do us any good. Everyone's closed their places for the season, and had the phone company suspend service until they reopen them in the spring."

Fifty yards from the cabin, Steph let out a sharp yelp as her ankle buckled. Before she could fall, I scooped her up in my arms, pain flaring in my shoulder again. "Dan!" she yelped and a second later said, "You don't have to carry me."

I flexed my arms in a gentle squeeze and smiled. "Maybe I want to."

"Any other time I wouldn't object." She kissed my cheek. "But it's not doing your shoulder any good now. Put me down and let me walk. I can make it from here."

I did and the fire searing my wound subsided, but I hooked an arm around her waist in case she stumbled again, and we ambled on.

A ten-foot band of trees separated Steph's cabin from her neighbor. I stopped before we stepped clear of it. She looked at me, puzzled. "What?"

"Being cautious." I checked my cell. The screen showed four bars but halfway through dialing Andy's number, the no signal icon filled the screen. No way to get help. We were on our own. I put my phone away. "I want to check out the cabin, see if Lisa's there, before we go walking up to it."

"I'm coming with you."

"No, you're going to sit and rest your ankle." I pushed down gently on her shoulders, and she settled at the base of a maple tree. I spent a few seconds eyeing the glass wall facing the lake. If anyone was waiting for us, that's where they'd most likely be. I didn't see any movement, so I moved on, keeping far enough back in the trees I hoped someone inside couldn't see me.

I checked each window as I worked my way around the cabin. My heart beat a little faster with every step, thumping as hard as a sledgehammer by the time I was opposite the door. I watched for several moments but didn't see anyone inside. Heading back, I detoured to the road to look for the Volvo, didn't spot it, and continued my hike back to Steph.

"Well?" she asked as I stepped out of the woods.

I shrugged. "I didn't see anyone inside."

"What do we do now?"

"Wait and see if Lisa or someone shows themselves. Or wait by the road and hope one of Boston's officers drives by. Or we can risk it and go into the cabin."

A flicker of pain danced across Steph's eyes. "My arm is really hurting and I'm getting a little chilled."

"The cabin it is then." I helped her to her feet. 'But let's be smart about it. This way." I led her through the woods around the cabin until we were opposite the door. We paused there while I checked again for movement. Seeing none, we crossed to the porch, I opened the door, we entered the cabin, and Steph gasped.

Lisa Styles stood in the great room, a wild gleam in her eye, the deadly looking silver automatic in her hand aimed at Steph.

Chapter 58

09/13/2003 – One Final Surprise

I stepped in front of Steph. She immediately moved to my side. "Lisa, what are you—"

Lisa pointed the automatic at me. "Close the door. And put the gun on the table."

I eased the pistol from my front pocket slowly and laid it on the table by the door.

"Sit on the sofa." Lisa waggled her pistol. "Move."

We sat, Steph to my left. Lisa took the chair facing us across the coffee table and pointed the small automatic at Steph. "Where's Jeffrey?"

She didn't flinch. I admired her coolness, but her straight back signaled tension. I'd perched on the edge of the seat, so I slid back an inch to match her composure. "Lying on the trail with a shattered leg."

A confused expression flashed across Lisa's face, replaced by coldness a second later. "You're lying! He's on his way here."

"Lisa, listen to me," Steph said. "He's not. He tried to kill me." She raised her injured arm. "That's how I got this. If Dan hadn't shot him, he would have killed me. He's bleeding badly." She wiggled her cell out of a hip pocket. "Let me call 9-1-1 and get him some help."

"No!" Lisa pointed with the gun, her hand shaking. "Put it on the table! Now!"

"Okay." Steph raised her hand in a 'stop' gesture and set the cell down. "But I'm telling you the truth."

Lisa swung the gun my way. "You, too. Phone on the table."

I pried my cell out of my front left pocket and set it next to Steph's. She asked, "What are you doing, Lisa? What's going on?"

Lisa aimed at her. "You're not taking Jeffrey's partnership from us."

"How do you plan to stop us?" I asked.

"I...we..." The confused expression returned. "Jeffrey will tell you. As soon as he gets here."

Good. I wanted her confused enough that she was unsure what to do but not so off balance that she snapped. "Jeff's not coming. Not with a bullet in his leg. It's all on you now, Lisa. What's the plan? How are you going to stop us?"

"You're going to have a lovers' quarrel that goes out of control. You kill her," she pointed her little gun at Steph, shifted it to me, "then yourself in remorse." She said it as calmly as she would an invitation to dinner.

Steph paled. "Oh, God!"

I eased my hand back and gripped the pistol tucked in my belt. "Give it up, Lisa. It's all coming apart on you and Jeff. Holding us at gunpoint is only making it worse. Killing us will make it your worst nightmare come true."

"It's *not* coming apart." She glared at me. "It's under control."

I slipped the pistol from my belt onto the cushion by my butt. "The cops know everything."

"They don't know anything!"

"They know you took Alex Hopper's Jeep from his garage the night of Tom's accident, used it to run him off the road, then parked it in your garage overnight. They know you took it to Scott Harris the next day to fix the side you tore up hitting Tom's car then returned it to Alex's garage days before he got back from Disneyworld. They know Jeff hired Scott and Eddie Harris to break into Steph's house and crash into her car at the mall, plant drugs in my shops and set it on fire, and take shots at both of us."

Steph gasped. "Dan?"

"I only found out this morning." I eased the pistol alongside my thigh.

"And you didn't tell me?" Fire in her eyes.

I sighed. "I didn't want you worried unnecessarily."

She lifted her injured arm. "And now I have this!"

"I'm sorry. I—"

"Shut up!" Lisa screamed. "Just...shut...up! Let me think."

"It's over, Lisa. The cops are coming. If they see a gun in your hand when they get here, they'll blow through that door," I pointed, "like a hurricane, shoot first and ask questions later."

"Lisa," Steph said, "put it down. Please." A tremor colored her voice. "Before it's too late. Before you get hurt."

"No!" She lowered her automatic and looked away. "You don't know what it's like." Pain filled her voice. "Nothing Jeffrey ever did, no matter how hard he tried, was good enough to please Lawrence. Tom was his favorite, his golden boy." She sneered the words. "He was getting the partnership that should have been

334

Jeffrey's. So I did what I had to do."

"You killed Tom just so Jeff could make partner? God, Lisa, what is wrong with you?"

"Jeffrey deserved it after putting up with his father's *crap* all these years. Tom was going to get it, so I stopped him." She pointed her pistol at Steph. "You aren't going to take it away from Jeff, either!" Her finger turned white against the trigger.

I propped my gun on my thigh, pointing at her. "Lisa. Look at me."

She cringed at the gun in my hand.

"If you kill Steph, I'll kill you."

She swung the gun my way. "Then I'll shoot you first."

"And I'll shoot you. Either way, you lose."

She aimed at Steph. I stiff-armed her sideways an instant before Lisa fired, shot my pistol a nanosecond later. Her bullet brushed my sleeve. My bullet hit her chest, the impact knocking her and the chair over. I dropped my gun on the table and knelt by Steph sprawled on the floor. "Are you hurt?"

"No." She saw the blood on Lisa's blouse. "Dan! We have to help her! Get me some towels!" She crawled to her friend and pressed a hand over her wound. "Hold on, Lisa. Help is on the way."

I admired her compassion for the friend who moments ago had tried to kill her. I doubted I could be as caring. Grabbing all the towels in the bathroom, I dumped them at her side.

Then I called 9-1-1.

Within minutes, Buckley Township police cars and EMS ambulances clotted the cabin's driveway. One EMT team worked on Lisa, two more accompanied by four police officers headed up the trail for Jeff and Holland, while Steph and I described the three attacks on us to Chief Boston and Officer Knowles. Ten minutes later, one ambulance raced off with Lisa and twenty minutes after that two more carried Jeff and Holland away.

Epilogue

May 11, 2004 – All Is Well

The surgeons did their best that September day to save Lisa, but she died in the OR. That same evening, Chief Boston arrested Holland Carter and Jeff Styles on two counts each of conspiracy, assault with a deadly weapon, attempted murder, and several other charges for attacking us. When Boston finished, Andy arrested Carter on stalking charges and Jeff as an accessory to first-degree murder in Tom's death once he admitted Lisa ran him off the road with Hopper's Jeep.

After treating our wounds, the doctors admitted Steph for overnight observation but discharged me. I spent the night there anyway, sitting at her bedside and holding her hand.

A week after Jeff and Holl's arrests, Leland and Helen Mercer offered me a five-figure reward for unmasking their son's killer. I refused it, suggesting they use it to establish a scholarship in his name at the University of Pennsylvania.

Steph and I were in court today when, under agreements worked out between the DAs and their lawyers, Jeff Styles and Holland Carter pled guilty to all the charges against them. The judge, irate that two members of the bar engaged in such heinous acts, sentenced them both to twelve to forty years in state prison.

As the bailiffs led them away, Steph leaned against me and took my hand. "It's over."

A word about the author...

I've had a deep interest in reading as far back as I can remember and first dabbled in writing in 1970 but only really got bitten by the writing bug around 1995. Since then I have worked and studied hard to improve my writing skills. You can reach me through my FaceBook page: David A Freas – Author

Thank you for purchasing
this publication of The Wild Rose Press, Inc.

For questions or more information
contact us at
info@thewildrosepress.com.

The Wild Rose Press, Inc.
www.thewildrosepress.com

CPSIA information can be obtained
at www.ICGtesting.com
Printed in the USA
JSHW010140210623
43402JS00002B/37